❧∙❧

I PLACED ONE HAND IN his and put my cheek on his chest. He rested his chin on my head as we spun to the music of the rain. In that moment I felt sure we could make it. If we could do this, we'd somehow always find our way back to each other.

❧∙❧

ALSO BY KIERA CASS

The Selection

The Elite

The Heir

The Selection Stories: The Prince & The Guard

The Queen (available as an ebook only)

THE ONE

KIERA CASS

An Imprint of HarperCollinsPublishers

HarperTeen is an imprint of HarperCollins Publishers.

The One

Copyright © 2014 by Kiera Cass

Library of Congress Cataloging-in-Publication Data

Cass, Kiera.

The one / Kiera Cass. — First edition.

    pages cm

    Summary: "As her Selection approaches its finish, America must decide where her heart truly lies—and Prince Maxon must pick one winner to wear the crown"— Provided by publisher.

    ISBN 978-0-06-206000-6

    [1. Marriage—Fiction. 2. Contests—Fiction. 3. Social classes—Fiction. 4. Princes—Fiction. 5. Love—Fiction. 6. Revolutionaries—Fiction.] I. Title.

PZ7.C2685133One 2014   2013021356

[Fic]—dc23   CIP

                                                                        AC

Typography by Sarah Hoy
20 PC/LSCH   20
❖
First paperback edition, 2015

For Callaway,
the boy who climbed into the tree house in my heart
and let me be the crown on his.

CHAPTER 1

THIS TIME WE WERE IN the Great Room enduring another etiquette lesson when bricks came flying through the window. Elise immediately hit the ground and started crawling for the side door, whimpering as she went. Celeste let out a high-pitched scream and bolted toward the back of the room, barely escaping a shower of glass. Kriss grabbed my arm, pulling me, and I broke into a run alongside her as we made our way to the exit.

"Hurry, ladies!" Silvia cried.

Within seconds, the guards had lined up at the windows and were firing, and the bursts of sound echoed in my ears as we fled. Whether they came with guns or stones, anyone showing the smallest level of aggression within sight of the palace would die. There was no more patience left for these attacks.

"I hate running in these shoes," Kriss muttered, a heap of dress draped over her arm, eyes focused on the end of the hall.

"One of us is going to have to get used to it," Celeste said, her breath labored.

I rolled my eyes. "If it's me, I'll wear sneakers every day. I'm already over this."

"Less talking, more moving!" Silvia yelled.

"How do we get downstairs from here?" Elise asked.

"What about Maxon?" Kriss huffed.

Silvia didn't answer. We followed her through a maze of hallways, looking for a path to the basement, watching as guard after guard ran in the opposite direction. I found myself admiring them, wondering at the courage it took to run *toward* danger for the sake of other people.

The guards passing us were completely indistinguishable from one another until a set of green eyes locked with mine. Aspen didn't look afraid or even startled. There was a problem, and he was on his way to fix it. That was simply who he was.

Our gaze was brief, but it was enough. It was like that with Aspen. In a split second, without a word, I could tell him *Be careful and stay safe.* And saying nothing, he'd answer *I know, just take care of yourself.*

While I could easily be at peace with the things we didn't need to say, I had no such luck with the things we'd said out loud. Our last conversation wasn't exactly a happy one. I had been about to leave the palace and had asked him to give me some space to get over the Selection. And then I'd ended up staying and had given him no explanation as to why.

Maybe his patience with me was falling short, his ability to see only the best in me running dry. Somehow I would have to fix that. I couldn't see a life for me that didn't include Aspen. Even now, as I hoped Maxon would choose me, a world without Aspen felt unimaginable.

"Here it is!" Silvia called, pushing a mysterious panel in a wall.

We started down the stairs, Elise and Silvia heading the charge.

"Damn it, Elise, pick up the pace!" Celeste yelled. I wanted to be irritated that she said it, but I knew we were all thinking the same thing.

As we descended into the darkness, I tried to reconcile myself to the hours that would be wasted, hiding like mice. We continued on, the sound of our escape covering the shouts until one man's voice rang out right on top of us.

"Stop!" he yelled.

Kriss and I turned together, watching as the uniform became clear. "Wait," she called to the girls below. "It's a guard."

We stood on the steps, breathing heavily. He finally reached us, gasping himself.

"Sorry, ladies. The rebels ran as soon as the shots were fired. Weren't in the mood for a fight today, I guess."

Silvia, running her hands over her clothes to smooth them, spoke for us. "Has the king deemed it safe? If not, you're putting these girls in a very dangerous position."

"The head of the guard cleared it. I'm sure His Majesty—"

"You don't speak for the king. Come on, ladies, keep moving."

"Are you serious?" I asked. "We're going down there for nothing."

She fixed me with a stare that might have stopped a rebel in his tracks, and I shut my mouth. Silvia and I had built a friendship of sorts as she unknowingly helped me distract myself from Maxon and Aspen with her extra lessons. After my little stunt on the *Report* a few days ago, it seemed that had dissolved into nothing. Turning to the guard, she continued. "Get an official order from the king, and we'll return. Keep walking, ladies."

The guard and I shared an exasperated look and parted ways.

Silvia showed absolutely no remorse when, twenty minutes later, a different guard came, telling us we were free to go upstairs.

I was so irritated by the whole situation, I didn't wait for Silvia or the other girls. I climbed the stairs, exiting somewhere on the first floor, and continued to my room with my shoes still hooked on my fingers. My maids were missing, but a small silver platter holding an envelope was waiting on the bed.

I recognized May's handwriting instantly and tore open the envelope, devouring her words.

Ames,

We're aunts! Astra is perfect. I wish you were here to meet her in person, but we all understand you need to be at the palace right now. Do you think we'll be together for Christmas? Not that far away! I've got to get back to helping Kenna and James. I can't believe how pretty she is! Here's a picture for you. We love you!

May

I slipped the glossy photo from behind the note. Everyone was there except for Kota and me. James, Kenna's husband, was beaming, standing over his wife and daughter with puffy eyes. Kenna sat upright in the bed, holding a tiny pink bundle, looking equal parts thrilled and exhausted. Mom and Dad were glowing with pride, while May's and Gerad's enthusiasm jumped from the image. Of course Kota wouldn't have gone; there was nothing for him to gain from being present. But I should have been there.

I wasn't though.

I was here. And sometimes I didn't understand why. Maxon was still spending time with Kriss, even after all he'd done to get me to stay. The rebels unrelentingly attacked our safety from the outside, and inside, the king's icy words did just as much damage to my confidence. All the while, Aspen orbited me, a secret I had to keep. And the cameras came and went, stealing pieces of our lives to entertain the people. I was being pushed into a corner from every angle, and I was missing out on all the things that had always mattered to me.

I choked back angry tears. I was so tired of crying.

Instead I went into planning mode. The only way to set things right was to end the Selection.

Though I still occasionally questioned my desire to be the princess, there was no doubt in my mind that I wanted to be Maxon's. If that was going to happen, I couldn't sit back and wait for it. Remembering my last conversation with the king, I paced as I waited for my maids.

I could hardly breathe, so I knew eating would be a waste. But it would be worth the sacrifice. I needed to make some progress, and I needed to do it fast. According to the king, the other girls were making advances toward Maxon—physical advances—and he'd said I was far too plain to have a chance of matching them in that department.

As if my relationship with Maxon wasn't complicated enough, there was a whole new issue of rebuilding trust. And I wasn't sure if that meant I wasn't supposed to ask questions or not. While I felt pretty sure he hadn't gone that far physically with the other girls, I couldn't help but wonder. I'd never tried to be seductive before—pretty much every intimate moment I'd had with Maxon came about without intention—but I had to hope that if I was deliberate, I could make it clear that I was just as interested in him as the others.

I took a deep breath, raised my chin, and walked into the dining hall. I was purposely a minute or two late, hoping everyone would already be seated. I was right on that count. But the reaction was better than I'd hoped.

I curtsied, swinging my leg around so the slit in the dress fell open, leading nearly all the way up my thigh. The dress was a deep red, strapless and practically backless, and I was almost positive my maids had used magic to make it stay up at all. I rose, locking eyes with Maxon, who I noticed had stopped chewing. Someone dropped a fork.

Lowering my gaze, I walked to my seat, settling in next to Kriss.

"Seriously, America?" she whispered.

I tilted my head in her direction. "I'm sorry?" I replied, feigning confusion.

She put her silverware down, and we stared at each other. "You look trashy."

"Well, you look jealous."

I'd hit pretty close to the mark, because she flushed a bit before returning to her food. I took limited bites of my own, already miserably constricted. As dessert was being set in front of me, I chose to stop ignoring Maxon, and as I had hoped, his eyes were on me. He reached up and grabbed his ear immediately, and I demurely did the same. My gaze flickered quickly toward King Clarkson, and I tried not to smile. He was irritated, another trick I'd managed to get away with.

I excused myself first, giving Maxon a chance to admire the back of the dress, and scurried to my room. I closed the door to my room behind me and unzipped the gown immediately, desperate for a breath.

"How'd it go?" Mary asked, rushing over.

"He seemed stunned. They all did."

Lucy squealed, and Anne came to help Mary. "We'll hold it up. Just walk," she ordered. I did as I was told. "Is he coming tonight?"

"Yes. I'm not sure when, but he'll definitely be here." I perched on the edge of my bed, arms folded around my stomach to keep the open dress from falling down.

Anne gave me a sad face. "I'm sorry you'll have to be uncomfortable for a few more hours. I'm sure it'll be worth it though."

I smiled, trying to look like I was fine dealing with the pain. I'd told my maids I wanted to get Maxon's attention. I'd left out my hope that, with any luck, this dress would be on the floor pretty soon.

"Do you want us to stay until he arrives?" Lucy asked, her enthusiasm bubbling over.

"No, just help me zip this thing back up. I need to think some things through," I answered, standing so they could help me.

Mary took hold of the zipper. "Suck it in, miss." I obeyed, and as the dress cinched me in again, I thought of a soldier going to war. Different armor but the same idea.

Tonight I was taking down a man.

CHAPTER 2

I OPENED THE BALCONY DOORS, letting the air sweeten my room. Even though it was December, the breeze was light and tickled my skin. We weren't allowed to go outside at all anymore, not without guards by our sides, so this would have to do.

I scurried around the room, lighting candles, trying to make the space inviting. The knock came at the door, and I blew out the match, bolted over to the bed, picked up a book, and fanned out my dress. *Why yes, Maxon, this is how I always look when I read.*

"Come in," I offered, barely loud enough to be heard.

Maxon entered, and I lifted my head delicately, catching the wonder in his eyes as he surveyed my dimly lit room. Finally he focused on me, his gaze traveling up my exposed leg.

"There you are," I said, closing the book and standing to greet him.

He shut the door and came in, his eyes locked on my curves. "I wanted to tell you that you look fantastic tonight."

I flicked my hair over my shoulder. "Oh, this thing? It was just sitting in the back of the closet."

"I'm glad you pulled it out."

I laced my fingers through his. "Come sit with me. I haven't seen you much lately."

He sighed and followed. "I'm sorry about that. Things have been a bit tense since we lost so many people in that rebel attack, and you know how my father is. We sent several guards to protect your families, and our forces are stretched thin, so he's worse than usual. And he's pressuring me to end the Selection, but I'm holding my ground. I want to have some time to think this through."

We sat on the edge of the bed, and I settled close to him. "Of course. You should be in charge of this."

He nodded. "Exactly. I know I've said it a thousand times, but when people push me, it makes me crazy."

I gave him a little pout. "I know."

He paused, and I couldn't read his face. I was trying to figure out how to move this forward without being pushy, but I wasn't sure how to manufacture a romantic moment.

"I know this is silly, but my maids put this new perfume on me today. Is it too strong?" I asked, tilting my neck so he could lean in and breathe.

He came near, his nose hitting a soft patch of skin. "No,

dear, it's lovely," he said into the curve that led to my shoulder. Then he kissed me there. I swallowed, trying to focus. I needed to have some level of control.

"I'm glad you like it. I've really missed you."

I felt his hand snake around my back, and I brought my face down. There he was, eyes looking into mine, our lips millimeters apart.

"How much have you missed me?" he breathed.

His stare, combined with his voice being so low, was doing funny things to my heartbeat. "So much," I whispered back. "So, so much."

I leaned forward, aching to be kissed. Maxon was confident, pulling me closer with one hand and stringing the other through my hair. My body wanted to melt into the kiss, but the dress stopped me. Then, suddenly nervous again, I remembered my plan.

Sliding my hands down Maxon's arms, I guided his fingers to the zipper on the back of my dress, hoping that would be enough.

His hands lingered there for a moment, and I was seconds away from just asking him to unzip it when he burst out laughing.

The sound sobered me up pretty quickly.

"What's so funny?" I asked, horrified, trying to think of an inconspicuous way to check my breath.

"Of everything you've done, this is by far the most entertaining!" Maxon bent over, hitting his knee as he laughed.

"Excuse me?"

He kissed me hard on my forehead. "I always wondered what it would be like to see you try." He started laughing again. "I'm sorry; I have to go." Even the way he stood held a sense of amusement. "I'll see you in the morning."

And then he left. He just left!

I sat there, completely mortified. Why in the world did I think I could pull that off? Maxon may not know everything about me, but at the very least he knew my character—and this? It wasn't me.

I looked down at the ridiculous dress. It was way too much. Even Celeste wouldn't have gone this far. My hair was too perfect, my makeup too heavy. He knew what I was trying to do from the second he walked through the doorway. Sighing, I went around the room, blowing out candles and wondering how I was supposed to face him tomorrow.

CHAPTER 3

I DEBATED CLAIMING THE STOMACH flu. Or an incapacitating headache. Panic attack. Really, anything to get out of going to breakfast.

Then I thought of Maxon and how he always talked about putting on a brave face. That wasn't a particular strength of mine. But if I went downstairs at least, if I could just be present, maybe he'd give me some credit.

In hopes that I could erase some of what I'd done, I asked my maids to put me in the most demure dress I had. Based on that request alone, they knew not to ask about the night before. The neckline was a bit higher than the ones we typically wore in the warm Angeles weather, and it had sleeves that went nearly to my elbows. It was flowery and cheerful, the opposite of last night's getup.

I could barely look at Maxon when I entered the dining

hall, but I walked tall at least.

When I finally peeked at him, he was watching me, grinning. As he chewed his food, he winked at me; and I ducked my head again, pretending to be very interested in my quiche.

"Glad to see you in actual clothes today," Kriss spat.

"Glad to see you in such a good mood."

"What in the world has gotten into you?" she hissed.

Dejected, I gave up. "I'm not up for this today, Kriss. Just leave me alone."

For a moment, she looked as if she might fight back, but I guessed I wasn't worth it. She sat up a little straighter and continued eating. If I'd had any level of success last night, then I could justify my actions; as it was, I couldn't even fake being proud.

I risked another glance at Maxon, and even though he wasn't watching me, he was still suppressing a smug expression as he cut his food. That was it. I wasn't going to suffer through a day like this. I was about to swoon or clutch my stomach or do anything to get me out of the room when a butler came in. He carried an envelope on a silver platter, and he bowed before placing it in front of King Clarkson.

The king took the letter and read it quickly. "Damn French," he muttered. "Sorry, Amberly, it looks like I'll be leaving within the hour."

"Another problem with the trade agreement?" she asked quietly.

"Yes. I thought we'd settled all this months ago. We need

to be firm on this one." He stood, throwing his napkin on his plate, and made his way to the door.

"Father," Maxon called, standing. "Don't you want me to come?"

It had struck me as odd that the king didn't bark out a command for his son to follow when he exited, seeing as that was his usual method of instructing. Instead he turned to Maxon, his eyes cold and his voice sharp.

"When you're ready to behave the way a king should, you'll get to experience what a king does." Without saying anything more, he left us.

Maxon stood for a moment, shocked and embarrassed by his father's choice to call him out in front of everyone. As he sat down, he turned to his mother. "Wasn't really looking forward to that flight, if I'm being honest," he said, joking away the tension. The queen smiled, as of course she must, and the rest of us ignored it.

The other girls finished their breakfasts and excused themselves to the Women's Room. When it was just Maxon, Elise, and me remaining at our tables, I looked up at him. We both tugged our ears at the same time, then smiled. Elise finally left, and we met in the middle of the room, not bothered by the maids and butlers cleaning up around us.

"It's my fault he's not taking you," I lamented.

"Perhaps," he teased. "Trust me, this isn't the first time he's tried to put me in my place, and he has a million reasons in his head why he thinks he should. It wouldn't surprise me if his only motive this time was spite. He doesn't want to lose control, and the closer I am to picking a wife, the more of a likelihood that is for him. Though we both know he'll never truly let go."

"You might as well just send me home. He's never going to let you pick me." I still hadn't told Maxon about how his father had cornered me, threatening me in the middle of the hall after Maxon talked him into letting me stay. King Clarkson had made it clear I was to keep my mouth shut about our conversation, and I didn't want to cross him. At the same time, I hated keeping it from Maxon.

"Besides," I added, crossing my arms, "after last night, I can't imagine you're that keen on keeping me anyway."

He bit his lips. "I'm sorry I laughed, but really, what else could I do?"

"I had plenty of ideas," I muttered, still embarrassed at my attempt to seduce him. "I feel so stupid." I buried my head in my hands.

"Stop," he said gently, pulling me in for an embrace. "Trust me when I say, it was very tempting. But you're not that girl."

"But shouldn't I be? Shouldn't that be part of what we are?" I whined into his chest.

"Don't you remember the night in the safe room?" he said, his voice low.

"Yes, but that was basically us saying good-bye."

"It would have been a fantastic good-bye."

I stepped away and swatted at him. He laughed, happy to have broken through the uneasiness.

"Let's forget about it," I proposed.

"Very well," he agreed. "Besides, we have a project to work on, you and I."

"We do?"

"Yes, and since my father is gone, this will be a convenient time to start brainstorming."

"All right," I said, excited to be a part of something that was just between the two of us.

He sighed, making me nervous about what he was planning. "You're right. Father doesn't approve of you. But he might be forced to bend if we can manage one thing."

"Which is?"

"We have to make you the people's favorite."

I rolled my eyes. "*That* is what we're working on? Maxon, that's never going to happen. I saw a poll in one of Celeste's magazines after I tried to save Marlee. People can hardly stand me."

"Opinions change. Don't let that one moment bring you down too much."

I still felt hopeless, but what could I say? If this was my only option, I had to at least try.

"Fine," I said. "But I'm telling you, this won't work."

With an impish grin on his face, he came very close and gave me a long, slow kiss. "And I'm telling you it will."

CHAPTER 4

I WALKED INTO THE WOMEN'S Room, thoughts focused on Maxon's new plan. The queen hadn't shown up yet, and the girls were all laughing in a clump by the windows.

"America, come here!" Kriss said urgently. Even Celeste turned back smiling, waving me over.

I was a little uneasy about what could be waiting for me, but I walked to the huddle anyway.

"Oh, my goodness!" I squealed.

"I know," Celeste sighed.

There, running laps in the garden without their shirts on, were half of the guards in the palace. Aspen had told me that all guards got injections to help keep them strong, but apparently they also did a lot of work to keep their bodies in peak condition.

While we were all devoted to Maxon, the sight of cute

boys was something we couldn't ignore.

"The guy with blond hair," Kriss said. "Well, I think he's a blond. Their hair is so short!"

"I like this one," Elise said quietly as another guard ran past our window.

Kriss giggled. "I can't believe we're doing this!"

"Oh, oh! That guy, right there with the green eyes," Celeste said, pointing to Aspen.

Kriss sighed. "I danced with him at Halloween, and he's as funny as he is good-looking."

"I danced with him, too," Celeste bragged. "Easily the most gorgeous guard in the palace."

I had to laugh a little. I wondered how she would feel if she knew he used to be a Six.

I watched him run and thought about the hundreds of times those arms had embraced me. The distance growing between Aspen and me felt unavoidable, but even now I had to wonder if there was a way to keep some piece of what we had. What if I needed him?

"What about you, America?" Kriss asked.

The only one who really caught my eye was Aspen, and after feeling that ache for him, this felt kind of stupid. I dodged the question.

"I don't know. They're all kind of nice."

"Kind of nice?" Celeste echoed. "You have to be kidding! These are some of the best-looking guys I've ever seen."

"It's only a bunch of boys without their shirts on," I countered.

"Yeah, why don't you enjoy it for a minute before it's just the three of us you have to look at," she said snippily.

"Whatever. Maxon looks just as good without his shirt on as any of those guys."

"What?" Kriss shrieked.

A second after the words slipped out of my mouth, I realized what I'd said. Three sets of eyes focused in on me.

"When were you and Maxon topless, exactly?" Celeste demanded.

"I wasn't!"

"But he was?" Kriss asked. "Was that what that god-awful dress was about yesterday?"

Celeste gasped. "You slut!"

"Excuse me!" I yelled.

"Well, what else would you expect?" she snapped, crossing her arms. "Unless you want to tell us all what happened and why we're so wrong."

But there was no way to explain this. Undressing Maxon hadn't exactly been a romantic moment, but I couldn't tell them I'd been tending to wounds on his back specifically delivered by his father. He'd spent his life guarding that secret. If I betrayed him now, it would be the end of us.

"Celeste was half-naked up against him in a hallway!" I accused, pointing a finger at her.

Her mouth popped open. "How did you know?"

"Has everyone been getting naked with Maxon?" Elise asked, horrified.

"We weren't naked!" I shouted.

"Okay," Kriss said, putting out her arms. "We need to clear this up. Who has done what with Maxon?"

Everyone was quiet for a moment, not wanting to speak up first.

"I've kissed him," Elise said. "Three times, but that's it."

"I haven't kissed him at all," Kriss confessed. "But that's by my own choosing. He would kiss me if I'd let him."

"Really? Not once?" Celeste asked, shocked.

"Not once."

"Well, I've kissed him plenty." Celeste flipped her hair, deciding to be proud instead of embarrassed. "The best was in the hallway one night." She eyed me. "We kept whispering about how exciting it was that we might get caught."

Finally all eyes were on me. I thought of the king's words, suggesting that maybe the other girls were being much more promiscuous than I was prepared to be. But now I knew it was one more weapon in his arsenal, a way to make me feel insignificant. I came clean.

"I was Maxon's first kiss, not Olivia. I didn't want anyone to know. And we've had a few . . . more intimate moments, and one of those times Maxon's shirt came off."

"Came off? Like it magically flew over his head?" Celeste pressed.

"He took it off," I admitted.

Not satisfied, Celeste pushed on. "He took it off or *you* took it off?"

"I guess we both did."

After a charged moment, Kriss started again. "Okay, so

now we all know where we stand."

"And where is that?" Elise asked.

No one answered.

"I just want to say . . . ," I started. "All of those moments were really important to me, and I care about Maxon."

"Are you implying that we don't?" Celeste barked.

"I know that *you* don't."

"How dare you?"

"Celeste, it's no secret that you want someone with power. I'm willing to bet you like Maxon well enough, but you're not in love with him. You're shooting for the crown."

Without denying it, she turned on Elise. "What about this one? I've never seen a speck of emotion out of you!"

"I'm reserved. You should try it sometime," Elise fired back quickly. Seeing a spark of anger in Elise made me like her more. "In my family, all the marriages are arranged. I knew what was coming for me, and that's all this is. I may not be head over heels for Maxon, but I respect him. Love can come later."

Sympathetically, Kriss spoke. "That actually sounds kind of sad, Elise."

"It's not. There are bigger things than love."

We stared at Elise, her words echoing. I fought for my family out of love, and for Aspen, too. And now, though it scared me to think it, I was sure that all my actions where Maxon was concerned—even when they were hopelessly stupid—were driven by that feeling. Still, what if there was something more important here than that?

"Well, I'll say it: I love him," Kriss blurted. "I love him, and I want him to marry me."

Snapped back into the discussion at hand, I ached to melt into the carpet. What had I started?

"All right, America, fess up," Celeste demanded.

I froze, breathing shallowly. It took me a moment to find the right words.

"Maxon knows how I feel, and that's all that matters."

She rolled her eyes at my answer but didn't press any further. No doubt she was worried I would do the same to her if she did.

We stood there, looking at one another. The Selection had been going on for months, and now we could finally see the real lines of competition. We'd all gotten a peek into everyone else's relationship with Maxon—at least one aspect of it—and could look at them side by side.

Moments later the queen walked in, wishing us a good morning. After curtsying to her, we all retreated. Into corners, into ourselves. Maybe it was always supposed to come to this. There were four girls and one prince, and three of us would be leaving soon with little more than an interesting story of how we spent our fall.

CHAPTER 5

I WAS WRINGING MY HANDS as I paced the downstairs library, trying to put the words together in my head. I knew I needed to explain what had just happened to Maxon before he heard about it from the other girls, but that didn't mean I was looking forward to the conversation.

"Knock, knock," he said, coming in. He took in my worried expression. "What's wrong?"

"Don't get mad," I warned as he approached.

His pace slowed, and the concerned look on his face became guarded instead. "I'll try."

"The girls know I saw you without your shirt on." I saw the question coming to his lips. "I didn't say anything about your back," I vowed. "I wanted to, because now they just think we were in the middle of some big make-out fest."

He smiled. "It did end up that way."

"Don't joke, Maxon! They hate me right now."

The light didn't leave his eyes as he hugged me. "If it's any consolation, I'm not mad. So long as you kept my secret, I don't mind. Though I am a little shocked you told them. How did it even come up?"

I buried my head in his chest. "I don't think I can tell you."

"Hmm." His thumb rubbed up and down my back. "I thought we were supposed to be working on our trust."

"We are. I'm asking you to trust that this will only get worse if I tell you." Maybe I was wrong, but I was pretty sure confessing to Maxon that we were checking out half-dressed, sweaty guards would get us all into some kind of trouble.

"Okay," he finally said. "The girls know you've seen me partly undressed. Anything else?"

I hesitated. "They know I was your first kiss. And I know everything you have and haven't done with them."

He pulled back. "What?"

"After I let the whole shirtless thing slip, there was a lot of finger-pointing, and everyone came clean. I know you've spent plenty of time kissing Celeste and that you would have kissed Kriss long before now if she would have let you. It all came out."

He wiped his hand over his face, taking a few paces as he processed this. "So I have absolutely no privacy anymore? None? Because the four of you had to check scores with each other?" His frustration was clear.

"You know, for someone concerned with honesty, you ought to be grateful."

He stopped and stared. "I beg your pardon?"

"Everything is out in the open now. We all have a pretty good idea of where we stand, and I, for one, am thankful."

He rolled his eyes. "Thankful?"

"If you had told me that Celeste and I were at about the same point with you physically, I would never have tried to come on to you like I did last night. Do you know how humiliated I was?"

He scoffed and started pacing again. "Please, America, you've said and done so many foolish things, I'm surprised you can even be embarrassed anymore."

Maybe it was because I had been raised with less of an articulate education, but it took a second for the full impact of his words to hit me. Maxon had always liked me, or so he'd said. I knew it was against the better judgment of other people. Was it also against his?

"I'll go then," I said quietly, unable to look him in the eye. "Sorry I let the whole shirt thing out." I started walking away, feeling so small I wondered if he even noticed.

"Come on, America. I didn't mean it like—"

"No, it's fine," I mumbled. "I'll watch my words better."

I made my way upstairs, unsure of whether I wanted Maxon to come after me or not. He didn't.

When I got to my room, Anne, Mary, and Lucy were in

there, changing my sheets and dusting the shelves.

"Hello, my lady," Anne greeted. "Would you like some tea?"

"No, I'm just going to sit on the balcony for a moment. If any visitors come, tell them I'm resting."

Anne frowned a bit but nodded. "Of course."

I spent some time taking in the fresh air, then went over the assigned reading Silvia had prepared for us. I took a short nap and played my violin for a little while. So long as I could avoid the other girls and Maxon, I really didn't care what I was doing.

With the king away, we were allowed to take our meals in our rooms, so I did. Halfway through my lemon-and-pepper chicken, a knock came at the door. Maybe I was being paranoid, but I was sure it was Maxon. There was no way I could see him right now. I grabbed Mary and Anne and headed to the bathroom.

"Lucy," I whispered. "Tell him I'm taking a bath."

"Him? A bath?"

"Yes. Don't let him in," I instructed.

"What's this all about?" Anne asked as I closed the door, pressing my ear up against it.

"Can you hear anything?" I asked.

They both put their ears to the door, too, waiting to see if something intelligible came through.

I heard Lucy's muffled voice, but then I put my ear to the crack of the door and the following conversation was much clearer.

"She's in the bath, Your Majesty," Lucy answered calmly. It *was* Maxon.

"Oh. I was hoping she'd be eating still. I thought maybe I could have my dinner with her."

"She decided to take a bath before she ate." There was a tiny waver in her voice, uncomfortable with being dishonest.

Come on, Lucy. Hold it together.

"I see. Well, maybe you could have her send for me when she's done. I'd like to speak with her."

"Umm . . . it might be a very long bath, Your Majesty."

Maxon paused. "Oh. Very well. Then could you please let her know I came by and tell her to send for me if she'd like to talk. Tell her not to worry about the hour; I'll come."

"Yes, sir."

It was quiet for a long time, and I was starting to think he had left.

"Um, thank you," he said finally. "Good night."

"Good night, Your Majesty."

I hid for a few seconds longer to make sure he was gone. When I came out, Lucy was still standing by the door. I looked at all my maids, seeing the questions in their eyes.

"I just want to be alone tonight," I said vaguely. "In fact, I think I'm ready to wind down. If you could take my dinner tray, I'm going to get ready for bed."

"Do you want one of us to stay?" Mary asked. "In case you decide to send for the prince?"

I could see the hope in their eyes, but I had to let them down.

"No, I just need some rest. I'll see Maxon in the morning."

It was strange tucking myself into bed, knowing something was hanging between Maxon and me, but I didn't know how to talk to him right now. It didn't make sense. We'd already been through so many ups and downs together, so many attempts to make this relationship real; but it was clear that if that was going to happen, we still had a very long way to go.

I was gruffly awoken before dawn. The light from the hallway flooded my room, and I rubbed my eyes as a guard entered.

"Lady America, wake up, please," he said.

"What's wrong?" I asked, yawning.

"There's an emergency. We need you downstairs."

At once my blood turned cold. My family was dead; I knew it. We'd sent guards; we'd warned those at home this was possible, but the rebels were too much. The same thing had happened to Natalie. She left the Selection an only child after the rebels killed her little sister. None of our families was safe anymore.

I threw off the covers and grabbed my robe and slippers. I ran down the hall and stairs as quickly as I could, nearly slipping twice on the steps.

When I got to the first floor, Maxon was there, talking intently to a guard. I ran up to him, forgetting about everything from the last two days.

"Are they all right?" I asked, trying not to cry. "How bad is it?"

"What?" he asked, taking me in for an unexpected hug.

"My parents, my brothers and sisters. Are they okay?"

Quickly Maxon held me at arm's length and looked me in the eye. "They're fine, America. I'm sorry; I should have realized that's what you would have thought of first."

I nearly started weeping I was so relieved.

Maxon seemed a bit confused as he continued. "There are rebels in the palace."

"What?" I shrieked. "Why aren't we hiding?"

"They're not here to attack."

"Then why *are* they here?"

He sighed. "It's only two rebels from the Northern camp. They're unarmed, and they're specifically asking to speak to me . . . and to you."

"Why me?"

"I'm not sure; but I'm going to talk to them, so I thought I would give you the chance to speak to them as well."

I looked down at myself and ran my hand over my hair. "I'm in my nightgown."

He smiled. "I know, but this is very informal. It's fine."

"Do *you* want me to talk to them?"

"That is truly up to you, but I'm curious as to why they want to speak with you in particular. I'm not sure they'll tell me if you're not there."

I nodded, weighing this in my head. I wasn't sure I wanted to talk to rebels. Unarmed or not, they were probably far deadlier than I could ever be. But if Maxon thought I could do it, maybe I should. . . .

"Okay," I said, pulling myself up. "Okay."

"You won't get hurt, America. I promise." His hand was still on mine, and he gave my fingers a tiny squeeze. He turned to the guard. "Lead the way. Keep your holster unlocked, just in case."

"Of course, Your Majesty," he answered, and escorted us around the corner into the Great Room, where two people were standing, surrounded by more guards.

It took me seconds to find Aspen in the crowd.

"Could you call off your dogs?" one of the rebels asked. He was tall and slim and blond. His boots were covered in mud, and his outfit looked like something a Seven might wear: a pair of heavy pants taken in to fit him closely and a patched-up shirt beneath a beaten leather jacket. A rusting compass on a long chain swung around his neck, moving as he shifted. He looked rugged without being terrifying, which wasn't what I'd expected.

Even more unexpected was that his companion was a girl. She, too, wore boots; but as if she was trying to be resourceful and fashionable at the same time, she had on leggings and a skirt constructed from the same material as the male's pants. Her hip jutted out confidently to the side despite her being surrounded by guards. Even if I hadn't recognized her face, I would have remembered her jacket. Denim and cropped, covered with what looked like dozens of embroidered flowers.

Making sure I remembered who she was, she gave me a little curtsy. I made a sound that was somewhere between a laugh and a gasp.

"What's wrong?" Maxon asked.

"Later," I whispered.

Confused but calm, he gave me a comforting squeeze and focused again on our guests.

"We've come to speak to you in peace," the man said. "We are unarmed, and your guards have searched us. I know asking for privacy would be inappropriate, but we have things to discuss with you that no one else should hear."

"What about America?" Maxon asked.

"We want to speak with her as well."

"To what end?"

"Again," the young man said, almost cockily, "we need to be out of earshot of these guys." He playfully gestured around the room.

"If you think you can harm her—"

"I know you're skeptical of us, and for good reason, but we have no cause to hurt either of you. We want to talk."

Maxon deliberated for a minute. "You," he said, looking toward one of the guards, "pull down one of the tables and four chairs. Then all of you, please stay back to give our guests some room."

The guards obeyed, and we were all silent for a few uncomfortable minutes. When the table was finally down from the stack and in the corner with two chairs on either side, Maxon gestured that the pair should join us over there.

As we walked, the guards stepped back, wordlessly forming a perimeter around the room and focusing their eyes on the two rebels as if they were prepared to fire at a second's notice.

As we reached the table, the male stuck out his hand. "Don't you think introductions are in order?"

Maxon eyed him warily but then relented. "Maxon Schreave, your sovereign."

The young man chuckled. "Honored, sir."

"And you are?"

"Mr. August Illéa, at your service."

CHAPTER 6

MAXON AND I LOOKED AT each other, then back to the rebels.

"You heard me right. I'm an Illéa. And by birth, too. This one will be by marriage sooner or later," August said, nodding to the girl.

"Georgia Whitaker," she said. "And of course, we know all about you, America."

She gave me another smile, and I returned it. I wasn't sure I trusted her, but I certainly didn't hate her.

"So Father was right." Maxon sighed. I looked over to him, confused. Maxon knew there were direct descendants of Gregory Illéa walking around? "He said you'd come for the crown one day."

"I don't want your crown," August assured us.

"Good, because I intend to lead this country," Maxon shot back. "I've been raised for it, and if you think you can come in here claiming to be Gregory's great-great-grandson—"

"I don't want your crown, Maxon! Destroying the monarchy is more up the Southern rebels' alley. We have other goals." August sat at the table, leaning back in his seat. Then as if it was his home we'd stepped into, he swept his arm across the chairs, inviting us to sit.

Maxon and I eyed each other again and joined him, Georgia following quickly. August looked at us awhile, either studying us or trying to decide where to start.

Maxon, perhaps reminding us who was in charge, broke the tension. "Would you like some tea or coffee?"

Georgia lit up. "Coffee?"

In spite of himself, Maxon smiled at her enthusiasm and turned behind him to get a guard's attention. "Could you have one of the maids bring some coffee, please? For goodness' sake, make sure it's strong." Then he focused again on August.

"I can't begin to imagine what you want from me. It seems you made a point to come while the palace was asleep, and I'm guessing you'd like to keep this visit as secretive as possible. Say what you must. I can't promise to give you what you want, but I will listen."

August nodded and leaned forward. "We've been looking for Gregory's diaries for decades. We knew they existed long ago and had a recent confirmation from a source I cannot reveal." August looked at me. "It wasn't your presentation on the *Report* that gave it away, just so you know."

I sighed in relief. The second he mentioned the diaries,

I began silently cursing myself and bracing for later when Maxon would add this to the list of stupid things I'd done.

"We have never desired to take down the monarchy," he said to Maxon. "Even though it came about in a very corrupt way, we have no problem with having a sovereign leader, particularly if that leader is you."

Maxon was still, but I could sense his pride. "Thank you."

"What we would like are other things, specific freedoms. We want nominated officials, and we want to end the castes." August said all this as if it was easy. If he'd seen my presentation get cut off on the *Report*, he ought to know better.

"You act like I'm already the king," Maxon answered in frustration. "Even if it was possible, I can't simply give you what you're asking for."

"But you're open to the idea?"

Maxon raised his hands and dropped them to the table. "What I'm open to is irrelevant at the moment. I am not king."

August sighed, looking over to Georgia. They seemed to communicate wordlessly, and I was impressed at their easy intimacy. Here they were, in a very tense situation—one they'd entered maybe suspecting they wouldn't be able to get out of—and their feelings for each other were so close to the surface.

"Speaking of kings," Maxon added, "why don't you explain to America who you are. I'm sure you'd do a better job than I would."

I knew this was a way for Maxon to stall, to think of a

way to get control of this situation, but I didn't mind. I was dying to understand.

August smiled humorlessly. "That *is* an interesting story," he promised, the vibrancy in his voice hinting at how exciting his tale would be. "As you know, Gregory had three children: Katherine, Spencer, and Damon. Katherine was married off to a prince, Spencer died, and Damon was the one who inherited the throne. Then when Damon's son, Justin, died, his cousin Porter Schreave became prince, marrying Justin's young widow, who had won the Selection barely three years earlier. And now the Schreaves are the royal family. No more Illéas ought to exist. But we do."

"We?" Maxon asked, his tone calculated, like he was hoping for numbers.

August only nodded. The click of heels announced that the maid was coming. Maxon put a finger to his lips, like August would dare to say more with her in hearing distance. The maid set down the tray and poured coffee for all of us. Georgia's hands were on her cup immediately, waiting for it to be filled. I didn't really care for coffee—it was too bitter for my tastes—but I knew it would help me wake up, so I braced myself to take a drink.

Before I could even sip, Maxon slid the bowl of sugar in front of me. Like he knew.

"You were saying?" Maxon prompted, taking his coffee black.

"Spencer didn't die," August said flatly. "He knew what his father had done to take over the country, he knew his older sister had basically been sold into marriage, and he knew the same was expected of him. He couldn't do it, so he ran."

"Where did he go?" I asked, speaking for the first time.

"He hid with relatives and friends, eventually making a camp with some like-minded people in the north. It's colder up there, wetter, and so hard to navigate that no one tries. We live there quietly most of the time."

Georgia nudged him, her face a little shocked.

August came to his senses. "I suppose I've now given you directions to invade us yourself. I want to remind you that we've never killed any of your officers or staff, and we avoid injuring them at all costs. All we ever wanted was to put an end to the castes. To do that we needed proof that Gregory was the man we'd always been told he was. We have that now, and America hinted at it enough that we feel we could exploit that if we wanted to. We really don't though. Not if we don't have to."

Maxon took a deep swig and set down his cup. "I'm honestly not sure what I'm supposed to do with this information. You're a direct descendant of Gregory Illéa, but you don't want the crown. You've come looking for things only the king could provide, but you asked for an audience with me and one of the Elite. My father isn't even here."

"We know," August said. "This was deliberate timing."

Maxon huffed. "If you don't want the crown and only want things I can't give you, why are you here?"

August and Georgia looked at each other, perhaps preparing themselves for their biggest request yet.

"We came to ask you for these things because we know you're a reasonable man. We've watched you all your life, and we can see it in your eyes. I can see it now."

I tried to be inconspicuous as I studied Maxon's reaction to these words.

"You don't like the castes either. You don't like the way your father holds the country under his thumb. You don't want to fight wars you know are nothing more than a distraction. More than anything, you want peace during your lifetime.

"We're guessing that once you're king, things could really change. And we've been waiting a long time for that. We're prepared to wait longer. The Northern rebels are willing to give you our word never to attack the palace again and to do our best to stop or slow the Southern rebels. We see so much that you can't from behind these walls. We would swear our allegiance to you, without question, if you would be willing to give us a sign of your readiness to work with us toward a future that would finally give the people of Illéa a chance to live their own lives."

Maxon didn't seem to know what to say, so I spoke up.

"What do the Southern rebels want anyway? Just to kill us all?"

August moved his head in a motion that was neither a shake nor a nod. "That's part of it, sure, but only so they'll have no one to combat them. Too much of the population is oppressed, and this growing cell has bought in to the idea that they could rule the country themselves. America, you're a Five; I know you've seen your share of people who hate the monarchy."

Maxon discreetly moved his eyes my way. I gave a brief nod.

"Of course you have. Because when you're on the bottom, your only choice is to blame the top. In this case, they've got good reason—after all, it was a One who sentenced them to their lives with no real hope for bettering them. Those in charge of the Southern rebels have convinced their disciples that the way to get back what they think is theirs is to take it from the monarchy. But I've had people defect from the Southerner rebel leadership and end up with me. I know for a fact that once the Southerners get control, they have no intention of sharing the wealth. When in history has that ever happened?

"Their plan is to obliterate what Illéa has, take over, make a bunch of promises, and leave everyone in the same place they are now. For most people, I'm sure it'll get worse. The Sixes and Sevens won't move up, except for a select few the rebels will manipulate for the sake of the show. Twos and Threes will have everything stripped from them. It'll make a bunch of people feel vindicated, but it won't fix anything.

"If there are no pop stars churning out those mind-numbing songs, then there are no musicians in the booths backing them up, no clerks running back and forth with tapes, no shop owners selling the music. Taking out one person at the top destroys thousands at the bottom."

August paused for a moment, looking consumed with

worry. "It'll be Gregory all over again, only worse. The Southerners are prepared to be far more cutthroat than you could ever be, and the chances of the country bouncing back are slim. It'll be the same old oppression under a brand-new name . . . and your people will suffer like never before." He looked into Maxon's eyes. They seemed to have some understanding between them, something that maybe came from being born to lead.

"All we need is a sign, and we'll do everything we can to help you change things, peacefully and fairly. Your people deserve a chance."

Maxon looked at the table. I couldn't imagine the debate in his head. "What kind of sign?" he asked hesitantly. "Money?"

"No," August said, nearly laughing. "We have more funds than you might guess."

"How is that possible?"

"Donations," he replied simply.

Maxon nodded, but I was surprised. Donations meant there were people—who knew how many—supporting them. How big was the Northern rebel force when those supporters were taken into account? How much of the country was asking for exactly what these two had come here requesting?

"If not money," Maxon said finally, "what do you want?"

August flicked his head toward me. "Pick her."

I buried my face in my hands, knowing how Maxon would take this.

There was a long moment of silence before he lost his temper. "I will not have anyone else telling me who I can and cannot marry! This is my life you're playing games with!"

I looked up in time to see August stand across the table. "And the palace has been playing with other people's lives for years. Grow up, Maxon. You're the prince. You want your damn crown, then keep it. But responsibilities come with that privilege."

Guards were cautiously walking our way, alerted by Maxon's tone and August's aggressive stance. Certainly they could hear everything by now.

Maxon stood to counter him. "You don't get to choose my wife. End of story."

August, completely undeterred, stepped back and crossed his arms. "Fine! We have another option if this one doesn't work."

"Who?"

August rolled his eyes. "As if I would tell you, given how calmly you reacted the first time."

"Come off it."

"This one or that one doesn't really matter. We just need to know you'll have a partner who'll be on the same page for this plan."

"My name is America," I said fiercely, standing and looking him straight in the eye, "not *This One*. I'm not some toy in your little revolution. You keep talking about everyone in Illéa having a chance at the life they want. What about me? What about my future? Do I not count in that plan?"

I searched their faces, waiting for an answer. They were silent. I noticed the guards, surrounding us, on edge.

I lowered my voice. "I'm all for killing off the castes, but I'm not something to be played with. If you're looking for a pawn, there's one girl upstairs so in love with him, she'd do anything you asked if it meant a proposal at the end of the day. And the other two . . . between duty and prestige, they'd be game, too. Go get one of them."

Without waiting to be excused, I turned to leave, storming away as best I could in a robe and slippers.

"America! Wait!" Georgia called. I got out the door before she caught up with me. "Stop for a minute."

"What?"

"We're sorry. We thought you two were in love. We didn't realize we were asking for something he'd be opposed to. We were sure he'd be on board."

"You don't understand. He's so tired of being bullied and bossed around. You have no idea what he's been through." I felt the tears rising, and I blinked them away, focusing on the designs on Georgia's jacket.

"I know more than you think," she said. "Maybe not everything, but a lot. We've been watching the Selection very closely, and it looks like you two get along so well. He seems so happy around you. And then . . . we know about how you rescued your maids."

It took me a second to realize what that meant. Who was watching us on their behalf?

"And we saw what you did for Marlee. We saw you fight.

And then your presentation a few days ago." She stopped to laugh. "That took some guts. We could use a girl with guts."

I shook my head. "I wasn't trying to be a hero. Most of the time, I don't feel anything close to brave."

"So? It doesn't really matter how you feel about your character; it just matters what you do with it. You, more than the others, act on what's right before thinking about what it will mean for yourself. Maxon has some great candidates up there, but they won't get their hands dirty to make things better. Not like you."

"A lot of that was selfish. Marlee was important to me, and so are my maids."

She stepped closer. "But didn't those actions come with consequences?"

"Yes."

"And you probably knew they would. But you acted for those who couldn't speak up for themselves. That's special, America."

This was different praise from what I was used to. I could handle my dad telling me I was a beautiful singer or Aspen saying I was the prettiest thing he'd ever seen . . . but this? It was almost overwhelming.

"Honestly, with some of the stuff you've done, I can't believe the king let you stay. The whole thing on the *Report* . . ." She let out a whistle.

I laughed. "He was so angry."

"I was shocked you made it out alive!"

"It was by the skin of my teeth, let me tell you. And most

days I feel like I'm only seconds away from being kicked out."

"But Maxon likes you, right? The way he guards you . . ."

I shrugged. "There are days when I feel so sure and then others where I have no idea. Today isn't a good day. Neither was yesterday. Or the day before, if I'm honest."

She nodded. "Well, we're pulling for you, all the same."

"Me and someone else," I corrected.

"True."

Again she gave no clue as to her other favorite.

"What was the deal with that curtsy in the woods? Just messing with me?" I asked.

She smiled. "I know it might not seem like it by the way we act sometimes, but we really do care about the royal family. If we lose them, the Southern rebels will win. If they get true control . . . well, you heard August." She shook her head. "Anyway, I'd felt certain I was looking at my future queen, so I figured the least you deserved was a curtsy."

Her reasoning was so silly, it made me laugh again. "I can't tell you how nice it is to talk to a girl I'm not competing with."

"Getting a bit old?" she asked with a sympathetic expression.

"As it's gotten smaller, it's gotten worse. I mean, I knew it would, but . . . it feels like it's moving away from trying to be the girl that Maxon would pick to making sure the *other* girls won't be the one he picks. I don't know if that makes sense."

She nodded. "It does. But, hey, this is what you signed up for."

I chuckled. "Actually, I didn't. I was sort of . . . encouraged to put my name in. I didn't want to be a princess."

"Really?"

"Really."

She smiled. "Not wanting the crown means you're probably the best person to have it."

I stared at her, convinced by her wide eyes that she believed that without a doubt. I hoped to ask more, but Maxon and August came out of the Great Room, looking surprisingly calm. A single guard followed at a distance. August was looking at Georgia like it had hurt him to be away from her even for a few minutes. Maybe that was the only reason she was here today.

"Are you okay, America?" Maxon asked.

"Yes." My ability to look him in the eye had disappeared again.

"You should go get ready for the day," he commented. "The guards have been sworn to secrecy, and I'd appreciate the same from you."

"Of course."

He seemed displeased with my coolness, but how else was I supposed to act right now?

"Mr. Illéa, it was a pleasure. We'll talk again soon." Maxon held out his hand. August took it easily.

"If there's anything you need, don't hesitate to ask. We

truly are on your side, Your Majesty."

"Thank you."

"Georgia, let's go. Some of these guards look a little too trigger-happy."

She chuckled. "See you around, America."

I nodded, sure I'd never see her again and sad because of it. She walked past Maxon and slid her hand into August's. With a guard in tow, they walked out the gaping doors of the palace, leaving Maxon and me alone in the foyer.

His eyes rose to mine. I mumbled something and pointed upstairs, moving as I did so. His quick objection to choosing me only drove home the pain of his words yesterday in the library. I thought after the safe room there was some kind of understanding between us. But it seemed as if everything had gotten even more muddled than it had been when I was still trying to decide how much I liked Maxon in the first place.

I didn't know what this meant for us. Or if there was still an *us* worth worrying about.

CHAPTER 7

FOR AS FAST AS I was at getting to my room, Aspen was faster. I shouldn't have been surprised. Aspen knew the palace so well, this was probably nothing to him now.

"Hey," I started, a little unsure of what to say.

Quickly, he wrapped his arms around me, then pulled away. "That's my girl."

I smiled. "Yeah?"

"You put 'em in their place, Mer." Risking his life, Aspen ran a thumb down my cheek. "You do deserve to be happy. We all do."

"Thank you."

Smiling, he dropped his hand to move the bracelet Maxon had brought me from New Asia and reached underneath to touch the one I'd made of a button he'd given me. His eyes looked sad as he stared at our little memento.

"We'll talk soon. Really talk. There's a lot we need to work out."

With that, Aspen moved down the hall. I sighed and put my head in my hands. Did he assume my rejection meant that I was pushing Maxon away for good? Did he think I wanted to rekindle things with him?

Then again, *hadn't* I just pushed Maxon away?

Hadn't I thought yesterday that Aspen needed to stay in my life?

So then why did everything feel awful?

The mood in the Women's Room was dark. Queen Amberly sat writing her letters, and from time to time, I'd notice her peek up to take in the four of us. After yesterday, we were avoiding doing anything that might require us to interact with one another. Celeste had a pile of magazines and was stretched out on the couch. In a very wise move, Kriss had taken her journal and settled in to write, once again positioning herself near the queen. Why hadn't I thought of that? Elise had gotten out a collection of drawing pencils and was working on something by the window. I was in a wide chair near the door, reading a book.

As it was, we didn't even have to make eye contact.

I tried to concentrate on the words in front of me, but mostly I wondered who the Northern rebels wanted as princess if they couldn't have me. Celeste was very popular, and it would be easy to get people to follow her. I wondered if they were aware of how manipulative she could be. If they knew things about me, maybe they did. Was there more to Celeste than I'd guessed?

Kriss was sweet, and according to that poll a while back, she was one of the people's favorites. Her family didn't have much sway, but she was more of a princess than the rest of us. She had that air about her. Maybe that was her big draw; she wasn't perfect, but she was so lovable. There were days when even I wanted to follow Kriss.

The one I suspected the least was Elise. She'd admitted she didn't love Maxon and that she was here because of duty. I genuinely thought that when she spoke of duty she meant to her family or to her New Asian roots, not to the Northern rebels. Besides that, she was so stoic and calm. There was nothing close to rebellious about her.

And that was why I was suddenly positive she was their favorite. She seemed to be trying the least to compete and had openly admitted her coolness toward Maxon. Maybe she didn't *have* to try because, at the end of the day, she had a quiet army of supporters to put her under the crown anyway.

"That's it," the queen said suddenly. "All of you, come here." She pushed her little table away and stood as we all walked over nervously.

"Something's wrong. What is it?" she demanded.

We looked at one another, none of us wanting to explain. Finally too-perfect Kriss piped up.

"Your Majesty, we've just suddenly realized how intense this competition is. We're a bit more aware of where we each stand with the prince, and it's difficult to let it sink in and still want to chat right now."

The queen nodded in understanding. "How often do you all think of Natalie?" she asked. Natalie had been gone barely a week. I thought of her nearly every day. I also thought of Marlee all the time, and some of the other girls would pop into my head at random as well.

"Always," Elise said quietly. "She was so lighthearted."

A smile came to her lips as she said this. I had always assumed that Natalie got on Elise's nerves since she was so reserved and Natalie was so spacey. But maybe it was one of those opposites-attract kinds of friendships.

"Sometimes she would laugh over the littlest thing," Kriss added. "It was contagious."

"Exactly," the queen said. "I've been where you are, and I know how difficult it is. You second guess the things you do; you second guess everything he does. You wonder over every conversation, trying to read into the breaths between sentences. It's exhausting."

It was as though I could see a weight lifting from everyone. Someone got us.

"But know this: as much tension as you feel with one another now, you will ache every time one of you leaves. No one will ever understand this experience like the other girls who have been through it, the Elite especially. You may fight, but that's what sisters do. These girls," she said, pointing to each of us, "will be the ones you call nearly every day for the first year, terrified of making a mistake and needing their support. When you have parties, these are the names you'll put at the top of your guest lists, just under the names of your family members. Because that's what you are now. You'll never lose these relationships."

We looked at one another. If I was the princess and something was happening where I needed a rational perspective, I'd call Elise first. If I was fighting with Maxon, Kriss would remind me of every good thing about him. And Celeste . . . well, I wasn't so sure, but if anyone was ever going to tell me to toughen up about something, it would be her.

"So take your time," she advised. "Adjust to where you are. And let it go. You don't choose him; he chooses you. There's no point in hating the others for that."

"Do you know who he wants the most?" Celeste asked. And for the first time, I heard worry in her voice.

"I don't," Queen Amberly confessed. "Sometimes I think I could guess, but I don't pretend to understand everything Maxon feels. I know who the king would choose, but that's about it."

"Who would you choose?" I asked, then cursed myself for being so blunt.

She smiled kindly. "I honestly haven't let myself think about it. It would break my heart to start loving one of you like a daughter and then lose you. I couldn't bear it."

I lowered my eyes, not sure if those words were meant to be a comfort or not.

"I will say I'd be happy to have any of you in my family." I looked up and watched as she took the time to meet each set of eyes. "For now, there's work to do."

We stood there silently, soaking in her wisdom. I'd never taken the time to look at the competitors in the last Selection, to find their pictures or anything. I knew a handful of names, mostly because older women would drop them into conversations when I sang at parties. It was never that important to me; we already had a queen, and even as a girl, the possibility of becoming a princess never crossed my mind. But now I wondered how many of the women who showed up to visit the queen or came for Halloween were her former competition, now her closest friends.

Celeste walked away first, heading back to the comfort of the couch. It didn't seem as if Queen Amberly's words meant much to her. For some reason that was the tipping point for me. Everything from the last few days crashed back onto my heart, and I could feel it was seconds away from cracking.

I curtsied. "Excuse me, please," I mumbled, before moving swiftly to the door. I didn't have a plan. Maybe I could go sit in the bathroom for a minute or tuck myself away in one of the numerous parlors downstairs. Maybe I would just go to my room and cry my eyes out.

Unfortunately, it looked like the universe was plotting against me. Just outside the Women's Room, Maxon was pacing back and forth, looking as if he was trying to solve a riddle. Before I could hide somewhere, he saw me.

Of everything I wanted to do right now, this was the last thing on my list.

"I was debating asking you to come out," he said.

"What do you need?" I answered shortly.

Maxon stood there, still working up the nerve to say something that was obviously driving him crazy. "So there's one girl who loves me beyond reason?"

I crossed my arms. After the last few days, I should have seen his change of heart coming. "Yes."

"Not two?"

I looked up at him, almost irritated that he needed me to explain. *Don't you already know how I feel?* I wanted to scream. *Don't you remember the safe room?*

But, honestly, I needed some confirmation right now, too. What had happened to make me so unsure so quickly?

The king. His insinuations about what the other girls had done, his praise of their merits made me feel small. And it was compounded by all my missteps with Maxon this week. The only way we would have ever been brought together was because of the Selection; but it seemed that as long as it went on, there was no way for anything to feel certain.

"You told me you didn't trust me," I accused. "The other day you made a point of humiliating me, and yesterday you basically said I was an embarrassment. And not a few hours ago, the suggestion of marrying me sent you into a rage. Forgive me for not feeling so secure in our relationship right now."

"You forget that I've never done this, America," he said passionately, but without any anger. "You have someone to compare me to. I don't even know how to have a typical relationship, and I only get one chance. You've had at least two. I'm going to make mistakes."

"I don't mind mistakes," I shot back. "I mind the uncertainty. Most of the time I can't tell what's going on."

He was quiet for a moment, and I realized that we'd come to a very serious crossroad. We'd implied so many things, but we couldn't go on like this for much longer. Even if we ended up together, these moments of insecurity would haunt us.

"We keep doing this," I breathed, exhausted with this game. "We get close and then something happens and it falls apart, and you never seem to be able to make a decision. If you want me as much as you've always claimed to, why isn't this over?"

Even though I'd accused him of not caring about me at all, his frustration melted into sadness. "Because half the time I've been sure you loved someone else and the other half I've doubted you could love me at all," he answered, making me feel positively awful.

"Like I haven't had my own reasons to doubt? You treat Kriss like she's heaven on earth, and then I catch you with Celeste—"

"I explained that."

"Yes, but it still hurt to see."

"Well, it hurts me to see how quickly you shut down. Where does that even come from?"

"I don't know, but maybe you should stop thinking about me for a while."

The silence was abrupt.

"What does that mean?"

I shrugged. "There are three other girls here. If you're so worried about your one shot, you might want to make sure you're not wasting it on me."

I walked away, angry with Maxon for making me feel this way . . . and angry with myself for making things so much worse.

CHAPTER 8

I WATCHED AS THE PALACE was transformed. Almost overnight, lush Christmas trees lined the hallways of the first floor, garlands were strung down the stairways, and all the floral arrangements were changed to include holly or mistletoe. The strange thing was, if I opened my window, it still felt like the edge of summer outside. I wondered if the palace could somehow manufacture snow. Maybe if I asked Maxon, he'd look into it.

Then again, maybe not.

Days passed. I tried not to be upset that Maxon was doing exactly what I'd asked, but as the space between us grew icy, I regretted my pride. I wondered if this was always bound to happen. Was I destined to say the wrong thing, make the wrong choice? Even if Maxon was what I wanted, I was never going to get myself together long enough for it to be real.

The whole thing just felt tired; it was the same problem I'd been facing since Aspen walked through the doorway of the palace. And I ached from it, from feeling so torn, so confused.

I'd taken to walking around the palace during the afternoons. With the gardens off-limits, the Women's Room day after day was too confining.

It was while I was walking that I felt the shift. As if some unseen trigger had set off everyone in the palace. The guards stood a bit stiller, and the maids walked a bit faster. Even I felt strange, like I wasn't quite so welcome here as I was only moments ago. Before I knew what it was I was feeling, the king rounded the corner, a small entourage behind him.

Then it all made perfect sense. His absence made the palace warmer, and now that he was home, we were all subject to his whims again. No wonder the Northern rebels were excited about Maxon.

I curtsied as the king approached. While he walked, he put up a hand, and the men behind him paused as he came close, leaving us with a small bubble of space in which to speak.

"Lady America. I see you're still here," he said, his smile and his words at odds with each other.

"Yes, Your Majesty."

"And how have you been in my absence?"

I smiled. "Silent."

"That's a good girl." He started to walk away but then remembered something and came back. "It was brought to my attention that of the girls left, you're the only one still receiving money for your participation. Elise gave hers up voluntarily almost immediately after the payments were stopped for the Twos and Threes."

That didn't surprise me. Elise was a Four, but her family owned high-end hotels. They weren't hurting for money the way the shopkeepers back in Carolina were.

"I think that should end," he announced, snapping me back into the moment.

My face fell.

"Unless, of course, you're here for a payout and not because you love my son." His eyes burned into me, daring me to challenge his decision.

"You're right," I said, hating the way the words felt in my mouth. "It's only fair."

I could see he was disappointed not to get more of a fight. "I'll see to it immediately."

He walked away, and I stood there, trying not to feel sorry for myself. Really, it was fair. How did it look that I was the only one getting checks? It would all end eventually anyway. Sighing, I headed toward my room. The least I could do was write home and warn them that the money wouldn't be coming anymore.

I opened my door, and, for the first time, I was completely ignored by my maids. Anne, Mary, and Lucy were in the back corner, hovering over a dress that they appeared to be working on, bickering about their progress.

"Lucy, you said you were going to finish this hem last night," Anne said. "You left early to do it."

"I know, I know. I got sidetracked. I can do it now." Her eyes were pleading. Lucy was already a bit sensitive, and I knew Anne's rigid manner sometimes got to her.

"You've been getting sidetracked an awful lot these last few days," Anne commented.

Mary held out her hands. "Calm down. Give me the dress before you mess it up."

"I'm sorry," Lucy said. "Just let me take it now, and I'll get it done."

"What's going on with you?" Anne demanded. "You've been acting so funny."

Lucy looked up at her, eyes frozen. Whatever her secret was, she looked terrified to share it.

I cleared my throat.

They whipped their heads in my direction, all curtsying in turn.

"I don't know what's going on," I said as I walked toward them, "but I highly doubt the queen's maids argue like that. Besides, we're wasting time if there's work to be done."

Anne, still angry, pointed her finger at Lucy. "But she—"

I silenced her with a small gesture of my hand, a bit surprised that it worked so easily.

"No arguing. Lucy, why don't you take that down to the workroom to finish, and we can all get some room to think."

Lucy happily scooped up the fabric, so grateful for the means to escape that she practically ran from the room. Anne watched her go, a full pout on her face. Mary looked worried but dutifully went to work without another word.

It took all of two minutes for me to realize that the mood in my room was too dreary for me to focus. I grabbed some paper and a pen and headed back downstairs. I wondered if I'd done the right thing, sparing Lucy. Maybe they'd all be fine if I'd let them air out whatever was happening. Perhaps my meddling would shake their resolve in helping me. I'd never really bossed them around like that before.

I paused outside the Women's Room. That didn't feel like the right place either. I moved down the main hallway, finding a little nook with a bench. That seemed nice. I ran into the library and picked up a book to lean on and went back to the nook, finding myself practically hidden by the large plant beside the bench. The wide window looked into the garden, and, for a minute, the palace didn't seem so small. I watched birds fly outside the window and tried to form the kindest way to tell my parents there wouldn't be any more checks.

"Maxon, can't we go on a real date? Somewhere outside the palace?" I recognized Kriss's voice immediately. Hmm. The Women's Room might not have been so full after all.

I could hear the smile in his voice as he answered. "I wish we could, sweetheart, but even if things were calm, that would be difficult."

"I want to see you somewhere where you're not the prince," she whined lovingly.

"Ah, but I'm the prince everywhere."

"You know what I mean."

"I do. I'm sorry I can't give that to you, really. I think it would be nice to see you somewhere where you weren't an Elite. But this is the life I live."

His voice grew a little sad.

"Would you regret it?" he asked. "For the rest of your life, it would be like this. Beautiful walls, but walls all the same. My mother scarcely leaves the palace more than once or twice a year." Through the thick leaves of the planted shrub, I watched as they passed me, completely unaware. "And if you think the public is intrusive now, it would be much worse when you're the only girl they're watching. I know your feelings for me run deep. I feel it every day. But what about the life that comes along with me? Do you want that?"

It seemed as if they'd stopped somewhere in the hallway, as Maxon's voice wasn't fading.

"Maxon Schreave," Kriss started, "you make it sound like it's a sacrifice for me to be here. Each day I'm *thankful* for being chosen. Sometimes I try to imagine what it would have been like if we'd never met. . . . I'd rather lose you now than have gone a lifetime without this."

Her voice was getting thick. I didn't think she was crying, but she was close.

"I need you to know I'd want you without the beautiful clothes and the gorgeous rooms. I'd want you without the crown, Maxon. I just want you."

Maxon was momentarily speechless, and I could imagine him holding her close or wiping away the tears that might have come by now.

"I can't tell you what it means to me to hear that. I've been dying for someone to tell me that I was what mattered," he confessed quietly.

"You are, Maxon."

There was another quiet moment between them.

"Maxon?"

"Yes?"

"I . . . I don't think I want to wait anymore."

Even though I knew I'd regret it, at those words I silently put down my paper and pen, slipped off my shoes, and scurried to the end of the hall. I peeked around and saw the back of Maxon's head as Kriss's hand slid just barely into the neck of his suit. Her hair fell to the side as they kissed, and, for her first, it seemed like it was going really well. Better than Maxon's, that was for sure.

I ducked back around the corner and heard her giggle a second later. Maxon let out a sigh that was half triumph and half relief. I walked to my seat quickly, angling myself toward the window again, just in case.

"When can we do that again?" she asked quietly.

"Hmm. How about in as much time as it takes to get from here to your room?"

Kriss's laugh faded as they moved down the hallway. I sat there for a minute, then I picked up my pen and paper, finding the words easily now.

Mom and Dad,

There's so much to do these days, I have to keep this short. In an effort to show my devotion to Maxon and not to the luxuries of being in the Elite, I've given up receiving payments for my participation. I realize this is short notice, but I'm sure with everything we've been given by now, there's not much more we could want for.

I hope you won't be too disappointed by this news. I miss you and hope we'll get to see each other again soon.

I love you all.

America

CHAPTER 9

THE *REPORT* WAS LACKING MATERIAL following what the public would see as a rather uneventful week. After the brief updates from the king on his visit to France, the floor was turned over to Gavril, who was now interviewing the remaining Elite in a casual manner about things that didn't seem to matter at this point in the competition.

Then again, the last time they'd asked us about something that *did* matter, I suggested dissolving the castes and nearly got thrown out of the competition.

"Lady Celeste, have you seen the princess's suite?" Gavril asked jovially.

I grinned to myself, grateful he didn't ask me the same question. Celeste's perfect smile managed to widen, and she flipped her hair over her shoulder playfully before answering.

"Well, Gavril, not yet. But I'm certainly hoping to earn the privilege. Of course, King Clarkson has provided us with the most beautiful accommodations, I can't imagine anything better than what we already have. The, um . . . the beds are so . . ."

Celeste stammered just a bit as her eyes caught two guards rushing into the studio. Our seats were arranged in such a way that I could see them as they ran to the king, but Kriss and Elise had their backs to the action. They both tried to turn their heads discreetly, but it did them no good.

"Luxurious. And it would be more than I could dream of to . . ." Celeste continued, not totally focused on her answer.

But it appeared she didn't need to be. The king stood and came over, cutting her off.

"Ladies and gentlemen, I apologize for the interruption, but this is very urgent." He clutched a piece of paper in one hand as he smoothed his tie with the other. He was composed as he spoke. "Since our country's birth, the rebel forces have been the bane of our society. Over the years, their means of attacking the palace, not to mention the common man, have become far more aggressive.

"It appears they have sunk to new lows. As you may well know, the four remaining young ladies of the Selection represent a wide range of castes. We have a Two, a Three, a Four, and a Five. We're honored to have such a varied group, but this has given a strange incentive to the rebels."

The king looked over his shoulder at us before continuing.

"We are prepared for attacks on the palace, and when the rebels attack the public, we intercede as best we can. And I would not worry you if I thought that I, as your king, could protect you, but . . ."

"The rebels are attacking by caste."

The words hung in the air. In an almost friendly gesture, Celeste and I shared a confused glance.

"They have wanted to end the monarchy for a long time. Recent attacks on the families of these young girls have shown the lengths that they're prepared to go to, and we've sent guards from the palace to protect the Elite's loved ones. But now that is not enough. If you are a Two, Three, Four, or Five—that is, in the same caste as any of these ladies—you may be subject to an attack from the rebels based on that fact alone."

I covered my mouth and heard Celeste suck in a breath.

"Beginning today, the rebels intend to attack Twos and work their way down the castes," the king added solemnly.

It was sinister. If they couldn't get us to abandon the Selection for our families, they would get a very large portion of the country to want us out. The longer we held on, the more the people would hate *us* for risking *their* lives.

"That is sad news, indeed, my king," Gavril said, breaking the silence.

The king nodded. "We will seek a solution, of course. But we have reports of eight attacks today in five different provinces, all of them against Twos and all of them resulting in at least one death."

The hand that had been frozen over my mouth dropped to my heart. People had died today at our expense.

"For now," King Clarkson continued, "we encourage you to stay close to home and to take any security measures possible."

"Excellent advice, my king," Gavril said. He turned to us. "Ladies, anything you'd like to add?"

Elise merely shook her head.

Kriss took a deep breath. "I know that Twos and Threes are being targeted, but your homes are safer than most of the ones for lower castes. If you can take in a family of Fours or Fives that you know well, I think that would be a good idea."

Celeste nodded. "Stay safe. Do what the king says."

She turned to me, and I realized I needed to say something. When I was on the *Report* and feeling a bit lost, I tended to look to Maxon, as if he could silently give me advice. Falling into that habit, I searched for his eyes. But all I saw was his blond hair as he stared into his lap, his dejected frown the only thing visible.

Of course he was worried about his people. But this was about more than protecting his citizens. He knew we might leave.

And shouldn't we? How many Fives could lose their lives because I sat on my stool in the bright lights of the palace studio?

But how could I—or any of the girls—shoulder that burden? We weren't the ones taking their lives. I remembered everything August and Georgia said to us, and I knew there was only one thing we could do.

"Fight," I said to no one in particular. Then remembering where I was, I turned to the camera. "Fight. The rebels are bullies. They're trying to scare you into doing what they want. And what if you do? What kind of future do you think they'll offer you? These people, these tyrants, aren't going to suddenly stop being violent. If you give them power, they're going to be a thousand times worse. So fight. However you can, fight."

I felt blood and adrenaline pulsing through me, like I was ready to attack the rebels myself. I'd had enough. They'd kept us all in terror, victimized our families. If one of those Southern rebels was in front of me right now, I wouldn't run.

Gavril started speaking again, but I was so angry, all I could hear was my heart beating in my ears. Before I knew it, the cameras were off and the lights were powering down.

Maxon went over to his father and whispered something to which the king shook his head.

The girls stood and started to leave.

"Go straight to your rooms," Maxon said gently. "Dinner will be brought up, and I'll be visiting you all soon."

As I walked past them, the king put a single finger on my arm, and in that small gesture, I knew he meant for me to stop.

"That wasn't very smart," he said.

I shrugged. "What we're doing isn't working. Keep this up and you won't have anyone left to rule over."

He flicked his hand, dismissing me, fed up with me again.

Maxon quietly knocked on my door, letting himself in. I was already in my nightgown, reading in my bed. I'd begun to wonder if he was going to come at all.

"It's so late," I whispered, though there was no one to disturb.

"I know. I had to speak with all the others, and it's been extremely taxing. Elise was very shaken. She's feeling particularly guilty. I wouldn't be surprised if she left in the next day or two."

Even though he'd expressed his lackluster feelings for Elise more than once, I could see just how much this hurt him. I curled my legs to my chest so he could sit.

"What about Kriss and Celeste?"

"Kriss is almost too optimistic. She's sure that people will be careful and protect themselves. I don't see how that's possible if there's no way to tell when or where the rebels will attack next. They're all over the country. But she's hopeful. You know how she is."

"Yeah."

He sighed. "Celeste is fine. She's concerned, of course; but as Kriss pointed out, the Twos are most likely to be the safest during all this. And she's always so determined." He laughed to himself, staring at the floor. "Mostly she seemed concerned that I would be upset with her if she stayed. As if I could hold it against her for choosing this over going home."

I sighed. "It's a good point. Do you want a wife who isn't worried about her subjects being threatened?"

Maxon looked at me. "You're worried. You're just too smart to be worried the way everyone else is." He shook his head and smiled. "I can't believe you told them to fight."

I shrugged. "It seems like we do a whole lot of cowering."

"You're absolutely right. And I don't know if that will scare the rebels off or make them more determined, but there's no doubt you changed the game."

I cocked my head. "I don't think I'd call a group of people trying to kill the population at random a game."

"No, no!" he said quickly. "I can't think of a word bad enough to call that. I meant the Selection." I stared at him. "For better or worse, the public got a real glimpse into your character tonight. They can see the girl who drags her maids to safety, who stands up to kings if she thinks she's right. I'll bet everyone will look at you running after Marlee in an entirely different light now. Before this, you were just the girl who yelled at me when we met. Tonight, you became the girl who's not afraid of the rebels. They'll think of you differently now."

I shook my head. "That's not what I was trying to do."

"I know. For all the planning I was doing to get you to show the people who you are, it turns out you just do it on an impulse. It's so you." There was a look of astonishment in his eyes, as if he should have been expecting this all along.

"Anyway, I think it was the right thing to say. It's about time we did more than hide."

I looked down at my bedspread, tracing the seams with my finger. I was glad he approved, but the way he spoke—as if it was one more of my little quirks—felt too intimate at the moment.

"I'm tired of fighting with you, America," he said quietly. I looked up and saw the sincerity in Maxon's eyes as he continued. "I like that we disagree—it's one of my favorite things about you, actually—but I don't want to argue anymore. Sometimes I have a bit of my father's temper. I fight it, but it's there. And you!" he said with a laugh. "When you're upset, you're a force!"

He shook his head, probably remembering a dozen things at the same time I did. A knee to the groin, the whole thing with the castes, Celeste's busted lip when she talked about Marlee. I'd never thought of myself as temperamental, but apparently I was. He smiled, and I did, too. It was kind of funny when I thought about all my actions piled up like that.

"I'm looking at the others, and I'm being fair. It makes me nervous to feel some of the things I do. But I want you to know, I'm still looking at you, too. I think you know by now I can't help it." He shrugged, seeming so boyish at that moment.

I wanted to say the right thing, to let him know that I still wanted him to look at me. But nothing felt right, so I slid my hand into his. We sat there quietly, looking at our hands. He toyed with my two bracelets, seeming very concerned with them, and spent a little while rubbing the back of my hand with his thumb. It was nice to have a still moment, just the two of us.

"Why don't we spend the day together tomorrow?" he asked.

I smiled. "I'd like that."

CHAPTER 10

"So, LONG STORY SHORT: MORE GUARDS?"

"Yeah, Dad. Lots more." I laughed into the phone, though the situation was hardly a funny one. But Dad had a way of making the toughest things light. "We're all staying. For now anyway. And even though they say they're starting with Twos, don't let anyone be careless. Warn the Turners and the Canvasses to stay safe."

"Aw, kitten, everyone knows to be careful. After what you said on the *Report*, I think people will be braver than you'd guess."

"I hope so." I looked down at my shoes and had a funny flashback. Right now my feet were covered with jeweled heels. Five months ago they were wearing dingy flats.

"You made me proud, America. Sometimes I'm surprised

at the things you say, but I don't know why. You were always stronger than you knew."

Something about his voice then was so genuine that I was humbled. No one's opinion of me mattered as much as his.

"Thanks, Dad."

"I'm serious, now. Not every princess would say something like that."

I rolled my eyes. "Uh, Dad, I'm not a princess."

"Matter of time," he shot back playfully. "Speaking of which, how is Maxon?"

"Good," I said, fidgeting with my dress. The silence grew. "I really like him, Dad."

"Yeah?"

"Yeah."

"Why exactly?"

I thought for a minute. "I'm not really sure. But part of it is that he makes me feel like me, I think."

"Did you ever feel like not you?" Dad joked.

"No, it's like . . . I've always been aware of my number. Even when I came to the palace, I obsessed about it for a while. Was I a Five or a Three? Did I want to be a One? But now I'm not conscious of it at all. And I think it's because of him.

"He screws up a lot, don't get me wrong." Dad chuckled. "But when I'm with him I feel like I'm America. I'm not a caste or a project. I don't even think of him as elevated, really. He's just him, and I'm just me."

Dad was quiet for a moment. "That sounds really nice, kitten."

Boy talk with my dad was a little awkward, but he was the only one back home who I thought saw Maxon more like a person than a celebrity; no one else would get it like he would.

"Yeah. It's not perfect though," I added as Silvia poked her head in the doorway. "I feel like there's always something going wrong."

She gave me a pointed look and mouthed *Breakfast*. I nodded.

"Well, that's okay, too. Mistakes mean it's real."

"I'll try to remember that. Listen, Dad, I've got to go. I'm late."

"Can't have that. Take care, kitten, and write your sister soon."

"I will. Love you, Daddy."

"Love you."

As the girls exited after breakfast, Maxon and I lingered in the dining room. The queen passed, winking in my direction, and I felt my cheeks redden. But the king came along soon after, and the look in his eyes took away any lingering blush.

Once we were alone, Maxon walked over to me and laced his fingers through mine. "I'd ask what you want to do today, but our options are pretty limited. No archery, no hunting, no riding, no anything outside."

I sighed. "Not even if we took a slew of guards?"

"I'm sorry, America." He gave me a sad smile. "But what about a movie? We can watch something with spectacular scenery."

"It's not the same." I pulled on his arm. "Come on. Let's go make the best of it."

"That's the spirit," he said. Something about that actually made me feel better, like we were in this together. It had been a while since it really felt that way.

We went into the hallway and were headed toward the stairway to the theater when I heard the musical clinks on the window.

I turned my head to the sound and gasped in wonder. "It's raining."

I let go of Maxon's arm and pressed my hand against the glass. In the months I'd been at the palace, it had yet to rain, and I'd wondered if it ever would. Now that I could see it, I realized I missed it. I missed the ebb and flow of seasons, the way things changed.

"It's so beautiful," I whispered.

Maxon stood behind me, wrapping an arm around my waist. "Leave it to you to find beauty in something others would say ruins a day."

"I wish I could touch it."

He sighed. "I know you do, but it's just not—"

I turned to Maxon, trying to see why he cut himself off. He looked up and down the hall, and I did the same. Besides a couple of guards, we were alone.

"Come on," he said, grabbing my hand. "Let's hope we're not seen."

I smiled, ready for whatever adventure he had in mind. I loved when Maxon was like this. We wound our way up the stairs, heading for the fourth floor. For a moment, I got nervous, worried he'd show me something similar to the hidden library. That hadn't turned out so well for me.

We walked down to the middle of the floor, passing one guard on his rounds but no one else. Maxon pulled me into a large parlor and steered me to the wall next to a wide, dormant fireplace. He reached inside the lip of the fireplace and, sure enough, found a hidden latch. He pushed open a panel in the wall, and it led to yet another secret stairwell.

"Hold my hand," he said, stretching his out to me. I did so, following him up the dimly lit steps until we came to a door. Maxon undid the simple lock, pulled open the door . . . and there was a wall of rain.

"The roof?" I asked over the sound.

He nodded. There were walls surrounding the entrance, leaving an open space about as large as my bedroom to walk on. It didn't matter that all I could see were walls and sky. At least I was outside.

Positively beside myself, I stepped forward, reaching into the water. The drops were fat and warm as they collected on my arm and ran down to my dress. I heard Maxon laugh once before shoving me out into the downpour.

I gasped, soaked in seconds. Turning around, I grabbed

his arm, and he smiled as he pretended to fight. His hair fell in strands around his eyes as we were both quickly drenched, and he was still grinning as he pulled me over to the edge of the wall.

"Look," he said into my ear.

I turned, noticing our view for the first time. I stared in awe as the city spread out in front of me. The web of streets, the geometry of buildings, the array of colors—even dimmed in the gray hue of rain, it was breathtaking.

I found myself feeling attached to it all, as if it belonged to me somehow.

"I don't want the rebels to take it, America," he said over the rain, as if he was reading my mind. "I don't know how bad the death toll is, but I can tell that my father is keeping it a secret from me. He's afraid I'll call off the Selection."

"Is there a way to find out the truth?"

He debated. "I feel like, if I could get in touch with August, he'd know. I could get a letter to him, but I'm afraid of putting too much in writing. And I don't know if I could get him into the palace."

I considered that. "What if we could get to him?"

Maxon laughed. "How do you suggest we do that?"

I shrugged playfully. "I'll work on it."

He stared at me, quiet for a minute. "It's nice to say things out loud. I'm always watching what I say. I feel like no one can hear me up here, I guess. Just you."

"Then go ahead and say anything."

He smirked. "Only if you will."

"Fine," I answered, happy to play along.

"Well, what do you want to know?"

I wiped the wet hair from my forehead, starting with something important but impersonal. "Did you really not know about the diaries?"

"No. But I'm up to speed now. Father made me read them all. If August had come two weeks ago, I would have thought he was lying about everything, but not anymore. It's shocking, America. You only scratched the surface with what you read. I want to tell you about it, but I can't yet."

"I understand."

He stared me down, determined. "How did the girls find out about you taking off my shirt?"

I looked at the ground, hesitating. "We were watching the guards work out. I said you looked as good as any of them without your shirt on. It slipped out."

Maxon threw back his head and laughed. "I can't be mad about that."

I smiled. "Have you ever brought anyone else up here?"

He looked sad. "Olivia. One time, and that's it."

I actually remembered that, come to think of it. He'd kissed her up here, and she'd told us all about it.

"I kissed Kriss," he blurted out, not looking at me. "Recently. For the first time. It seems only right that you should know."

He peeked down, and I gave him a small nod. If I hadn't

seen them kiss myself, if this had been how I found out, I might have broken down. And even though I already knew, it hurt to hear him say it.

"I hate dating you this way." I fidgeted, my dress getting heavy with water.

"I know. It's just how it is."

"Doesn't make it fair."

He laughed. "When has anything in either of our lives ever been fair?"

I gave him that. "I'm not supposed to tell you—and if you let on that you know, he'll get worse, I'm sure—but . . . your father's been saying things to me. He also took away the payments for my family. None of the other girls has them anymore, so I guess it looked bad anyway."

"I'm sorry," he said. He looked out over the city. I was temporarily distracted by the way his shirt was sticking to his chest. "I don't think there's a way to undo that one, America."

"You don't have to. I just wanted you to know it was happening. And I can handle it."

"You're too tough for him. He doesn't understand you." He reached down for my hand, and I gave it to him freely.

I tried to think of anything else I might want to know, but it mostly pertained to the other girls, and I didn't want to bother with that. I was sure at this point I could guess close enough to the truth, and if I was wrong, I didn't think I wanted that to ruin this.

Maxon looked down at my wrist. "Do you . . ." He looked

up at me, seeming to rethink his question. "Do you want to dance?"

I nodded. "But I'm awful."

"We'll go slow."

Maxon pulled me close, placing a hand on my waist. I put one hand in his and used the other to pick up my soaking dress. We swayed, barely moving. I settled my cheek on Maxon's chest, he rested his chin on my head, and we spun to the music of the rain.

As he made his grip on me a little bit tighter, it felt like all the bad had been erased and Maxon and I were stripped to the core of our relationship. We were friends who realized they didn't want to be without each other. We were the other's opposite in many ways but also so very similar. I couldn't call our relationship fate, but it did seem bigger than anything I'd known before.

I raised my face to Maxon's, placing a hand on his cheek, pulling him down for a kiss. His lips, wet, met mine with a brush of heat. I felt both his hands wrap around my back, holding me to him as if he'd fall apart otherwise. While the rain pummeled the roof, the whole world went silent. It felt like there wasn't enough of him, not enough skin or space or time.

After all these months of trying to reconcile what I wanted and hoped for, I realized then—in this moment Maxon created just for us—that it would never make sense. All I could do was move forward and hope that whenever we drifted, we would somehow find a way back to each other.

And we had to. Because . . . because . . .

For as long as it took to get to this moment, when it came it was fast.

I loved Maxon. For the first time, I could feel it solidly. I wasn't keeping the feeling at a distance, holding on to Aspen and all the what-ifs that went along with him. I wasn't walking into Maxon's affections while keeping one foot out the door in case he let me down. I simply let it come.

I loved him.

I couldn't pinpoint what made me so certain, but I knew it then, as surely as I knew my name or the color of the sky or any fact written in a book.

Could he feel it, too?

Maxon broke the kiss and looked at me. "You're so pretty when you're a mess."

I laughed nervously. "Thank you. For that and for the rain and for not giving up."

He ran his fingers along my cheek and nose and chin. "You're worth it. I don't think you get that. You're worth it to me."

I felt as if my heart was on the edge of bursting, and I just wanted everything to end today. My world had settled onto a new axis, and it felt like the only way to handle how dizzy it made me was for us to finally be real. I felt certain now that it would come. It would have to. Soon.

Maxon kissed the tip of my nose. "Let's go get dry and watch a movie."

"Sounds good."

I carefully tucked my love for Maxon away in my heart, a little afraid of this feeling. Eventually, it would have to be shared, but for now it was my secret.

I tried to wring out my dress in the little canopy where the door was, but it was hopeless. I was going to leave a little trail of water back to my room.

"I vote for a comedy," I said as we went down the stairs, Maxon leading the way.

"I vote for action."

"Well, you just said I was worth it, so I think I'm going to win this one."

Maxon laughed. "Nicely done."

He chuckled again as he pushed on the panel that led us back into the parlor only to stop dead in his tracks a second later.

I peeked over his shoulder to see King Clarkson standing there, looking as irritated as ever.

"I'm assuming this was your idea," he said to Maxon.

"Yes."

"Do you have any idea how much danger you put yourself in?" he demanded.

"Father, there are no rebels waiting on the roof," Maxon countered, trying to sound rational but looking a bit ridiculous in his dripping clothes.

"One well-aimed bullet is all it would take, Maxon." He let the words hang in the air. "You know we're stretched tight, sending guards to watch the girls' homes. And dozens of those who've been sent have gone AWOL. We're vulnerable." He glared past his son at me. "And why is it that when anything happens these days, she's got her hands all over it?"

We stood there, silent, knowing there was nothing we could say anyway.

"Get cleaned up," the king ordered. "You have work to do."

"But I—"

A single look from his father told Maxon that any plans he'd had for the day were done.

"Very well," he said, caving.

King Clarkson took Maxon's arm and pushed him away, leaving me behind. Over his shoulder, Maxon mouthed the word *Sorry,* and I gave him a little smile.

I wasn't afraid of the king. Or the rebels. I knew how much Maxon meant to me, and I was sure that it was all going to work, somehow.

CHAPTER 11

AFTER ENDURING MARY'S SILENT SMIRK as she made me back up, I went to the Women's Room, happy the rain was still coming down. It would always mean something special to me now.

But while Maxon and I could escape for a little while, once we were out of our bubble, the tension of the ultimatum the rebels had placed on the Elite was thick. All the girls were distracted and anxious.

Celeste wordlessly painted her nails at a nearby table, and I could see the slight tremor in her hand from time to time. I watched as she cleaned up her mistakes and tried to carry on. Elise held a book in her hands, but her eyes were trained on the window, lost in the downpour. None of us could quite manage to finish even the smallest task.

"How do you think it's going out there?" Kriss asked me,

her hand paused over the needlepoint pillow she was working on.

"I don't know," I answered quietly. "It doesn't seem like they'd threaten something huge and then do nothing." I was penciling out a melody I'd had in my head on some sheet music. I hadn't written anything original in nearly six months. There wasn't much point to it. At parties, people preferred the classics.

"Do you think they're hiding the number of deaths from us?" she wondered.

"It's possible. If we leave, they win."

Kriss did another stitch. "I'm going to stay no matter what." Something about the way she said it seemed to be directed specifically at me. Like I needed to know she wasn't giving up on Maxon.

"Same here," I promised.

The next day was much of the same, though I'd never been disappointed to see the sun shine before. The worry was so heavy that it was all we could do to stay put. I ached to run, to put some of the energy into *something*.

After lunch, our return to the Women's Room was staggered. Elise was reading as I sat with my sheet music, but Kriss and Celeste were missing. Maybe ten minutes later, Kriss walked in with full arms. She sat down with drawing paper and a collection of colored pencils.

"What are you working on?" I asked.

She shrugged. "Whatever keeps me busy."

She sat for a long time with a red pencil in her hand, hovering over the paper.

"I don't know what I'm doing," she finally said. "I know that people are in danger, but I love him. I don't want to leave."

"The king won't let anyone die," Elise offered comfortingly.

"But people already have died." Kriss wasn't argumentative, only worried. "I just need to think about something else."

"I bet Silvia would have work for us," I offered.

Kriss gave a single chuckle. "I'm not that desperate." She put the tip of the pencil down, making a smooth curve across the page. It was a start. "Everything will be fine. I'm sure of it."

I rubbed my eyes, looking at my music. I needed to switch things up.

"I'm going to hop over to one of the libraries. I'll be right back."

Elise and Kriss each gave me a cursory nod as they attempted to focus on their tasks, and I stood to leave.

I wandered down the hall to one of the rooms on the far end of the floor. There were a few books on those shelves I'd been wanting to read. The door of the parlor swung open quietly, and I realized I wasn't alone. Someone was crying.

I searched for the source and found Celeste, hugging her knees to her chest, sitting on the wide perch of a windowsill. I felt immediately awkward. Celeste *did not* cry. Up until this moment, I hadn't even been sure she was capable.

The only thing to do was leave, but as she wiped her eyes, she caught sight of me.

"Ugh!" she whined. "What do you want?"

"Nothing. Sorry. I was looking for a book."

"Well, get it and go. You get everything you want anyway."

I stood there blankly for a moment, confused by her words. She heaved a sigh and pushed herself up from her seat. Snatching one of her many magazines, she flung the glossy pages at me, and I caught it clumsily.

"See for yourself. Your little speech on the *Report* pushed you over the top. They love you." Her voice was angry, accusing. As if I'd planned this all along.

I turned the magazine right side up, finding half of the page full of pictures of the four remaining girls with a graph beside our photos. Above the image, an elegant headline asked *Who do YOU want as Queen?* Next to my face, a wide line shot out, showing thirty-nine percent of the people were pulling for me. It wasn't as high as I thought it should be for whoever won, but it was much higher than the others!

Quotes from those polled edged the graph, saying that Celeste was positively regal, though she was in third. Elise was so poised, it said, but she also only had eight percent of the population pulling for her. By my picture were opinions that made me want to cry.

"Lady America is just like the queen. She's a fighter. It's more than wanting her; we need her!"

I stared at the words. "Is . . . is this real?"

Celeste snatched back the magazine. "Of course it's real. So go ahead, marry him or whatever. Be princess. Everyone will love it. The sad little Five gets a crown."

She started walking away, her sour mood ruining the most incredible news I'd gotten during the entirety of the Selection.

"You know, I don't even see why this matters so much to you. Some very happy Two is going to marry you anyway. And you're still going to be famous when this is over," I accused.

"As a has-been, America."

"You're a model, for goodness' sake!" I yelled. "You've got everything."

"But for how long?" she shot back. Then quieter. "How long?"

"What do you mean?" I said, my voice becoming softer. "Celeste, you're beautiful. You're a Two for the rest of your life."

She was shaking her head before I was even done speaking. "You think you're the only one who's ever felt trapped by your caste? Yes, I'm a model. I can't sing. I can't act. So when my face isn't good enough anymore, they're going to forget all about me. I've got maybe five years left, ten if I'm lucky."

She stared at me. "You've spent your whole life in the background. I can see you miss it sometimes. Well, I've spent mine in the spotlight. Maybe it's a stupid fear to you, but it's real for me: I don't want to lose it."

"That makes sense, actually."

"Yeah?" she dabbed under her eyes, gazing out the window.

I walked over and stood beside her. "Yeah. But, Celeste, did you ever even like him?"

She tilted her head to the side, thinking. "He's cute. And a great kisser," she added with a smile.

I grinned back. "I know."

"I know you do. That was a serious blow to my plan, when I found out how far you two had gone. I thought I had him in the palm of my hand, making him dream about the possibility of more."

"That's no way to get to someone's heart."

"I didn't need his heart," she confessed. "I just needed him to want me enough to keep me. Fine, it's not love. I need the fame more than I need the love."

For the first time, she wasn't my enemy. I understood that now. Yes, she was conniving when it came to the competition, but that was her being desperate. She simply felt she had to intimidate us out of something that most of us *wanted* but that she felt she *needed*.

"First of all, you do need the love. Everyone does. And it's okay to want that right along with the fame."

She rolled her eyes but didn't interrupt.

"Second of all, the Celeste Newsome I know doesn't need a man to get fame."

She laughed out loud at that. "I have been a bit vicious,"

she said, more playful than ashamed.

"You ripped my dress!"

"Well, at the time I needed it!"

And suddenly all of it was funny. All the arguing, the wicked faces, the little tricks—they felt like a really long joke. We stood there for a minute, laughing over the past few months, and I found myself wanting to look after her the way I did Marlee.

Surprisingly, her laughter faded away quickly, and she averted her eyes as she spoke.

"I've done so many things, America. Horrible, shameful things. Part of it was not reacting well to the stress of this, but mostly it was because I was ready to do anything to get that crown, to get to Maxon."

I was a little shocked as I watched my hand rise up to pat her on the shoulder.

"Honestly," I started, "I don't think you need Maxon to get anything you want out of life. You've got the drive, the talent; and probably, most importantly, you've got the ability. Half of the country would give anything to have what you have."

"I know," she said. "It's not that I'm completely unaware of how lucky I am. It's just hard to accept the possibility of . . . I don't know, being less."

"Then don't accept it."

She shook her head. "I didn't stand a chance, did I? It's been you the whole time."

"Not only me," I admitted. "Kriss. She's at the top, too."

"Do you need me to break her leg? I could make it happen." She chuckled to herself. "I'm kidding."

"You want to come back with me? It's hard to sit through the days right now, and you do add a little something to the mix."

"Not right now. I don't want the others to know I was crying." She gave me a pleading look.

"Not a word, I promise."

"Thanks."

There was a tense pause, as if one of us ought to say more. It felt significant, this moment of finally, truly seeing Celeste. I wasn't sure if I could let go of everything she'd done to me, but at least I understood now. There was nothing to add, so I gave her a little wave and left.

Only once I closed the door did I realize that I'd forgotten to grab a book. And then I thought of the glossy chart with my smiling face and the huge number beside it. I'd have to tug my ear at dinner. Maxon needed to know about this. I hoped that maybe if he knew how the people felt about me, it would raise his feelings a little closer to the surface.

As I reached the corner to turn toward the Women's Room, a familiar face reminded me that I had even bigger plans to think about right now. I'd told Maxon that I'd find us a way to get to August, and I felt certain our only shot was coming my way.

Aspen walked down the hall, seeming even bigger and taller than the last time I'd seen him.

I looked around, seeing if we were alone. There were a

few guards down the hall just past him, but they were out of earshot.

"Hey," I said, beckoning him over. I bit my lip, hoping that Aspen would be as able as I thought he was. "I need your help."

Without batting an eye, he responded. "Anything."

CHAPTER 12

I was right. Aspen had every corner of the palace memorized, and he knew exactly how to get us out of it.

"Are you quite sure about this?" Maxon asked as we got dressed in my room the following evening.

"We need to know what's going on. I have no doubt we'll be safe," I assured him.

We spoke through the cracked-open bathroom door as he dropped the pieces of his suit to the floor and climbed into the denim and cotton a Six would wear. Aspen's clothes were going to be a bit big on Maxon, but they would do. Thankfully, Aspen had found a smaller guard to borrow clothes from for me, but even then I had to roll up the hem of the pants several times to find my feet.

"You seem to trust this guard a lot," Maxon commented,

and I couldn't figure out the tone he was using. Perhaps he was anxious.

"My maids say he's one of the best you have. And he got me to the safe room that time the Southerners came, when everyone was running late. He always looks ready to go, even when things are quiet. I have a good feeling about him. Trust me."

I heard the rustling of clothes as he continued. "How did you know he could get us out of the palace?"

"I didn't. I just asked."

"And he simply told you?" Maxon replied, astonished.

"Well, I told him it was for you, of course."

He made a sound, something like a sigh. "I still don't think you should come."

"I'm going, Maxon. Are you done yet?"

"Yes. I need to get my shoes on."

I opened the door, and after a quick once-over, Maxon started laughing. "I'm sorry. I'm used to seeing you in gowns."

"You look a bit different when you're not in a suit yourself." And he did, but not in any way that was close to comical. Even though Aspen's clothes were too big, Maxon looked good in plain old denim. The shirt had short sleeves, and I got a peek at those strong arms I'd only ever seen the one time in the safe room.

"These pants are far too heavy. Why are you so partial to jeans?" he asked, remembering my request from my very first day in the palace.

I shrugged. "I just like them."

He smiled at me, shaking his head a bit. He walked over to my closet, not asking if it was all right to open it. "We need something to hold your pants up or it's going to be a very scandalous evening. Well, more so than it already is."

Maxon pulled out a dark-red sash and returned to me with it, lacing it through my belt loops.

I couldn't say why, but this felt meaningful. My heart pounded, and for a minute I wondered if he could hear it shouting how much I loved him. If so, he ignored it in favor of the business at hand.

"Listen," he said, making a little knot in the sash, "what we're doing is very dangerous. If something happens, I want you to run. Don't even try to get back to the palace. Find a family who will hide you through the night."

Maxon stepped back and looked into my worried eyes. I tilted my head. "Right now, asking a family to hide me is almost as dangerous as facing the rebels. People might be upset that we girls aren't leaving the competition."

"If the article Celeste showed you is right, then people might be proud of you."

I wanted to tell Maxon I disagreed, but a knock at the door interrupted us. He went over to answer it, and quickly Aspen and a second guard walked into my dimly lit room.

"Your Majesty," Aspen said with a small bow. "Lady America has informed me that you need to get outside the palace walls."

Maxon sighed deeply. "Yes. And I hear you're the man to

help me. Officer . . ." He looked for Aspen's badge. "Leger."

Aspen nodded. "It's not very difficult, actually. The secrecy might be more of an issue than getting out in the first place."

"How so?"

"Well, I have to assume there's a reason for you to be doing this at night, without the king's knowledge. If we're specifically asked," Aspen said, glancing over to the other guard, "I don't think we could lie to him."

"And I wouldn't ask you to. I'm hoping to be able to reveal this to my father soon enough, but, for tonight, discretion is imperative."

"It shouldn't be a problem." Aspen hesitated. "I don't think the lady should go."

As if he'd won the argument, Maxon looked at me with a face that said *See!*

I stood as tall as I could manage. "I'm not just going to sit here. I've been chased by rebels once already, and I'm fine."

"But those weren't Southerners," Maxon countered.

"I'm going," I said. "And we're wasting time."

"To be clear, no one agrees with you."

"To be clear, I don't care."

Sighing, Maxon pulled the knit hat over his hair. "So what do we need to do?"

"The plan is pretty simple," Aspen said decisively. "Twice a week, a truck is sent out for groceries. Sometimes the kitchen staff simply falls short of the needs for the week, so the truck goes out again to pick up whatever's lacking. Usually people from the kitchen go, along with a few guards."

"And no one will suspect?" I asked.

Aspen shook his head. "These runs are often done at night. If the cook says we need more eggs for breakfast, well, we'd better go before sunup."

Maxon ran over to his suit pants, rummaging through his pocket. "I did manage to get a note out to August. He said we should meet him at this address." Maxon handed the paper to Aspen, who shared the note with the other guard.

"You know where this is?" Aspen asked.

The guard—a dark-skinned young man whose name tag I finally noticed said AVERY—nodded. "Not the best part of town, but close enough to the food storage area that we shouldn't raise any alarm."

"All right," Aspen said. He looked at me. "Tuck your hair beneath your hat."

I grabbed my hair and twisted it up, hoping it would all fit beneath the knit hat Aspen had provided. I pushed up the last strands and looked to Maxon. "Well?"

He choked on a laugh. "Great."

I gave him a playful punch in the arm before turning to follow Aspen's next instructions.

I saw the hurt in his eyes to see me so casual with Maxon. And maybe it went beyond that. We'd hid in a tree house for two years, but here I was wandering into the streets, past curfew, with the man the Southern rebels wanted to see dead more than anyone.

This moment was a slap in the face of everything we were.

And even though I wasn't in love with Aspen, he still mattered to me, and I didn't want to cause him pain.

Before Maxon probably even noticed, Aspen straightened his face. "Follow us."

Slipping into the hallway, Aspen and Officer Avery took us down the stairway that led to the massive safe room reserved for the royal family. Instead of heading toward the great steel doors, we moved quickly across the length of the palace, where we ascended another spiral staircase. I had assumed we would be heading to the first floor, but we exited into the kitchen.

Immediately, I was hit with billowing warmth and the sweet smell of bread rising. For a split second, it felt like home. I expected something clinical, professional, like the big bakeries we had in Carolina on the nice end of town. But there were huge wooden tables with vegetables laid out, ready to be prepped. Notes were left in places, reminding whoever was on duty next of what had to be done. All in all, the kitchen seemed cozy, even for as big as it was.

"Keep your heads down," Officer Avery whispered to Maxon and me.

We studied the floor as Aspen called out. "Delilah?"

"Hold on, honey!" someone shouted back. Her voice was rich and had the slight drawl of a southern accent that I'd heard sometimes back in Carolina. Heavy footsteps came around the corner, but I avoided looking up to see the woman's face. "Leger, you cutie, how've you been?"

"Been good. Just heard there was a delivery to pick up,

and I was wondering if you had a list for me."

"Delivery? Not that I know of."

"That's funny. I was sure."

"Might as well drive out," she said, no hint of worry or suspicion in her voice. "Don't want to miss something."

"Good point. Shouldn't be too long," Aspen answered. I heard the swift sound of him catching a set of keys. "See you later, Delilah. If you're asleep, I'll put the keys on the hook."

"Okay, honey. You come see me soon. It's been too long."

"Will do."

Aspen was already walking, and we followed him wordlessly. I smiled to myself. The woman, Delilah, had a deeper voice, mature sounding. But even she was sweet on Aspen.

We walked around a corner and up a wide incline to a set of broad doors. Aspen undid the lock and pushed the doors open. Waiting in the dark was a large black truck.

"There's nothing to hold on to, but I think you two should get in the back," Avery said. I looked at the large cargo space. At least we wouldn't be recognized.

I went around to the back, where Aspen was already opening the doors. "My lady," he said, offering me his hand, which I took. "Your Majesty," he added as Maxon passed, refusing assistance.

There were a couple of crates inside and a shelving unit along one wall, but otherwise it was an empty metal box. Maxon passed me, surveying the area.

"Come here, America," he said, pointing to the corner. "We'll wedge ourselves against the shelf."

"We'll try to drive smoothly," Aspen called.

Maxon nodded. Aspen gave us both a solemn look before shutting the doors.

In the pitch-dark, I pushed myself against Maxon.

"Are you scared?" he asked.

"No."

"Me neither."

But I was pretty sure we were both lying.

CHAPTER 13

I COULDN'T TELL HOW LONG we'd been traveling, but I was very aware of every move the giant truck made. Maxon, in an effort to keep us stable, had pushed his back against the shelf and braced a leg across me on the wall, caging me in. But even with that, we both slid a bit against the metal floor at every turn.

"I don't like not knowing where I am," Maxon said, trying to secure us again.

"Have you ever been out in Angeles before?"

"Only in a car," he confessed.

"Is it strange that I feel better going into a den of rebels than I did when I had to entertain the women of the Italian royal family?"

Maxon laughed. "Only you."

It was hard talking over the rumble of the engine and the squeal of the wheels, so we were quiet for a while. In the dark, the sounds felt bigger. I inhaled deeply, trying to focus myself, and noticed a hint of coffee in the air. I couldn't tell if it was some lingering scent in the truck or if we were passing a shop on the road. After what felt like a very long time, Maxon put his lips to my ear.

"I wish you were safe at home, but I'm really glad you're here." I laughed quietly. I doubted he could hear it, but he probably felt it, we were so close. "Promise me that you'll run though."

I decided that I'd be of no help to Maxon if something really bad happened anyway. I searched and put my mouth by his ear. "I promise."

We went over a pretty jarring bump, and he grabbed me. I felt our noses brush in the dark, and the urge to kiss him came unexpectedly fast. Though our kiss on the roof had only been three days ago, it felt like an eternity. He held me close, and I could feel his breath on my skin. It was coming; I was sure of it.

Maxon used his nose, nudging at my cheek, bringing our lips closer together. The same way I could smell coffee and hear every tiny squeak in the dark, the lack of light made me focus on the clean scent that hung around Maxon, feel the pressure of his fingers moving up my neck to the wisps of hair peeking out from under my cap.

In the second before our lips touched, the truck came

to an abrupt stop, flinging us forward. I knocked my head against the wall, and I was pretty sure I felt Maxon's teeth against my ear.

"Ow!" he exclaimed, and I felt him adjusting his position in the dark. "Are you hurt?"

"No. My hair and the hat took most of it." If I hadn't wanted that kiss so badly, I would have laughed.

As soon as we'd stopped, we started moving slowly in reverse. After a few seconds, the truck halted again and the engine cut off. Maxon switched positions, and it felt as if he was ducking low in a crouch, facing the door. I got into a similar position as one of Maxon's hands come back to protect me, just in case.

The light of the streetlamp coming into the cabin was shocking, and I squinted against it as someone climbed into the back of the truck.

"We're here," said Officer Avery. "Follow me closely."

Maxon stood and extended a hand to me. He let go to hop out of the truck, then reached up to help me down and immediately slid his hand back into mine. The thing I noticed right away was the large brick wall cornering us in the alley, followed by the stinging smell of something rotting. Aspen was standing in front of us, looking around intently, a gun held low in his hand.

He and Avery started moving toward the back entrance of the building, and we kept close to them. The walls surrounding us were high and reminded me of the apartment buildings back home with their fire escapes snaking down the sides, though this didn't seem like an area where people lived. Aspen knocked on the grime-covered door and waited. It cracked open, a small chain there to protect whoever was inside. But I saw August's eyes before the door was quickly shut again. The next time, it opened wide, and August ushered in all of us.

"Hurry," he said quietly.

In the shadowy room was a younger boy and Georgia. I could see she was just as anxious as we were, and I couldn't stop myself from bolting across the room to embrace her. She held me back, and I was happy to find I'd acquired an unexpected friend.

"Were you followed?" she asked.

Aspen shook his head. "No. But you should be quick."

Georgia pulled me over to a small table, and Maxon sat next to me, with August and the younger boy beside him.

"How bad is it?" Maxon asked. "I have a feeling my father is keeping the truth from me."

August gave a surprised shrug. "As best we can tell, the numbers are low. The Southerners are doing their typical destruction, but as far as the attacks on Twos specifically, it looks like it's less than three hundred people."

I gasped. Three hundred people? How could that be deemed low?

"America, it's not that bad, all things considered," Maxon comforted me, taking my hand again.

"He's right," Georgia said, her face warm. "It could have been so much worse."

"It's what I would expect from them: starting at the top and working their way down. We're guessing they'll pick it up before too long," August interjected. "It looks like the attacks are still isolated on the Twos, but we're watching and will alert you if or when that changes. We've got allies in every province, and they're all trying to keep watch. But there's only so much they can do without exposing themselves, and we all know what would happen if they did."

Maxon nodded soberly. They'd die, of course.

"Should we cave?" Maxon suggested. I looked over at him, surprised.

"Trust us," Georgia said. "They're not going to get any better if you give in."

"But there must be something more we can do," Maxon insisted.

"You've already done something pretty empowering. Well, she did," August said, dipping his head in my direction. "From what we're able to tell, farmers are keeping their axes with them if they leave their fields, seamstresses walk the street with scissors clutched in their hands, and you'll see Twos parading around with disarming spray. No matter the caste, everyone seems to have found some way to arm themselves, just in case. Your people don't want to live in fear, and they're not. They're fighting back."

I wanted to cry. For maybe the first time in all of the Selection, I'd done something right.

Maxon squeezed my hand, proud. "That's a comfort," he said. "Still, it doesn't feel like enough."

I nodded. I was so happy the public wasn't rolling over, but there had to be a way to stop this once and for all.

August sighed. "We've wondered if there was a way for us to attack them. They're not fighting with any sort of training—they just go after people. Our supporters are nervous about being identified, but they're everywhere. And they might be the best source for a surprise assault.

"In many ways, we're already an army of sorts, but we're essentially unarmed. We can't possibly beat the Southerners when the majority of our forces fight with bricks or rakes."

"You want weapons?"

"Wouldn't hurt."

Maxon considered this. "There are things you can do that we simply can't from the palace. But I don't like the idea of sending any of my people on a mission to take out these savages. Certainly they would die."

"That's possible," August confessed.

"There's also the small issue of me not being able to guarantee you won't use any weapons I give you against me eventually."

August snorted. "I don't know how to make you believe that we're on your side, but it's true. All we've ever wanted was to see an end to the castes, and we're prepared to support you to that end. I have no intentions of ever harming you, Maxon, and I think you know that." He and Maxon shared a very long look. "If you didn't, you wouldn't be here now."

"Your Majesty," Aspen said. "I'm sorry to interrupt, but there are some of us who would like to see the Southern

rebels gone as much as you would. I would personally vol-
unteer to train anyone in something more along the lines of
hand-to-hand combat."

My chest swelled with pride. That was my Aspen, always
trying to fix things.

Maxon nodded at him before turning back to August.
"That's something I'll need time to think about. I might be
able to provide training, but I couldn't arm you. Even if I
was sure of your intentions, if there's any link between us, I
can't imagine what my father would do."

Without thinking, Maxon flexed the muscles across his
back. It seemed to me that maybe he'd done that a lot in the
time I'd known him, only I hadn't understood its meaning.
Even now he was hyperaware of his secret.

"True. In fact, you should probably already be leaving. I'll
get word to you as soon as we have more information, but
for now it looks good. Well, as good as we could hope for."
August passed Maxon a note. "We have one landline. You
can call if there's something urgent. Micah here, he's on top
of those things."

August motioned to the boy who hadn't made a sound the
whole time. He pulled his lips into his mouth like he might
be biting them and gave us a small nod. Something about his
stance suggested he was both shy and eager at once.

"Very good. I'll use it with discretion." Maxon placed the
paper in his pocket. "I'll be in touch soon." He stood and I
followed suit, looking over at Georgia as I did so.

She came around the table to me. "Be safe getting back.

And that number is for you, too, you know."

"Thank you." I gave her a quick hug and headed out with Maxon, Aspen, and Officer Avery. I took one last glance at our strange friends before the door closed and was bolted behind us.

"Get away from the truck," Aspen said. I turned to see what he meant, as we weren't even close yet.

Then I saw that Aspen wasn't talking to me. A handful of men were circling the vehicle. One had a wrench in his hands, looking as if he was about to try and steal the tires. Another two were at the back, trying to open the metal doors.

"Just give us the food, and we'll go," one said. He looked younger than most of the others, maybe Aspen's age. His voice was cold and desperate.

I hadn't noticed back at the palace that the truck we were jumping into had a massive Illéa emblem on the side. As I stood there looking at the small crowd of haggard men, this seemed like an incredibly stupid oversight. And while Maxon and I weren't dressed like ourselves, that wouldn't help very much if anyone got too close. Even though I wouldn't have known the first thing to do with one, I wished I had a weapon.

"There is no food," Aspen said calmly. "And if there was, it wouldn't be yours to take."

"How well they train their puppets," another man remarked. As he gave us an amused smile, I could see that a few of his teeth were missing. "What were you before they turned you into this?"

"Step away from the truck," Aspen ordered.

"You couldn't have been a Two or a Three; you'd have bought your way out. So come on, little man, what were you?" the toothless man taunted, stepping closer.

"Back. Away." Aspen put one hand in front of himself, reaching down toward his hip with the other.

The man stopped, shaking his head. "You don't know who you're messing with, boy."

"Wait!" someone said. "That's her. That's one of the girls."

I turned my head to the voice, giving myself away.

"Get her!" the young one said.

Before I could even think, Maxon jerked me back. I saw a blur of Aspen and Officer Avery pulling out their guns as my head got whipped around by the force of Maxon's strong arms. I was moving sideways, stumbling to keep up while Aspen and Avery held the men at bay. Quickly, Maxon and I were against the brick wall, trapped.

"I don't want to kill you," Aspen said. "Leave. Now!"

The toothless man chuckled darkly, his hands raised in front of him as if he meant no harm. In a move so fast I nearly missed it, he reached down and drew a gun of his own. Aspen fired, and shots came in return.

"Come on, America," Maxon said urgently.

Come where? I thought, my heart pounding in terror.

I looked at him and saw that he had laced his fingers together, making a cradle for my foot. Suddenly understanding, I put my shoe in his hands, and he pushed me up as I grappled at the wall for some stability. I reached the top, and

I felt something funny in my arm as I crawled over.

I ignored it as I pulled my body across the ledge, lowering myself as much as I could before dropping to the concrete. I fell to the side, positive I'd messed up my hip or leg; but Maxon had instructed me to run if I was in danger, so I did.

I didn't know why I assumed he would be right behind me, but when I reached the end of the street and he wasn't there, I realized no one would be free to give him a boost. In that moment, I noticed that funny feeling in my arm was starting to burn. I looked down, and in the faint glow of a streetlight, I saw something wet coming from a rip in my sleeve.

I'd been shot.

I'd been shot?

There were guns and I was there, but it didn't seem real. Still, there was no denying the searing pain that was growing bigger every second. I cupped my hand over the wound, but that made it worse.

I looked around. The city was still.

Of course it was. We were out well after curfew. I'd gotten so used to the palace that I'd forgotten that the world outside stopped after eleven.

If an officer came by, I'd be thrown in jail. How was I supposed to explain that to the king? *How are you going to talk away a bullet wound, America?*

I started moving, staying to the shadows. I had no idea where to go. I didn't know if trying to get back to the palace was a good idea. Even if it was, I didn't know how to get there.

God, the burning. It was hard to think. I made my way past a narrow backstreet between two apartment buildings. That alone told me I wasn't in the best part of town. Generally, only Sixes and Sevens had to squeeze into apartments.

There was nowhere for me to go, so I walked down the poorly lit alley, tucking myself behind a tight pack of trash cans. The night was cool, but it had been a typical hot Angeles day, and the stink was rising from the metal bins. Between the smell and the pain, I felt myself on the edge of vomiting.

I peeled off my right sleeve, trying not to irritate the wound any more than necessary. My hands were trembling, either from fear or adrenaline, and just bending my arm made me want to scream. I bit my lips together to keep the sound in, but even with that my muffled whimpers escaped into the night.

"What happened?" a tiny voice asked.

I jerked my head up, looking for the source. There were two glittering eyes in the darker depths of the alley.

"Who's there?" I asked, voice trembling.

"I won't hurt you," she said, crawling out. "I'm having a bad night, too."

The girl, maybe fifteen if I had to guess, crept out of the shadows and came to look at my arm. She sucked in a breath at the sight.

"That looks really painful," she said sympathetically.

"I got shot," I blurted, ready to cry. It burned so badly.

"Shot?"

I nodded.

She looked at me hesitantly, like maybe she should run away. "I don't know what you did or who you are, but you don't mess with rebels, okay?"

"Huh?"

"I haven't been out here long, but I know that the only people who can get guns are rebels. Whatever you did to them, don't do it again."

In all the times they'd attacked us, I'd never considered that. No one was supposed to have a gun unless they were an officer. Only a rebel would be able to get around that. Even August had just said the Northerners were *essentially unarmed*. I wondered if he'd been carrying tonight.

"What's your name?" she asked. "I know you're a girl under there."

"Mer," I said.

"I'm Paige. Looks like you're new to being an Eight yourself. Your clothes are pretty clean." She was turning my arm gently, looking at the oozing wound as if she could do something even though we both knew better.

"Something like that," I hedged.

"You can starve out here if you're alone. You got anywhere to go?"

I shuddered with a roll of pain. "Not exactly."

She nodded. "It was just my dad and me. I was a Four. We had a restaurant, but my grandma had made some rule that he was supposed to leave it to my aunt when he died, not to me. I think she was worried my aunt wouldn't have anything or something like that. Well, my aunt hates me, always has. She got the restaurant, but she got me, too. Didn't like that.

"Two weeks after Dad died, she started hitting me. I had to sneak food because she said I was getting fat and wouldn't give me anything to eat. I thought about going to a friend's house, but my aunt would just be able to come and get me, so I left. I took some money, but not enough. Even if it was, I got robbed my second night out here."

I looked Paige over as she talked. I could see it, under the growing layer of grime. There was a girl in there who used to be very well taken care of. She was trying to be tough now. She had to be. What else was there for her?

"Just this week I found a group of girls. We work together and share all the profits. If you can forget what you're doing, it's not so bad. I have to cry afterward. That's why I was hiding back there. If the other girls see you cry, they make my aunt look like a saint. J. J. says they're just trying to toughen me up and that I better get that way fast, but it still hurts.

"Anyway, you're pretty. I know they'd be glad to have you."

My stomach rolled, processing her offer. In what seemed like a few weeks, she'd lost her family, her home, and herself.

And still she was sitting in front of me—a girl who'd been chased by a pack of rebels, a girl who could be nothing but danger—and she was kind.

"We can't get you a doctor, but there would be something

to ease the pain. And they could get you some stitches from this guy they know. You'd have to work it off though."

I focused on my breathing. Even though she was distracting, the conversation couldn't stop the pain.

"You don't talk much, do you?" Paige asked.

"Not when I've been shot."

She laughed, and the ease of it made me laugh a little, too. Paige sat down beside me for a little while, and I was glad I wasn't alone.

"If you don't want to come with me, I get it. It's dangerous and kind of sad."

"I . . . can we just be quiet for a minute?" I asked.

"Yes. Do you want me to stay with you?"

"Please."

And she did. Without question, she sat beside me, as silent as a mouse. It felt like an eternity was passing, though it couldn't have even been twenty minutes. The pain was becoming more severe, and I was getting desperate. Maybe I could get to a doctor. Of course, I'd have to find one. The palace would pay for it, but I had no clue how to get ahold of Maxon.

Was Maxon even okay? Was Aspen?

They were outnumbered, but they were armed. If the rebels recognized me so quickly, did they recognize Maxon, too? If so, what would they do to him?

I sat still, trying to talk myself out of the worry. It was all I could do to focus on myself. But what was I going to do if Aspen died? Or if Maxon—

"Shh!" I ordered, though Paige still hadn't made a sound. "Do you hear that?"

We both tuned our ears to the street.

". . . Max," someone yelled. "Come out, Mer; it's Max."

That would have been Aspen's idea, no doubt, using those names.

I scrambled to my feet and went to the edge of the alley, with Paige right behind me. I saw the truck coming down the street at a snail's pace, heads poking out of the windows, searching.

I turned around. "Paige, would you want to come with me?"

"Where?"

"I promise you, you'll have a real job and food, and no one will hit you."

Her heavy eyes filled with tears. "Then I don't care where it is. I'll go."

I took her with my good hand, my coat sleeve still hanging off the wounded arm. We made our way down the road, sticking close to the buildings.

"Max!" I called as we got closer. "Max!"

The massive truck skidded to a stop, and Maxon, Aspen, and Officer Avery came running out.

I dropped Paige's hand, seeing Maxon's open arms. He embraced me, hitting my wound, and I yelled.

"What's wrong?" he asked.

"I was shot."

Aspen parted us, grabbing my arm to see for himself.

"That could have been a lot worse. We need to get you back and find a way to treat you. I'm assuming we'll want to leave the doctor out of this?" He looked to Maxon.

"I don't want her to suffer," he insisted.

"Your Majesty," Paige said, dropping to her knees. Her shoulders started shaking like she might be crying.

"This is Paige," I said, offering nothing else. "Let's get in the back."

Aspen lowered a hand to Paige. "You're safe," he assured her.

Maxon put an arm around me, escorting me to the back of the truck.

"I was sure it would take all night to find you," he worried aloud.

"Me, too. But I was in too much pain to get very far. Paige helped."

"Then she'll be taken care of, I promise."

Maxon, Paige, and I crawled into the back of the truck, and the metal floor was strangely comforting as we sped back to the palace.

CHAPTER 14

IT WAS ASPEN WHO LIFTED me from the back of the truck and hurriedly carried me to a tiny room. The space was smaller than my bathroom and held two slim beds and a dresser. There were little notes and photos on the wall, which gave it some personality; but it was otherwise barren, not to mention incredibly cramped with Aspen, me, Officer Avery, Maxon, and Paige filling every spare inch.

Aspen laid me on a bed as gently as possible, but my arm continued to throb.

"We ought to get the doctor," he said. But I could tell he doubted his own words. Getting Dr. Ashlar would mean either telling the absolute truth or making up an outrageous lie, and neither of those options was something we wanted.

"Don't," I urged weakly. "I won't die from this. It'll just be a bad scar. We have to clean it up." I grimaced.

"You'll need something for the pain," Maxon added.

"She might get infected. That alley was really dirty, and I touched her," Paige said guiltily.

A sliver of fire burned across the wound, and I hissed. "Anne. Get Anne."

"Who?" Maxon asked.

"Her head maid," Aspen explained. "Avery, get Anne and a medical kit. We'll have to make do. And we need to do something with her," he added, nodding his head at Paige.

I watched Maxon's worried eyes finally move from my bloody arm to Paige's troubled face.

"Are you a criminal? A runaway?" he asked her.

"Not that kind of criminal. And I did run away, but there's no one looking for me."

Maxon considered her words. "Welcome aboard. Follow Avery down to the kitchens and tell a Mallory you'll be working with her on the prince's command. Instruct her to come to the officers' wing immediately."

"Mallory. Yes, Your Majesty." Paige gave him a deep curtsy and followed Officer Avery from the room, leaving me alone with Maxon and Aspen. I'd been with both of them all night, but this was the first time it was just the three of us. I could feel the weight of our secrets filling up the already restricting room.

"How'd you make it out?" I asked.

"August, Georgia, and Micah heard the gunshots and came running," Maxon said. "He wasn't kidding when he said they'd never hurt us." He paused, his eyes quickly distant and sad. "Micah didn't make it."

I turned my head away. I didn't know a thing about him, but he died tonight for us. I felt as guilty as if I'd taken his life myself.

I went to wipe a tear away, forgetting to use my left arm, and cried out.

"Calm down, America," Aspen said, forgetting to be formal.

"Everything's going to work out," Maxon promised.

I nodded, pursing my lips together to avoid crying anymore. What a waste.

We were quiet for what felt like a long time, but maybe it was the pain stretching out the minutes.

"It's wonderful to have such devotion," Maxon said suddenly.

At first I thought he was talking about Micah again. But Aspen and I looked over and saw him gazing at a space on the wall behind me.

I turned my head, happy to focus on anything that wasn't the searing pain in my arm. There, beside several pictures drawn by one of his younger siblings, was a note.

I'll always love you. I'll wait for you forever. I'm with you, no matter what.

My handwriting was a little sloppier a year ago when I'd left that note by my window for Aspen to find, and it was surrounded by silly little hearts that I would never put in a love letter now, but I could still feel the importance of those words. It was the first time I'd put them in writing, afraid of how much more I felt those things once they were on paper. I also remembered the fear of my mother finding that note surpassing any other worry about the enormity of knowing, without a doubt, that I loved Aspen.

Right now I feared Maxon recognizing my handwriting.

"It must be nice to have someone to write to. I've never had the luxury of love letters," Maxon said, a sad smile on his face. "Has she kept her word?"

Aspen was moving pillows from the other bed to prop under my head, avoiding eye contact with either Maxon or myself.

"Writing is difficult," he said. "But I do know she's with me, no matter what. I don't doubt it."

I looked at Aspen's short, dark hair—the only part of him I could really see—and I felt a new pain. In a way he was right. We would never truly leave each other. But . . . the words on that paper? That encompassing love that used to overwhelm me? It wasn't here anymore.

Was Aspen still counting on it?

My eyes flickered to Maxon, and the sadness on his face read a bit like jealousy. I wasn't surprised. I remembered telling Maxon that I'd been in love before; he'd looked as if he'd been cheated out of something, so unsure at that point if he would ever fall in love.

If he knew that the love I'd spoken about and the love

Aspen just shared were the same one, I was sure it would crush him.

"Write her soon," Maxon advised. "Don't let her forget."

"What's taking them so long?" Aspen muttered, and left the room, not bothering to acknowledge Maxon's words.

Maxon watched him go and turned back to face me. "I'm so useless. I have no idea how to help you, so I thought I'd at least try to help him. He saved both our lives tonight." Maxon shook his head. "Seems I only upset him."

"Everyone's just worried. You're doing fine," I assured him.

He gave an exasperated laugh, coming to kneel by the bed. "You're lying there with a seeping gash on your arm, and you're trying to comfort me. You're absurd."

"If you ever decide to write me a love letter, I'd lead with that," I joked.

He smiled. "Can't I do anything for you?"

"Hold my hand? Not too hard though."

Maxon placed his fingers in the loose grip of my palm, and even though it didn't change anything, it was nice to feel him there.

"I probably won't. Write you a love letter, that is. I try to stave off embarrassment as often as possible."

"You can't plan wars, don't know how to cook, and refuse to write love letters," I teased.

"That's correct. My list of faults is ever growing." He wiggled his fingers in my hand, and I was so grateful for the distraction.

"That's fine. I'll continue to guess at your feelings since you refuse to write me a note. With a purple pen. All the *i*'s dotted with hearts."

"Which is exactly how I would do it," he said in mock seriousness. I giggled but stopped quickly when the movement reignited the burning. "I don't think you have to guess at my feelings though."

"Well," I started, finding it harder and harder to breathe, "it's not like you've ever said it out loud."

Maxon opened his mouth to object and silenced himself. His eyes gazed toward the ceiling as he thought through our history, trying to pinpoint the moment when he'd told me he loved me.

In the safe room, it was suggested in every way. He'd let the feeling slip into a dozen romantic gestures or indicated it was there by dancing around the words . . . but the actual statement had never come. Not between us. I would have remembered, and I would have made them my reason never to question him, my reason to confess what I was feeling, too.

"My lady?" Anne said, her voice making its way through the door a moment before her worried face.

Maxon stepped back, letting go of my hand as he made space for her.

Anne's focused eyes took in the wound, and she touched it gingerly as she inspected how bad it was.

"You'll need stitches. I'm not sure we have anything that will completely numb you," she assessed.

"It's okay. Just do your best," I said. I felt calmer with her there.

She nodded. "Someone get some boiling water. We should have antiseptic in the kit, but I want water, too."

"I'll get it." By the door, Marlee was standing, her face lined with worry.

"Marlee," I whimpered, losing control. I put the Mallory thing together. Of course she and Carter couldn't go by their real names while they were hiding right under the king's nose.

"I'll be right back, America. Hold tight." She scurried away, but I felt a great relief knowing she would be with me.

Anne absorbed the shock of Marlee's presence in stride, and I watched as she pulled out a needle and thread from the medical kit. I took comfort in the fact that she sewed almost all my clothes. My arm shouldn't be a problem.

With incredible speed, Marlee was back with a pitcher of steaming water, an armful of towels, and a bottle of amber liquid. She set the pitcher and towels on top of the dresser, unscrewing the bottle as she came over.

"For the pain." She lifted my head so I could drink, and I obeyed.

The stuff in the bottle was a new kind of burning, and I coughed my way through swallowing it. She urged me to take another sip, and I did, hating it the whole time.

"I'm so glad you're here," I whispered.

"I'm always here for you, America. You know that." She smiled; and for the first time in our friendship, she seemed older than me, so calm and sure. "What in the world were you doing?"

I made a face. "It seemed like a good idea."

Her eyes became sympathetic. "America, you are full of nothing but bad ideas. Great intentions but awful ideas."

She was right, of course, and I should have known better by now. But having her here, even to tell me how dumb I'd been, made the whole thing less awful.

"How soundproof are these walls?" Anne asked.

"Pretty good," Aspen said. "Don't hear too much this deep in the palace."

"Good," she said. "Okay, I need everyone in the hall. Miss Marlee, I'm going to need some space, but you can stay."

Marlee nodded. "I'll keep out of your way, Anne."

Avery left first, with Aspen trailing close behind him, and Maxon was last. The look in his eyes reminded me of the day I'd told him I'd gone hungry before: sad to know about it and devastated that he couldn't undo it.

The door clicked shut, and Anne started working quickly. She'd already set up everything she needed and held out her hand to Marlee for the bottle.

"Gulp it," she ordered, lifting my head.

I braced myself. I had to come off the lip of the bottle and go back to it several times because of the coughing, but I managed to get a good amount of it down. Or at least it was good enough for Anne.

"Hold this," she said, passing me a small towel. "Bite down on it when things hurt."

I nodded.

"The stitches won't hurt like the cleaning will. I can see dirt from here, so I'm going to have to be thorough." She sighed, looking again at the wound. "You'll have a scar, but I'm going to make it as small as I can. We'll put loose sleeves on your dresses for a few weeks to cover it while you heal. No one will know. And seeing as you were with the prince, I won't ask questions. Whatever you did, I'll trust it was something important."

"I think so," I said, not really sure anymore.

She got a towel wet and held it inches away from the gash. "Ready?"

I nodded.

I bit into the towel, hoping it would muffle the screams. I was sure that everyone in the hall could hear, but no one else probably would. It felt as if Anne was poking every nerve in my arm, and Marlee crawled on top of me to keep me from writhing.

"It'll be over soon, America," she promised. "Think of something happy. Think about your family."

I tried. I fought to put May's laugh or my dad's knowing smile in the front of my thoughts, but they wouldn't stay. I could only catch them long enough to feel them slip away under a new wave of pain.

How in the world did Marlee make it through her caning alive?

Once my wound was clean, Anne started sewing me up. She was right: the stitches didn't hurt as much. I couldn't tell if it was because it was actually less painful or if the liquor they'd given me was finally kicking in. It did seem like the edges of the room weren't quite as sharp anymore.

Then people were back, talking about things, about me. Who should stay, who should go, what we would say in the morning . . . so many details that I couldn't contribute to.

In the end, it was Maxon who scooped me up to return me to my room. It took some effort to hold my head upright, but it made it easier to hear him.

"How are you feeling?"

"Your eyes look like chocolate," I mumbled.

He smiled. "And yours look like the morning sky."

"Can I have water?"

"Yes. Lots," he promised. "Let's get her upstairs," he said to someone else. And I fell asleep to the rocking of his steps.

CHAPTER 15

I WOKE WITH A HEADACHE. I moaned as I rubbed my temple, then yelped when the action sent a sharp pain across my arm.

"Here," Mary said, coming to sit on the edge of my bed. She held out two pills and a glass of water.

I slowly pushed myself up to take her offering, my head throbbing through all of it. "What time is it?"

"Nearly eleven," Mary said. "We sent word that you weren't feeling well and wouldn't be at breakfast. If we hurry, we could probably get you ready for lunch with the other Elite."

The thought of rushing or even eating didn't sound appealing, but I thought it was wisest to get back into a normal routine. It was becoming clear just how much we'd risked last night, and I didn't want to give anyone a reason to suspect anything at all had happened.

I gave Mary a nod, and we both stood. My legs weren't quite as reliable as I'd have liked, but I moved toward the bathroom anyway. Anne was just outside the door, cleaning, as Lucy sat in a wide chair sewing sleeves onto a dress that had probably been designed for simple straps.

She looked up from her handiwork. "Are you all right, miss? You gave us quite a scare."

"I'm sorry. I think I'm as good as I can be."

She smiled at me. "We're ready to do what we can to help you, miss. You only need to ask."

I wasn't completely sure what she was offering, but I would take her up on any help that might get me through the next few days.

"Oh, Officer Leger stopped by, as well as the prince. They both hoped you would let them know how you were feeling once you were up to it."

I nodded. "After lunch, I'll take care of that."

With no warning, my arm was in someone's hands. Anne was looking closely at the wound, gingerly peeking under the bandages to check my progress.

"It doesn't look infected. As long as we keep it clean, I think it will heal nicely. I wish I could have done something better. I know it'll leave a mark," she lamented.

"Don't worry. The best people all have some kind of scar." I thought of Marlee's hands and Maxon's back. They both held permanent marks of their bravery. I was honored to join them.

"Lady America, your bath is ready," Mary said from around the bathroom door.

I took in her face, then Lucy's, then Anne's. I'd always been close to my maids, had always trusted them. But something changed last night. It was the first time those bonds were tested; and in the light of day, they were still there, strong and holding.

I wasn't sure there was a way to prove that I was as loyal to them as they were to me. But I hoped an opportunity would show itself.

If I focused, I could lift my fork to my mouth without grimacing. It took an extraordinary amount of effort, to the point where I started sweating in the middle of the meal. I decided to stick to nibbling on bread. I didn't need my right arm to hold that.

Kriss asked how my headache was—which I guessed was the story circulating—and I told her I was fine now, though my head and arm were impossible to ignore. That was the extent of the questioning, and it looked as if no one had guessed that anything was out of the ordinary.

As I chewed a bite of bread, I debated how well the other girls would have done if they had gone in my place last night. I decided the only person who would have fared better was Celeste. Without a doubt, she'd have found a way to fight back, and I was a little jealous for a minute that I wasn't more like her.

Once our trays were carted out of the Women's Room, Silvia came in and asked for our attention.

"It's time for you ladies to shine again. In a week, we'll be

having a small tea party, and you all, of course, are invited!"
I sighed to myself, worried about who we were meant to entertain this time. "You won't be in charge of any preparations for this particular party, but you must be on your best behavior, because this will be filmed for the public."

I perked up a bit. I could handle that.

"You will each invite two people to be your personal guests at this tea party, and that will be your only responsibility. Choose wisely, and let me know your two contacts by Friday."

She walked away, leaving us all mentally scrambling. This was a test, and we knew it. Who in the room had the most impressive connections, the most valuable ones?

Maybe I was being paranoid, but it felt as if this task specifically targeted me. The king must be searching for ways to remind everyone I was useless.

"Who are you picking, Celeste?" Kriss asked.

She shrugged. "Not sure yet. But I promise they'll be spectacular."

If I had Celeste's list of friends at my disposal, I wouldn't be nervous either. Who was I going to invite? My mom?

Celeste turned to me, her voice warm. "Who do you think you'll bring, America?"

I tried to hide my shock. Even though we'd had a little breakthrough in the library, this was the first time she'd addressed me the same way she would a friend. I cleared my throat. "I have no idea. I'm not sure I know anyone who would be appropriate to invite. It might be better if I bring no one." I probably shouldn't have been so open about how disadvantaged I was, but it wasn't as if the others weren't aware.

"Well, if you really can't find anyone, let me know," Celeste said. "I'm positive I have more than two friends who would like to visit the palace, and I could make sure you at least have an idea of who they are. If you want to, that is."

I stared at her, tempted to ask her what the catch was; but, looking into her eyes, I didn't think there was one. Then I was sure of it when she winked at me with the eye that Elise and Kriss couldn't see. Celeste, the consummate fighter, was pulling for me.

"Thank you," I said, feeling truly humbled.

She shrugged. "No problem. If we're going to have a party, might as well make it a good one." She leaned back in her chair, smiling to herself, and I was sure she was picturing this event as her last hurrah. Part of me wanted to tell her not to give up, but I couldn't. Only one of us could have Maxon in the end.

By the afternoon, I had the rough outline of a plan, but it was dependent upon one big thing: I'd have to get Maxon's help.

I was sure we would find each other before the end of the day, so I didn't let myself worry about it too much. For the time being, I needed to rest again, so I headed back up to my room.

Anne was there, waiting with more pills and water. I

couldn't believe how calm she was about it all.

"I owe you one," I said, downing the medicine.

"No," Anne protested.

"Yes! Things would have been a lot different last night if you hadn't been there."

She gently took the glass from me. "I'm just glad you're okay."

She started walking to the bathroom to dispose of the water, and I followed her. "Isn't there anything I could do for you? Anything at all?"

She stood there at the counter, something clearly on her mind.

"Really, Anne. It would make me so happy."

She sighed. "Well, there's one thing. . . ."

"Please tell me."

Anne raised her eyes from the sink. "But you couldn't let it slip to anyone. Mary and Lucy would never let me live it down."

I creased my forehead. "What do you mean?"

"It's . . . it's very personal." She started fidgeting with her hands, something she never did, and I knew this was important to her.

"Okay, come talk to me about it," I encouraged, wrapping my good arm around her shoulder and ushering her to the table to sit with me.

She crossed her ankles and put her hands in her lap. "See, it's just that you get along with him so well. He seems to think so highly of you."

"You mean Maxon?"

"No," she whispered, a wild blush filling her cheeks.

"I don't understand."

She took a deep breath. "Officer Leger."

"Ooooh," I said, more shocked than I could express.

"You think it's hopeless, don't you?"

"Not hopeless," I insisted. I just didn't know how to tell the person who'd promised he'd always fight for me that he should pursue her instead.

"He's always speaking so kindly of you. I know if you maybe mentioned me to him, or could even find out if he's got a girlfriend at home . . ."

I sighed. "I can try, but I can't promise anything."

"Oh, I know. Don't worry. I've been telling myself it won't happen, but I can't stop thinking about him."

I tilted my head. "I know how that is."

She put a hand in front of her. "And it's not because he's a Two. If he was an Eight, I'd want someone like him."

"Lots of people would," I said. And that was true. Celeste noticed him, Kriss said he was funny, and even that Delilah woman sounded like she had a crush on him. That wasn't even taking into account all the girls back home who'd chased him. Hearing things like that didn't bother me so much anymore, not even from someone as close to me as Anne.

It was one more thing that made me sure that my feelings for Aspen were gone. If I was happy to suggest that someone else should take my place, then I really didn't belong with him.

Still, I wasn't sure how to broach the subject.

I reached over the polished wood and put my hand on hers. "I'll try, Anne. I swear."

She smiled but bit her lip anxiously. "Just please don't tell the others."

I held her hand tighter. "You've always kept my secrets. I'll always keep yours."

CHAPTER 16

IT WAS ONLY A FEW hours later when Aspen knocked on my door. My maids merely curtsied and exited, knowing without instruction that whatever we would say needed to be private.

"How are you feeling?"

"Not too bad," I said. "My arm throbs a bit and I have a headache, but otherwise I'm fine."

He shook his head. "I shouldn't have let you go."

I patted the space beside me on the bed. "Come sit."

He hesitated a bit. In my mind now, he was past suspicion. Maxon and my maids knew we communicated, and he'd led us out of the palace last night. Where was the risk? He must have thought the same thing, because he finally sat, choosing to keep a respectable distance just in case.

"I'm a part of this, Aspen. I couldn't have stayed behind.

And there's nothing wrong with me. I honestly owe that to you. You saved me last night."

"If I hadn't been fast enough, or if Maxon hadn't gotten you over that wall, you'd be a prisoner somewhere right now. I almost let you die. I almost let *Maxon* die." He shook his head at the floor. "Do you know what would have happened to Avery and me if you two hadn't made it back? Do you know what—" He paused, seeming to hold back tears. "Do you know what would have happened to me if we hadn't found you?"

Aspen looked at me, into me. The pain in his eyes was clear.

"But you did. You found me, you protected me, and you got me help. You were amazing." I put my hand on Aspen's back, running it up and down, trying to comfort him.

"I'm just realizing, Mer, that no matter what happens . . . there will always be a string tying you to me. I'll never not worry about you. I'll never not care about what you do. You'll always be something to me."

I took my hand and laced it through his arm, resting my head on his shoulder. "I know what you mean."

We stayed like that for a while, and I guessed that maybe Aspen was doing the same thing I was: replaying everything in his head. The way we avoided each other as children, the way we couldn't stop looking at each other when we were older, a thousand stolen moments in the tree house—all the things that made us who we were.

"America, I need to say something." I lifted my head, and Aspen turned to face me, holding me gently by my arms.

"When I told you that I would always love you, I meant it. And I . . . I . . ."

He couldn't manage to get the words out, and to be honest, I was grateful. Yes, I was tied to him, but we weren't that couple in the tree house anymore.

He gave a weak laugh. "I guess I need some sleep. I can't think straight."

"You and me both. And there's so much to think about."

He nodded. "Look, Mer, we can't do that again. Don't tell Maxon I'll help him with something so risky, and don't expect me to sneak you anywhere."

"I'm not sure it was worth it anyway. I can't imagine Maxon would want to go again."

"Good." He stood, then picked up my hand and kissed it. "My lady," he said, his voice teasing.

I smiled and squeezed his hand a little. And he did the same back. As we held hands, my grip tightening more every second, I realized that soon I'd need to let go. I'd need to really let go.

I looked into Aspen's eyes, and I could feel the tears threatening to come. *How do I say good-bye to you?*

He ran his thumb over the back of my hand and placed it on my lap. He bent and kissed my hair. "Take it easy. I'll come check on you tomorrow."

After a quick tug of my ear at dinner, Maxon knew I would be waiting for him tonight. I sat in front of my mirror, wishing the minutes would move faster. Mary brushed the length of my hair, calmly humming to herself. I vaguely recognized the tune as something I once played at someone's wedding. When I'd gotten chosen for the Selection, I'd wanted so badly to find my way back to that life. I wanted a world full of the music I'd always loved.

But, truly, that was never something I could have held on to. No matter which path I took in life now, music might only be something I pulled out at parties to entertain a guest or a way I relaxed on a weekend.

I looked at myself in the mirror and realized I wasn't bitter about that, not like I thought I'd be. I'd miss it, but it was just a piece of who I was now, not *everything* I was. There were possibilities in front of me no matter how the Selection unfolded.

I really was more than my caste.

Maxon's light knock pulled me from my thoughts, and Mary answered the door.

"Good evening," Maxon said to Mary as he entered, and she curtsied in response.

His eyes met mine briefly, and I wondered again if he could see how I felt about him, if it was as real to him as it was to me.

"Your Majesty," Mary greeted quietly. She was about to leave the room when Maxon held up a hand.

"Forgive me, but could you tell me your name?"

She stared at him for a moment, looked to me, and then

focused on Maxon again. "I'm Mary, Your Majesty."

"Mary. And Anne, we met last night." He gave her a small bow of his head. "And you?"

"Lucy." Her voice was small, but I could sense her joy in being acknowledged.

"Excellent. Anne, Mary, and Lucy. Lovely to properly meet you. I'm sure Anne has filled you both in on last night so you can serve Lady America the best way possible. I want to thank you for your dedication and discretion."

His eyes fell on each of them in turn. "I realize I've put you in a compromising position, and if anyone ever raises questions about what happened, feel free to send them directly to me. It was my decision, and you shouldn't be held responsible for any consequences that follow because of that."

"Thank you, Your Majesty," Lucy said.

I'd always sensed that my maids had a deep devotion to Maxon, but tonight I felt like it went beyond the typical obligation. It seemed to me in the past as if the highest level of loyalty was to the king, but now I wondered if that was true. More and more, I saw little things that made me think people preferred his son.

Maybe I wasn't the only one who saw King Clarkson's methods as barbaric, his way of thinking cruel. Maybe the rebels weren't the only ones ready for Maxon. Perhaps there were others out there who were looking for more.

My maids curtsied and left, leaving Maxon standing beside me.

"What was that about? Learning their names, I mean?"

He sighed. "Last night when Officer Leger said Anne's name and I didn't know who he meant . . . it was embarrassing. Shouldn't I know the people who tend to you better than some random guard?"

He's not that random. "To be fair, the maids all gossip about the guards. It wouldn't surprise me if the guards did the same."

"Still. They're with you every day. I should have known their names months ago."

I smiled at his reasoning and went to stand, though he looked uneasy about me moving at all.

"I'm fine, Maxon," I insisted, taking his outstretched hand.

"You were shot last night, if I remember correctly. You can't blame me for worrying."

"It wasn't like a real bullet wound. It only cut me."

"All the same, I won't quickly forget the sound of your muffled screams as Anne sewed you back together. Come, you should be resting."

Maxon ushered me to the bed, and I crawled in. He tucked me under the covers before lying down on top of them himself, facing me. I waited for him to talk about everything that had happened or to warn me of the coming fallout. But he didn't say anything. He lay there, brushing my hair back with his fingers, sometimes letting the tips linger on my cheek.

It felt as if we were the whole world just then.

"If something had happened—"

"But it didn't."

Maxon rolled his eyes, his voice getting serious. "It most certainly did! You came home bleeding. We nearly lost you in the streets."

"Look, I'm not upset with the choice I made," I said, trying to calm him. "I wanted to go, to hear for myself. Besides, it's not as if I could have let you go without me."

"I can't believe how unprepared we were, going out in a palace truck without more guards. And there are rebels just walking the streets. Since when are they not hiding? Where are they getting these guns? I feel clueless, helpless. I'm losing the country I love a little every day. I nearly lost you, and I—"

Maxon stopped himself, his frustration fading into something new. He moved his hand back to my cheek. "Last night, you said something . . . about love."

I looked down. "I remember." I tried to contain my blush.

"It's funny how you can think you've said something when you never really did."

I giggled, feeling that the words were coming in his very next breath.

"It's also funny how you can think you've heard something when you didn't either," he said instead.

All the humor vanished from the moment. "I know what you mean." I swallowed and watched as his hand moved from my cheek to lace his fingers through mine, knowing that he and I were both watching them. "Maybe, for some people, it would be hard to confess that. Like, if they worried they might not make it to the end."

He sighed. "Or it would be hard to say if you worried that someone might not *want* to make it to the end . . . maybe never quite gave up on someone else."

I shook my head. "That's not . . ."

"Okay."

For everything we'd said in the safe room, for everything we'd confessed to each other, for everything that had firmly settled in my heart, these small words were the most frightening things to pass between us. Because once they were out there, we could never take them back.

I didn't completely understand his reasons for hesitating, but I knew mine. If he ended up with Kriss after I'd put my heart out there, I would be upset with him, but I would *hate* myself. It was a risk I was too frightened to take.

The silence was making me uneasy, and when it became too much, I spoke.

"Maybe we could talk about this again when I'm feeling better?"

He sighed. "Of course. Completely thoughtless of me."

"No, no. There's just something else I wanted to ask you about." There were bigger things than us to consider right now.

"Go ahead."

"I had a thought about my guests for the upcoming tea party, but I would need your approval."

He looked at me, confused.

"And I want you to know everything I would intend to discuss with them. We might be breaking several laws, so I won't do it if you say not to."

Intrigued, Maxon propped himself up on one arm to listen. "Tell me everything."

CHAPTER 17

THE BACKDROP FOR OUR PHOTOS was plain and light blue. My maids put together a lovely dress for me, with little off-the-shoulder cuffs that just covered my scar. For now, my days of strapless gowns were gone.

Though I looked pretty good, I was completely overshadowed by Nicoletta, and even Georgia was dazzling in her gown.

"Lady America," the woman next to the camera called. "We remember Princess Nicoletta from when the women of the Italian royal family came to visit the palace, but who is your other guest?"

"This is Georgia, a dear friend of mine," I replied sweetly. "One of the things that I've learned from the Selection so far is that moving forward means joining your life before coming to the palace with the future that lies in front of you. I'm hoping to make another step in joining those two worlds today."

Some of those standing around let out satisfied noises as the cameras continued to capture the three of us.

"Excellent, ladies," the photographer said. "You can go enjoy the party. We'll be taking some candid shots later."

"Sounds fun," I answered, motioning for my guests to come with me.

Maxon had made it clear that of all days, today was one when I really needed to be on. I hoped to be the lead example of what an Elite should be, but it was hard for me to try and be so perfect.

"Tone it down, America, or rainbows are going to shoot out of your eyes." I loved that even though our friendship was brief, Georgia could see right through my act.

I laughed, and Nicoletta joined in. "She's right. You do seem a bit perky."

I sighed with a smile. "Sorry. Today is a high-stakes kind of day."

Georgia put an arm on my shoulder as we walked deeper into the room. "After everything you and Maxon have been through, I highly doubt he'll send you home over a tea party."

"That's not exactly what I mean. But we'll have to talk about it later." I turned to face them. "Right now, it would be a huge help to me if we could mingle. Once things settle down, we need to have a pretty serious discussion."

Nicoletta looked over at Georgia, then back to me. "What

kind of friend are you introducing me to here?"

"A valuable one. I swear. I'll explain later."

For their part, Georgia and Nicoletta made me shine. As a princess, Nicoletta was quite possibly the best guest in the room, and I saw in Kriss's eyes that she wished she had thought of that. Of course, she didn't have a direct line to Italian royalty like I did. Nicoletta herself had given me a phone number to contact her if I ever needed to.

No one knew who Georgia was, but when they'd heard my line—the one Maxon had specifically fed to me—about joining my past and my future, they thought that was a spectacular idea as well.

Elise's choices were predictable. Powerful but predictable. Two very distant cousins from New Asia representing her ties to the leaders of the nation paraded next to her in their traditional dresses. Kriss had chosen a professor from the college her father worked at and her mother. I was dreading my family hearing about that. When Mom or May realized they had a chance to be here, I was sure to get a very disappointed letter from them.

Celeste, true to her word, brought full-fledged celebrities. Tessa Tamble—who had allegedly given a show at Celeste's last birthday party—was there in a very short but glamorous dress. Celeste's other guest was Kirstie Summer, another musician who was mostly known for her outlandish concerts, and her outfit was more like a costume. My guess was that it was either something she usually performed in or an experiment in painted leather. Either way, I was surprised she got through the door, both because of the way she was dressed and the fact that if you passed within a foot of her, you could smell the alcohol radiating off her.

"Nicoletta," Queen Amberly said, approaching us. "How wonderful to see you again."

They exchanged kisses on both cheeks before Nicoletta spoke. "The joy is all mine. I was elated when I received America's invitation. We all had such a wonderful time on our last visit."

"I'm glad to hear that," the queen commented. "I'm afraid it's going to be a bit calmer today."

"I don't know," Nicoletta countered, pointing over to where Kirstie and Tessa were standing in a corner and talking loudly. "I'm betting those two will send me home with at least one story."

We all laughed, though I could see a little anxiety in the queen's eyes. "I suppose I should go introduce myself."

"Always the picture of bravery," I joked.

She smiled. "Please, relax and enjoy yourselves. I hope you get to meet some new acquaintances but, honestly, just take some time together with your friends."

I nodded, and Queen Amberly left to meet Celeste's guests. Tessa was looking fine, but Kirstie appeared to be picking up and smelling every finger sandwich on a nearby table. I made a mental note not to eat anything near where she'd been standing.

I surveyed the room. Everyone seemed busy eating or talking, so I decided now was as good a time as any.

"Follow me," I said, heading to a small table in the back. We sat, and a maid brought us tea. Once we were alone, I dived in, hoping this would go smoothly.

"Georgia, first, I haven't had a chance to apologize about Micah."

She was shaking her head even as I spoke. "He always wanted to be a hero. We all accept that things might . . . end like that. But I think he was proud."

"I'm still really sorry. Is there anything we can do?"

"No. Everything's taken care of. Trust me, he wouldn't have chosen a different end," she insisted.

I thought of the mouselike boy in the corner of the room that night. He willingly ran out into the fray for me, for all of us. Bravery hides in amazing places.

I turned back to the matter at hand. "Well, Georgia, as you can see, Nicoletta is the princess of Italy. She visited with us a few weeks ago." I looked between them. "At that time she made it clear that Italy would like to be an ally to Illéa if certain things changed."

"America!" Nicoletta hissed.

I held up a hand. "Trust me. Georgia here is a friend, but I don't know her from Carolina. She's one of the leaders of the Northern rebels."

Nicoletta sat up in her seat. Georgia gave her a timid nod, confirming what I'd said.

"She came to our aid recently. And lost someone close to her in the process," I explained.

Nicoletta placed her hand on Georgia's. "I'm sorry." Then

she turned to me, curious as to how all this tied together.

"What we say needs to stay among us, but I thought we might be able to talk about some things that would benefit everyone here," I explained.

"Are you trying to overthrow the king?" Nicoletta asked.

"No," Georgia assured her. "We're hoping to align ourselves with Maxon's reign, and work toward eliminating the castes. Maybe within his lifetime. He seems to have more compassion for his people."

"He does," I added.

"Then why do you attack the palace? And all those people?" Nicoletta accused sharply.

I shook my head. "They're not like the Southern rebels. They don't kill people. They sometimes deliver justice that they see as fit—"

"We've gotten unwed mothers out of jail, things like that," Georgia interjected.

"They *have* broken into the palace, but never with the intent to kill," I added.

Nicoletta sighed. "I'm not so bothered by that, but I'm not sure why you need me to know them."

"Neither am I," Georgia confessed.

I took a breath. "The Southern rebels are getting more and more aggressive. In the last few months alone, their attacks have increased, not just at the palace but across the country. They're merciless. I worry, as does Maxon, that they're very close to making a move we won't be able to recover from. Their idea of killing their way down the Elite's castes is pretty drastic, and we're all afraid those attacks are going to escalate."

"They already have," Georgia said, more to me than to Nicoletta. "When you invited me here, I was happy if only to be able to give you more news. The Southern rebels have moved to the Threes."

I placed a hand over my mouth, shocked that they were progressing so quickly. "Are you sure?"

"Positive," Georgia confirmed. "The numbers shifted yesterday."

After a moment of quiet worry, Nicoletta spoke. "Why are they doing this?"

Georgia turned to her. "To scare the Elite into leaving, to scare the royal family in general. It seems like they think that if they can stop the Selection from finishing and isolate Maxon, they'll only have to get rid of him in order to take over."

"And that's the real worry. If they come to power, there's nothing for Maxon to offer you as king. The Southern rebels would only oppress people further."

"So what do you propose?" Nicoletta asked.

I tried to walk lightly into the criminal territory in front of me. "Georgia and the other Northerners have a better opportunity to stop the Southern rebels than any of us in the palace. They can see their moves more easily and have had chances to confront them . . . but they're untrained and unarmed."

They both waited, not seeing what I was implying.

I lowered my voice. "Maxon can't siphon money from the palace to help them buy weapons."

"I see," Nicoletta finally said.

"It would be under the full understanding that these weapons would only be used to stop the Southerners. Never against an officer of any government-issued position," I said, looking at Georgia.

"That wouldn't be a problem." I saw in her eyes how much she meant that, and I already knew it in my own heart. If she'd wanted to, she could have taken me out when she found me in the woods or chosen not to come running into the alley after us. But that was never her goal.

Nicoletta was strumming her fingers across her lips, thinking. I knew we were asking a lot, but I wasn't sure how to move forward otherwise.

"If anyone found out . . . ," she said.

"I know. I've thought about that." If the king ever knew, a caning wouldn't be enough where I was concerned.

"If we could make sure there isn't a trail." Nicoletta kept fidgeting her fingers near her mouth.

"It would need to be cash, at least. That makes it harder," Georgia offered.

Nicoletta nodded and dropped her hand to the table. "I said if I could do anything for you, I would. We could use a strong friend, and if your country is lost, I fear we would only gain another enemy."

I gave her a sad smile.

She turned to Georgia. "I can get the cash today, but it

would need to be converted."

Georgia smiled. "We have means."

Over her shoulder I saw a photographer approaching. I picked up my teacup and whispered, "Camera."

"And I've always thought America was a lady. I think sometimes we miss those traits because we see Fives as performers and Sixes as housekeepers. But look at Queen Amberly. She's so much more than a Four," Georgia said kindly. Nicoletta and I both nodded.

"She's an incredible woman. It's been a privilege to live with her," I shared.

"Maybe you'll get to stay with her!" Nicoletta said with a wink.

"Smile, ladies!" the photographer instructed, and we all showed our brightest faces, hoping to cover our dangerous secret.

CHAPTER 18

THE DAY AFTER NICOLETTA AND Georgia left, I caught myself looking over my shoulder a lot. I was sure someone knew what I'd said, what I'd handed over to the rebels in a brief afternoon. I kept reminding myself that if anyone had overheard, I certainly would have been arrested by now. Seeing as I was still enjoying a wonderful breakfast with the other Elite and the royal family, I had to believe that everything was fine. Besides, Maxon would defend me if he had to.

After breakfast, I went back to my room to touch up my makeup. While I was in the bathroom, sweeping on another layer of lipstick, a knock sounded at the door. It was just Lucy and me, and she went to see who it was while I finished up. A minute later she popped her head around the corner.

"It's Prince Maxon," she whispered.

I whipped my head around. "He's here?"

She nodded, beaming. "He remembered my name."

"Of course he did," I replied with a smile. I put everything down and ran my fingers through my hair. "Lead me out, then leave quietly."

"As you wish, miss."

Maxon was standing tentatively by the door, uncharacteristically waiting for an invitation to enter. He held a small, thin box, and he drummed his fingers against it, fidgeting. "Sorry to interrupt. I was wondering if I could have a moment."

"Of course," I said, walking over. "Please come in." Maxon and I perched on the edge of my bed.

"I wanted to see you first," he said, getting situated. "I wanted to explain before the others came in bragging."

Explain? For some reason his words put me on edge. If the others were bragging, I was about to be excluded from something.

"What do you mean?" I realized I was biting my freshly glossed lip.

Maxon passed the box over to me. "I'll clarify, I promise. But first, this is for you."

I took the box and unhooked a small button in the front so I could open it. I think I inhaled every millimeter of air in the room.

Resting inside the box were a breathtaking set of earrings and matching bracelet. They coordinated beautifully, with blue and green gems woven into a subtle floral design.

"Maxon, I love it, but I can't possibly take this. It's too . . . too . . ."

"On the contrary, you must take them. It's a gift, and it's tradition that you wear them in the Convicting."

"The what?"

He shook his head. "Silvia will explain all that; but the point is, it's tradition for the prince to present the Elite with jewelry and for them to wear the pieces to the ceremony. There will be quite a few officials there, and you need to look your best. And unlike the things you've been presented with so far, these are all real and yours to keep."

I smiled. Of course we wouldn't have been given real jewelry to wear until now. I wondered how many girls had taken things home, thinking that if they hadn't gotten Maxon, at least they got a few thousand in jewelry.

"They're wonderful, Maxon. Just my taste. Thank you."

Maxon raised a finger. "You're welcome, and that's part of what I wanted to discuss. I chose the gifts for each of you personally and intended that they should all be equal. However, you prefer to wear the necklace from your father, and I'm sure it would be a comfort to you in the middle of something as big as the Convicting. So, while the others got necklaces, you have a bracelet."

He reached over to my hand and lifted it. "And I see you're attached to your little button, and I'm glad you still like the bracelet I brought back from New Asia, but they really aren't appropriate. Try this on so we can see how it rests."

I took off Maxon's bracelet and set it on the edge of my

nightstand. But I took Aspen's button and set it in my jar with its single penny. It seemed like it should be there for now.

I turned back and caught Maxon staring at the jar, something hard in his eyes. It disappeared swiftly enough, and he went to removing the bracelet from the box. His fingers tickled my skin, and when he moved away, I nearly gasped again at how beautiful his gift was.

"It really is perfect, Maxon."

"I hoped you'd think so. But that is precisely why I needed to talk to you. I set out to spend the same amount on all of you. I wanted to be fair."

I nodded. That sounded reasonable.

"The problem with that being, your tastes are much simpler than the others. And you have a bracelet as opposed to a necklace. I ended up spending half as much on you as the rest, and I wanted you to know that before you saw what I gave them. And I wanted you to know that it came from wanting to give you what I felt you would like the best, not because of your place or anything like that." Maxon's face was so sincere.

"Thank you, Maxon. I wouldn't have had it any other way," I said, placing a hand on his arm.

As always, he seemed so happy to be touched. "I suspected as much. Though thank you for saying so. I was afraid I might hurt you."

"Not at all."

Maxon's smile grew. "Of course, I still wanted to be fair,

so I had a thought." He reached into his pocket and pulled out a thin envelope. "Perhaps you would like to send the difference to your family."

I stared at the envelope. "Are you serious?"

"Of course. I want to be impartial, and I thought this would be the best way to handle the discrepancy. And I hoped it would make you happy." He placed the envelope in my hands, and I took it, still shocked.

"You didn't have to do that."

"I know. But sometimes it's about what you want to do, not what you have to."

Our eyes met, and I realized that he did a lot for me out of simply wanting to. Giving me pants when I wasn't allowed to wear them, bringing me a bracelet from the other side of the world . . .

Surely he loved me. Right? Why wouldn't he just say it?

We're alone, Maxon. If you say it, I'll say it back.

Nothing.

"I don't know how to thank you for this, Maxon."

He smiled. "Hearing you say it is nice." He cleared his throat. "I'm always interested in hearing how you feel."

Oh, no. Nope. I was not putting it out there first.

"Well, I'm very grateful. As always."

Maxon sighed. "I'm happy you like it." Unsatisfied, he took to watching the carpet. "I need to go. I still have to deliver the gifts to the others."

We stood together, and I escorted him to the door. As he left, he turned and kissed my hand. With a friendly nod of his head, he disappeared around the corner to visit the others.

I walked back to the bed and looked again at my gifts. I couldn't believe that something this beautiful was mine to keep, forever. I vowed to myself that, even if I went home and all the money ran out and my family was absolutely destitute, I would never sell these or give them away, or the bracelet he'd gotten me in New Asia. I would hold on to them no matter what.

"The Convicting is simple enough," Silvia said to us the next afternoon as we followed her to the Great Room. "It's one of those things that sounds much more challenging than it is, but above all it's symbolic.

"It will be a grand event. There will be several magistrates here, not to mention the extended members of the royal family, and enough cameras to make your heads spin," Silvia barked over her shoulder.

So far this was sounding anything but simple. We rounded the corner, and Silvia flung open the doors to the Great Room. In the middle of the space was Queen Amberly herself, giving instructions to men setting up rows of stadium seats. In another corner, someone was debating which carpet to roll out, and two florists were discussing which blossoms would be most appropriate. They apparently didn't think the Christmas decorations should stay. So much was happening, I almost forgot Christmas was coming at all.

Toward the back of the room a stage was set up with stairs

across the front of it, and three massive thrones were centered on the platform. To our right were four small stages with lone seats on them, looking beautiful but also very isolating. Those alone were enough to decorate the room, and I couldn't imagine how it would look once everything was in place.

"Your Majesty," Silvia said with a curtsy, and we all followed suit. The queen walked over to us, her face lit up with a smile.

"Hello, ladies," she said. "Silvia, how far have you gotten?"

"Not far at all, Majesty."

"Excellent. Ladies, let me enlighten you about your next task in the Selection process." She motioned for us to follow her inside the Great Room. "The Convicting is meant to be a symbol of your submission to the law. One of you will become the new princess, and someday queen. The law is how we live, and it will be your duty not only to live by it but to uphold it. And so," she said, stopping and facing us, "you will start with the Convicting.

"A man who has committed a crime, most likely a theft, will be brought in. These are cases that are worthy of a whipping, but these men will spend time in jail instead. And you will send them there."

The queen smiled at our bewildered expressions. "I know it sounds harsh, but it's not. These men have each committed a crime, and instead of facing the difficulties of a physical punishment, they'll be paying their debts with time.

You've seen firsthand how painful a caning can be. Being whipped isn't much better. You're doing them a favor," she said encouragingly.

I still didn't feel good about it.

Those who stole were penniless. Twos and Threes who broke laws paid their way out of punishment with money. The poor paid their way in flesh or time. I remembered Jemmy, Aspen's younger brother, leaning over a block while men took a handful of food out of his back in lashes. While I hated that, it was better than locking him away. The Legers needed him to work, young as he was, and it seemed that once you got above a Five, people forgot that.

Silvia and Queen Amberly walked us through the ceremony over and over until our lines were perfect. I tried to deliver mine with the grace that Elise or Kriss had, but they came out sounding flat every time.

I did not want to put a man in jail.

When we were dismissed, the other girls headed to the door together, but I went to the queen. She was finishing a conversation with Silvia. I should have used that time to come up with something more eloquent. Instead, when Silvia walked away and the queen addressed me, I just blurted it out.

"Please don't make me do this," I pleaded.

"I beg your pardon?"

"I can submit to the law, I swear. It's not that I'm trying to be difficult, but I can't put a man in jail. He didn't do anything to me."

Her expression was kind as she reached to touch my face. "But he did, dear girl. If you became the princess, you'd be the embodiment of the law. When someone breaks the smallest rule, they stab you. The only way to keep from bleeding out is to take a stand against those who have already harmed you so that others will not be so brazen."

"But I'm not the princess!" I implored. "No one's hurting me."

She smiled and lowered her head to mine, whispering, "You're not the princess today, but it wouldn't surprise me if that was a temporary issue."

Queen Amberly stepped back and winked.

I sighed, getting desperate. "Bring me someone else. Not some petty thief who probably only stole because they were hungry." Her face stiffened. "I'm not suggesting it's okay to steal. I know it's not. But bring me someone who did something really bad. Bring me the person who killed the guard that got Maxon and me into a safe room the last time the rebels came. That person should be locked up forever. And I'll say that happily. But I can't do this to some hungry Seven. I can't."

I could see she wanted to be gentle with me, but I could also see she wouldn't budge on this. "Allow me to be very blunt with you, Lady America. Of all the girls, you need to do this the most. People have seen you run to stop a caning, suggest undoing the castes on national television, and encourage people to fight when their lives are in serious danger." Her kind face was serious. "I'm not saying those were bad things, but they have given most people the impression that you run wild."

I fidgeted with my hands, knowing this was going to end with me doing the Convicting no matter what I said.

"If you want to stay, if you care about Maxon"—she paused, giving me a moment to consider—"then you need to do this. You need to show you have the ability to be obedient."

"I do. I just don't want to put someone in jail. That's not a princess's job. Magistrates do that."

Queen Amberly patted my shoulder. "You can do it. And you will. If you want Maxon at all, you need to be perfect. I'm sure you understand that there's opposition where you're concerned."

I nodded.

"Then do it."

She walked away, leaving me alone in the Great Room. I went up to my seat, practically a throne itself, and mumbled the lines again. I tried to tell myself that it wasn't a big deal. People broke laws and went to jail all the time. It was one person out of thousands. And I needed to be perfect.

Perfect was my only option.

CHAPTER 19

THE DAY OF THE CONVICTING I was a bundle of nerves. I was afraid I'd trip, or forget what to say. Even worse, I was afraid I'd fail. The one thing I didn't have to worry about was my clothes. My maids had to confer with the head dresser to make something suitable for me, though I wouldn't use a word as plain as *suitable* to describe it.

Following again on tradition, the dresses were all white and gold. Mine had a high waist and no strap on the left but did have a small, off-the-shoulder strap on the right, covering my scar and looking really lovely at the same time. The top was snug, but the skirt was billowing, kissing the floor with scallops of golden lace. It came together with pleats in the back that fell behind me in a short train. When I looked at myself in the mirror, it was the first time I actually thought I looked like a princess.

Anne grabbed the olive branch I was meant to carry and situated it in my arm. We were supposed to place the branches at the foot of the king as a sign of peace toward our leader and our willingness to yield to the law.

"You look beautiful, miss," Lucy said. I couldn't help but notice how calm and confident she seemed lately. I smiled.

"Thank you. I wish you were all going to be there," I said.

"Me, too." Mary sighed.

Ever proper, Anne turned the focus back in my direction. "Don't you worry, miss; you'll do perfectly. And we'll be watching with the other maids."

"You will?" That was encouraging, even though they wouldn't be downstairs.

"We wouldn't miss it," Lucy assured me.

A sharp knocking snapped us from our conversation. Mary opened the door, and I was happy to see it was Aspen.

"I'm here to escort you to the Convicting, Lady America," he said.

Lucy piped up. "What do you think of our handiwork, Officer Leger?"

He smiled slyly. "You've outdone yourselves."

Lucy giggled, and Anne quietly shushed her as she made final adjustments to my hair. Now that I knew about Anne's feelings for Aspen, it was obvious how perfect she tried to be in front of him.

I took a deep breath, remembering the masses waiting for me downstairs.

"Ready?" he asked.

I nodded, readjusted my branch, and went to the door, peeking back just once to see my maids' happy faces. I looped my arm through Aspen's and headed with him down the hall.

"How have you been?" I asked casually.

"I can't believe you're going through with this," he shot back.

I swallowed, immediately nervous again. "I don't have a choice."

"You always have a choice, Mer."

"Aspen, you know I don't like this. But in the end, it's only one person. And he's guilty."

"Just like the rebel sympathizers that the king demoted a caste. Just like Marlee and Carter." I didn't have to look up to see how disgusted he was.

"That was different," I mumbled, not sounding convincing at all.

Aspen stopped dead in his tracks and forced me to look at him. "It's never different with him."

His tone was so serious. Aspen knew more than most people did, because he'd stood guard during meetings or delivered orders himself. He was holding a secret right now.

"Are they thieves at all?" I asked quietly as we continued to move.

"Yes, but nothing deserving the years of jail they'll receive today. And it's going to be a pretty loud message to their friends."

"What do you mean?"

"They're people who've gotten in his way, Mer. Rebel sympathizers, men a bit too outspoken about what a tyrant he is. This is being broadcast everywhere. The people they've tried to sway will see this, will warn others about what happens to those who attempt to go against the king. This is deliberate."

I whipped my arm from his, hissing my words at him. "You've been here almost as long as I have. In all that time, did you ever not deliver one of the sentences you were ordered to?"

He considered. "No, but—"

"Then don't judge me. If he's not above putting his enemies in prison without real cause, what do you think he'll do to me? He hates me!"

Aspen's eyes were pleading. "Mer, I know it's scary, but you've—"

I put up my hand. "Do your job. Take me downstairs."

He swallowed once, turned forward, and put his arm out for me. I gripped it, and we walked on in silence.

Halfway down the stairs, as the buzz of conversation started to reach us, he spoke up again.

"I always wondered if they'd change you."

I didn't respond. What could I say anyway?

In the grand foyer, the other girls were staring into the distance, quietly moving their lips as they recited their lines. I detached myself from Aspen and moved to join them.

Elise had talked about her dress so much, I felt as if I'd already seen it. Gold and cream were woven together in a slim, sleeveless design, and her golden gloves looked dramatic. Her gifts from Maxon were deep, dark gems, and they made her slick hair and dark eyes pop.

Kriss once again managed to be the embodiment of all things royal, and it was like she wasn't even trying. Her dress was fitted through the waist and burst out like a flower blossoming toward the ground. And Maxon's necklace and earrings for her were iridescent, gently rounded, and perfect. It did, for a moment, make me sad that mine were so simple.

Celeste's dress . . . well, it would certainly be unforgettable. Her neckline was plunging, and it seemed a little inappropriate for the occasion. She caught me staring, and pushed her lips together and shook her shoulders at me.

I laughed once and put my hand to my forehead, feeling a little sick. I inhaled deeply, trying to calm myself.

Celeste met me halfway, swinging her branch with each step. "What's wrong?"

"Nothing. Just not feeling well, I guess."

"Do. Not. Puke," she ordered. "Especially not on me."

"I won't throw up," I assured her.

"Who threw up?" Kriss asked, joining the conversation; and Elise followed behind her.

"No one," I said. "I'm just tired or something."

"It won't last too long," Kriss reassured me.

It'll last forever, I thought. I looked at each of their faces. They'd come to my side just now. Wouldn't I have done the same for them? Maybe . . .

"Do any of you actually feel *good* about doing this?" I asked.

They all looked at one another or the floor, but no one answered.

"Then let's not do it," I urged.

"Not do it?" Kriss questioned. "America, it's tradition. We have to."

"No we don't. Not if we all decide not to."

"What would we do? Refuse to walk in there?" Celeste asked.

"That's one option," I offered.

"You want us to sit in there and do nothing?" Elise sounded appalled.

"I hadn't thought it through. I just know I don't think this is a good idea."

I could see that Kriss was genuinely considering it.

"It's a trick!" Elise accused.

"What?" How could she come to that conclusion?

"She's going last. If we all do nothing and then she follows through, she looks obedient while the rest of us look like idiots." Elise shook her branch at me as she spoke.

"America?" Kriss looked at me, disappointment filling her eyes.

"No, I swear; that's not what I was going to do!"

"Ladies!" We all turned toward Silvia's correcting tone. "I understand that you're nervous, but that's no reason to shout."

Her gaze hit each of us, and we all exchanged looks as

they decided whether to go in on this with me.

"All right," Silvia began. "Elise, you'll be first, just as we practiced. Celeste and Kriss, you will follow; and America, you'll be last. One at a time, carry your branch up the red carpet and place it at the feet of the king. Then come back and take your seat. The king will say a few words, and the ceremony will start."

She stepped over to what looked like a small box on a stand and turned it around to show a television monitor with a view of everything happening inside the Great Room. It was magnificent. Red carpeting divided the room into the seats for the press and guests, and the four seats delegated for us. In the back of the space, the thrones sat, waiting for the royal family.

As we watched, the side door to the Great Room opened, and the king, the queen, and Maxon came in to applause and trumpeting fanfare. Once they were seated, a slower, more dignified melody started playing.

"There it is. Now, head high," Silvia instructed. Elise gave me a pointed look and strode around the corner.

The music was dotted by the sound of hundreds of cameras taking her picture. It made for a strange rhythm section. She did great, though, as we could all see on the monitor Silvia was watching. Celeste followed, straightening her hair before she left. Kriss's smile looked absolutely genuine and natural as she paraded down the aisle.

"America," Silvia whispered. "Your turn."

I tried to wipe the worry off my face and focus on positive

things, but I realized there weren't any. I was about to kill a part of myself by punishing someone beyond what I thought was deserved and give the king something he wanted in a neat, short stroke.

The cameras clicked, the bulbs flashed, and people whispered their praises to one another as I walked quietly toward the royal family. I made eye contact with Maxon, who was the picture of calm. Was that his years of discipline or true happiness coming through? His face was reassuring, but I was certain he could see the anxiety in my gaze. I saw my open spot for the olive branch and curtsied before placing my offering at the king's feet, deliberately looking at anything in the room other than him.

As soon as I was in my place, the music came to a perfectly calculated stop. King Clarkson walked forward, standing on the edge of his stage, the circle of branches at his feet.

"Ladies and gentlemen of Illéa, today the final four beautiful young women of the Selection come before us all to present themselves to the law. Our great laws are what hold our nation together, the foundation for the peace we've so long enjoyed."

Peace? I thought. *Are you kidding?*

"One of these young ladies will stand before you soon, no longer a commoner, but a princess. And as a member of the royal family, it will be her job to hold on to what is right, not for her own benefit, but for yours."

. . . and how am I doing that now?

"Please join me in applauding their humility in their

submission to the law and their bravery in upholding it."

The king started clapping, and the room joined him. The applause continued as he stepped away, and I glanced down the row of girls. The only face I could really see was Kriss's. She shrugged and gave me a half smile before facing forward again and raising herself to her full height.

A guard by the door trumpeted into the room. "We call into the presence of His Majesty King Clarkson, Her Majesty Queen Amberly, and His Royal Highness Prince Maxon the criminal Jacob Digger."

Slowly, no doubt embarrassed by the spectacle, Jacob walked into the Great Room. His wrists were in handcuffs, and he flinched at the cameras' lights and went skittishly to bow in front of Elise. I couldn't see her very well without leaning too far forward, so I turned slightly and listened as she spoke the lines we all would in turn.

"Jacob, what is your crime?" she asked. She projected her voice really well, much better than usual.

"Theft, my lady," he answered meekly.

"And how long is your sentence?"

"Twelve years, my lady."

Slowly, not drawing attention to herself, Kriss looked my way. With hardly a change in her expression, she questioned what was happening. I nodded.

Small crimes of theft, we'd been told. If that was true, then this man would have been beaten in his town square, or, if he had been put in prison, it would have been for two or three years at the most. In two words, Jacob confirmed all my fears.

Subtly, I turned my eyes toward the king. There was no mistaking his pleasure. Whoever this man was, he wasn't just some thief. The king was delighting in his downfall.

Elise stood and walked down to Jacob, placing her hand on his shoulder. He hadn't truly looked her in the eye until that moment.

"Go, faithful subject, and pay your debt to the king." Her voice rang out in the quiet of the room.

Jacob nodded his head. He looked at the king, and I could see he wanted to do something. He wanted to fight or make an accusation, but he didn't. No doubt someone else would pay for any mistakes he made today. Jacob stood and exited the room as the audience applauded.

The next man had difficulty moving. As he turned to make his way down the carpet toward Celeste, he doubled over and fell. A collective gasp came from the room, but before he could garner too much sympathy, two guards came and walked him to Celeste. To her credit, her voice wasn't as sure as it usually was as she ordered the man to pay his debt.

Kriss looked as steady as ever until her criminal got closer. He was younger, probably around our age, and his steps were steady, almost determined. When he turned up the carpet to Kriss, I saw a tattoo on his neck. It looked like a cross, though it seemed as if whoever had done it messed up a bit.

Kriss delivered her lines well. Anyone who didn't know

her wouldn't be able to read the hint of regret in her voice. The room applauded, and she sat back down, her smile only slightly less bright than it usually was.

The guard yelled out the name Adam Carver, and I realized it was my turn. Adam, Adam, Adam. I needed to remember his name. Because I had to do this now, right? The other girls had. Maxon might forgive me if I failed, and the king would never like me either way; but I would certainly lose the queen, and that backed me into a corner. If I wanted a chance at all, I needed to deliver.

Adam was older, maybe my dad's age, and there was something wrong with his leg. He didn't fall, but it took him so long to reach me that it made the whole thing that much worse. I just wanted it to be done.

As Adam knelt in front of me, I focused on the few lines I needed to deliver.

"Adam, what is your crime?" I asked.

"Theft, my lady."

"And how long is your sentence?"

Adam cleared his throat. "Life," he squeaked out.

Around the room, murmurs began as people were sure they hadn't heard that right.

Though I hated to deviate from my lines, I too needed confirmation. "How long did you say?"

"Life, my lady." It was apparent in Adam's voice that he was on the verge of tears.

I peeked over at Maxon. He looked uncomfortable.

Wordlessly, I pleaded for help. His eyes conveyed how sorry he was that he couldn't guide me.

As I was about to focus again on Adam, my eyes flickered to the king, who had quickly shifted his weight. I watched him run his hand across his mouth in an effort to hide his smile.

He'd set me up.

Perhaps he suspected I would hate this part of the Selection and planned to do what he could to make me look disobedient. But even if I went through with it, what kind of person was I to put a man in prison forever? No one would love me now.

"Adam," I said softly. He looked up at me, tears threatening to fall at any moment. I noticed quickly that every whisper in the room ceased. "How much did you steal?"

People were trying to hear, but it was impossible.

He swallowed and darted his eyes toward the king. "Some clothes for my girls."

I spoke quickly. "But this isn't about that, is it?"

In a gesture so minute I almost missed it, Adam shook his head once.

So I couldn't do it. I *couldn't* do it. But I had to do something.

The idea hit me so quickly, and I was positive it was our only way out. I wasn't sure if it would gain Adam his freedom, and I tried not to think of how sad it would make me. It was simply right, and I had to do it.

I stood and made my way to Adam, touching him on his shoulder. He winced, waiting for me to tell him he was going to prison.

"Stand up," I said.

Adam looked at me, confusion in his eyes.

"Please," I said, and took one of his cuffed hands to pull him along.

Adam walked with me up the aisle, to the raised area where the royal family sat. When we got to the stairs, I turned to him and sighed.

I took off one of the beautiful earrings that Maxon had given me, then the other. I placed both in Adam's hands; and he stood there, dumbstruck, as my beautiful bracelet followed. And then—because, if I was truly going to do this, I wanted to give everything—I reached behind my neck and unclasped my songbird necklace, the one my dad had given me. I hoped he was watching and not hating me for giving his gift away. Once I dropped it into Adam's hand, I curled his fingers around the treasures, then stepped to the side so that he was standing directly in front of King Clarkson.

I pointed toward the thrones. "Go, faithful subject, and pay your debt to the king."

There were gasps and murmurs around the room, but I ignored them. All I could see was the sour expression on the king's face. If he wanted to play a game with my character, then I was prepared to answer in turn.

Adam slowly climbed the steps, and I could see both the joy and fear in his eyes. As he approached the king, he fell to his knees and held out his hands, full of jewels.

King Clarkson shot me a glance, letting me know this wouldn't be the end of it, but then reached out and took the jewelry out of Adam's hands.

The crowd erupted, but when I looked back, the other girls had mixed reactions on their faces. Adam backed away from the king quickly, perhaps afraid he'd change his mind. My hope was that, with so many cameras going and so many people writing articles about this, someone would follow up and make sure he made it home. When Adam got back to my level, he tried to hug me, even with the handcuffs on. He cried and blessed me, and went from the room looking like the happiest soul on earth.

CHAPTER 20

THE ROYAL FAMILY EXITED OUT the side door, and the other Elite and I left the way we'd come as the cameras and guests filmed and applauded.

Silvia's eyes when we came out the doorway were positively deadly. It looked like it was taking every last bit of strength she had to keep from throttling me. She led us around the corner to a small parlor.

"In," she ordered, as if anything more would push her past the brink. She shut the doors, not bothering to join us.

"Do you always have to be the center of attention?" Elise snapped.

"I didn't do anything except what I tried to ask you to do. You were the one who didn't believe me!"

"You act like such a saint. They were criminals. We weren't doing anything a magistrate wouldn't do; we just did it in pretty dresses."

"Elise, did you see those men? Some of them were sick. And the sentences for their crimes were way too long," I implored.

"She's right," Kriss said. "Life for theft? Unless he carted the palace away, what could he have possibly taken to deserve that?"

"Nothing," I vowed. "He took clothes for his family. Look, you guys are lucky. You were born into better castes. If you're in the lower ones, and you lose your main provider . . . things don't go well. I couldn't send him to jail for life and at the same time sentence his family to becoming Eights. I couldn't."

"Where is your pride, America?" Elise begged. "Where is your sense of duty or honor? You're just a girl; you aren't even the princess. And if you were, you wouldn't be allowed to make decisions like that. You are here to follow the king's rules, and you have never done that! Not even from the first night!"

"Maybe the rules are wrong!" I screamed, at perhaps the worst time possible.

The doors were flung open, and King Clarkson stormed in while Queen Amberly and Maxon stood in the hall. He grabbed my arm, hard—thankfully not my injured one— and dragged me out of the room.

"Where are you taking me?" I asked, fear making my breath come out in short bursts.

He didn't answer.

I looked over my shoulder at the girls as the king pulled me down the hall. Celeste wrapped her arms around herself, and Elise reached for Kriss's hand. For as upset as she was, Elise didn't seem happy to see me go.

"Clarkson, don't act in haste," the queen urged quietly.

We rounded a corner, and I was forced into a room. The queen and Maxon filed in behind us as the king shoved me toward a small couch.

"Sit," he commanded unnecessarily. He paced the floor, a lion in a cage. When he stopped, he faced Maxon.

"You swore!" he bellowed. "You said she was under control. First the outburst on the *Report*, then you nearly get yourself killed on the roof, and now this? It ends today, Maxon."

"Father, did you hear the cheers? People appreciate her sympathy. She's your greatest asset right now."

"I beg your pardon?" His voice was an iceberg, slow and deadly.

Maxon paused a moment at the chill but continued. "When she suggested that people defend themselves, the public responded positively. I daresay the reason more people aren't dead is because of her. And this? Father, I couldn't put a man in jail for life over what was supposed to be a petty crime. How can you expect that from someone who's probably seen more than her fair share of friends beaten for less? She's refreshing. The majority of the population is in the lower castes, and they relate to her."

The king shook his head and started walking again. "I let

her stay because she kept you alive. *You* are my most valuable asset, not her. If we lose you, we lose everything. And I don't just mean through death. If you aren't committed to this life, if you lose your focus, this will all fall apart." He waved his arms at the wide room, letting the silence hang.

"You're being brainwashed," the king accused. "You change a little every day. These girls, this one more than the others, are all useless."

"Clarkson, perhaps—" He silenced the queen with a look, and whatever her opinion was fell away.

The king turned back to Maxon. "I have a proposition for you."

"I'm not interested," he shot back.

King Clarkson raised his arms in front of him, gesturing that he meant no harm. "Hear me out."

Maxon sighed.

"These girls have been disastrous. Even the Asian's connections have done nothing for me. The Two is too concerned with fame; and the other, well, she's not entirely hopeless but not good enough, if you ask me. This one," he said, pointing at me, "whatever value she's had has been completely overshadowed by her inability to contain herself.

"This has all gone terribly wrong. And I know you. I know you're afraid of missing something, so this is my thought."

I watched the king walk around Maxon. "Let's call this off. Let's get rid of all the girls."

Maxon opened his mouth to protest, but the king held up a hand. "I'm not suggesting you stay single. I'm simply saying that we still have the entries of all the eligible girls in the country sitting around somewhere. Wouldn't it be nice if you got to handpick a few girls to come to the palace? Maybe find one who looks like the French king's daughter; remember how fond you were of her?"

I lowered my eyes. Maxon had never mentioned a French girl.

It genuinely felt as if someone took a chisel and chipped a crack in my heart.

"Father, I couldn't."

"Oh, but you could. You're the prince. And I think we've had enough outbursts that we could deem this lot unfit. You could have a real choice this time."

I looked up again. Maxon's eyes were focused on the floor. I could see he was struggling.

"This might even appease the rebels temporarily. Think of that!" the king added. "If we send these girls home, wait a few months like we're calling off the Selection, and then bring in a new group of lovely, educated, pleasant women . . . that could change a lot of things."

Maxon tried to say something but only closed his mouth again.

"Either way, you should ask yourself if that," he said, pointing to me again, "is someone you could really spend your life with. Dramatic, selfish, money hungry, and, to be quite honest, very plain. Look at her, son."

Maxon's eyes darted down to mine, holding them for a second before I had to turn away from humiliation.

"I'll give you a few days. For now there's the press to deal with. Amberly."

The queen scurried over, placing her arm through the king's, leaving us alone and speechless.

After a short pause, Maxon came to help me stand up.

"Thanks."

Maxon only nodded. "I should probably go with them. No doubt they'll have questions for me as well."

"That's a pretty nice offer," I commented.

"Maybe the most generous one he's ever made."

I didn't want to know if he was seriously considering this. There was nothing else to say, so I made my way past him, taking the back route to my room, hoping to outrun everything I was feeling.

My maids informed me that dinner would be on our own tonight, and when I couldn't be bothered to communicate with them, they graciously excused themselves. I lay on my bed, lost in my thoughts.

I'd done the right thing today, hadn't I? I believed in justice, but the Convicting wasn't justice. Still, I kept wondering if I'd actually accomplished anything. If that man was an enemy to the king somehow, which I had to believe he was, then surely he would be punished in some other way. Was it all for nothing?

And as frivolous as it was when I considered everything else going on, I couldn't stop thinking about this French girl. Why hadn't Maxon mentioned her? Was she here a lot? Why would he keep her a secret?

I heard the knock and assumed it was my food, even though it seemed a little early.

"Come in," I called, not wanting to get out of bed.

The door opened, and Celeste's dark hair swished into view.

"In the mood for some company?" she asked. Kriss peeked in behind her, and I saw the edge of Elise's arm hiding in the back.

I sat up. "Sure."

They ambled in, leaving the door open. Celeste, still shocking me every time she smiled so genuinely, climbed into my bed without even asking. Not that I minded. Kriss followed, sitting closer to my feet, and Elise balanced on the edge, ever the lady.

Kriss quietly asked what I was sure they were all wondering. "Did he hurt you?"

"No." Then I realized that wasn't entirely true. "He didn't hit me or anything; he just pulled me away a little too roughly."

"What did he say?" Elise fiddled with a piece of her dress as she spoke.

"He's not happy with my outburst. If it was the king choosing, I'd be long gone by now."

Celeste touched my arm. "But he's not. Maxon's fond of you, and so are the people."

"I don't know if that's enough." *For any of us,* I added in my head.

"Sorry I yelled at you," Elise said quietly. "It's frustrating. I try so hard to keep cool and confident, but I feel like nothing I do matters. You all outshine me."

"That's not true," Kriss argued. "At this point, we all mean something to Maxon. We wouldn't be here otherwise."

"He's afraid to get to the final three," Elise countered. "He's supposed to choose within, what, four days when it's down to three? He's holding on to me to keep from making that decision."

"Who's to say he's not holding on to me?" Celeste suggested.

"Listen," I said, "after today I'll probably be going home next. It was bound to happen sooner or later. I'm just not cut out for this."

Kriss giggled. "None of us is an Amberly, are we?"

"I like shocking people too much," Celeste said with a smile.

"And I'd rather hide than do half the things she has to." Elise ducked her head.

"I'm too wild." I shrugged my shoulders, embracing my faults.

"I'll never have her confidence," Kriss mourned.

"So there. We're all messed up. But Maxon has to pick one of us, so there's no point worrying anymore." Celeste toyed with the blanket. "But I think we can all agree that any of you would be a better choice than me."

After a heavy silence, Kriss spoke up. "What do you mean?"

Celeste looked across at her. "You know. Everyone does." She took a deep breath and continued. "I've kind of already had this discussion with America, and I broke down to my maids the other day, but I've never actually apologized to you two."

Kriss and Elise looked at each other briefly before focusing again on Celeste.

"Kriss, I ruined your birthday party," she blurted. "You were the only one who's been able to celebrate in the palace, and I took that moment from you. I'm so sorry."

Kriss shrugged. "It turned out okay in the end. Maxon and I had a great talk because of you. I forgave you a long time ago."

Celeste actually looked like she might cry, but she pushed her lips together into a tight smile. "That's generous considering I'm having a hard time forgiving myself." Celeste dabbed at her lashes. "I just didn't know how to hold his attention, so I stole it from you."

Kriss took a deep breath. "It felt awful at the time, but it really is all right. I'm fine. At least it wasn't like with Anna."

Celeste rolled her eyes shamefully. "Don't even get me started. Sometimes I wonder how far she would have made it if I hadn't . . ." She shook her head before moving her gaze to Elise. "I don't know how you could ever excuse all the things I've done to you. Even the ones you don't know were me."

Elise, ever poised, didn't explode like I might have in her place. "You mean the glass in my shoes, the ruined gowns hanging in my closet, the bleach in my shampoo?"

"Bleach!" I gasped, finding confirmation in Celeste's tired face.

Elise nodded. "I missed a morning in the Women's Room so my maids could dye it back." She turned from me to Celeste. "I knew it was you," she confessed calmly.

Celeste hung her head, absolutely mortified. "You didn't speak, you barely did anything. In my eyes, you were the easiest target, and I was shocked you never broke."

"I would never dishonor my family by quitting," Elise said. I loved her conviction, even if I didn't completely understand it.

"They should be proud of everything you've endured. If my parents had any idea how low I've sunk . . . I don't know what they'd say. If Maxon's parents knew, I'm sure they'd have kicked me out by now. I'm not fit for this." She breathed out, struggling to confess.

I leaned forward, putting my hands on hers. "I think this change of heart would prove otherwise, Celeste."

She tilted her head and gave me a sad smile. "All the same, I don't think he wants me. Even if he did," she added, pulling her hands from mine to tidy up her eye makeup, "someone recently reminded me that I don't need a man to get what I want out of life."

We shared a grin before she turned back to Elise.

"I can never begin to apologize for everything I've done to you, but I need you to know how sincerely I regret it. I'm sorry, Elise."

Elise didn't waver, staring Celeste down. I braced myself for her vicious words now that Celeste was finally at her mercy.

"I could tell him. America and Kriss would be my witnesses, and Maxon would have to send you home."

Celeste swallowed. How humiliating it would be to leave like that!

"I won't though," Elise said, finally. "I would never force Maxon's hand, and win or lose, I want to do it with integrity. So let's move forward."

It wasn't an actual statement of forgiveness, but it was above and beyond what Celeste was expecting. It was all she could do to keep herself together as she nodded and whispered her thanks to Elise.

"Wow," Kriss said, attempting to change the subject, "I mean, I didn't want to tell on you either, Celeste, but . . . I didn't think about honor being behind that choice." Kriss turned to Elise, thinking over the words.

"It's always on my mind," Elise confessed. "I have to hold on to it however I can, especially since I'll be an embarrassment to my family if I don't win."

"How is it your fault if he's the one doing the choosing?" Kriss asked, shifting her weight and settling back in. "How would that make you an embarrassment?"

Elise turned in more, moving from one worry to another. "Because of the arranged-marriage thing. The best girls get the best men and vice versa. Maxon is the height of perfection. If I lose, it means that I wasn't good enough. My family won't think about the feelings behind his choice, which is what I'm sure he'll judge by. They'll look at it logically. My breeding, my talents—I was raised to be worthy of the best, so if I'm not, then who will have me when I leave?"

I'd thought about how my life would change if I won or lost a million times, but I'd never considered what it would mean for the others. After everything with Celeste, I really should have.

Kriss put a hand on Elise's. "Almost all the girls who went home are already engaged to wonderful men. To be a part of the Selection at all makes you a prize. And you made it to the top four of the Elite at the very least. Trust me, Elise, guys will be lined up around the block for you."

Elise smiled. "I don't need a line. I just need one."

"Well, I need a line," Celeste said, making us all chuckle, even Elise.

"I'd like a handful," Kriss said. "A line does sound overwhelming."

They looked at me. "One."

"You're nuts," Celeste decided.

We talked for a while about Maxon, about home, about our hopes. We'd never really spoken like this, without any kind of wall between us. Kriss and I had been working on it, trying to be honest and upfront about the competition; but now that we could just talk about life, I could tell that our relationships would survive the palace. Elise was a surprise, but the fact that her perspective came from such a different place than mine made me think on a deeper level, opening me up.

And the bombshell: Celeste. If someone had told me that the brunette in the heels who walked over so menacingly that first day in the airport would be the girl I was happiest to have settled next to me at this very moment, I would have laughed in their face. The thought was almost as unbelievable as the fact that I was still here, one of the last girls and very heartbroken about how close I was to losing Maxon.

As we spoke, I could see her being accepted by the others as fully as she was now by me. She even looked different with the weight of her secrets cast off from her. Celeste had been raised to be a specific kind of pretty. That beauty depended on covering things up, shifting the light, and seeking to be perfect at all times. But there is a different kind of beauty that comes with humility and honesty, and she was glowing with it now.

Maxon must have walked up very quietly, because I had no idea how long he had been standing at the door, watching us. It was Elise who saw his figure on the edge of my room and stiffened first.

"Your Majesty," she said, bowing her head.

We all looked over, sure we'd misheard her.

"Ladies." He nodded his head back at us. "I didn't mean to interrupt. I think I just ruined something here."

We looked at one another, and I felt sure I wasn't the only one thinking, *No, you made something really amazing.*

"Everything's fine," I said.

"Again, I'm sorry to intrude, but I need to speak to America. Alone."

Celeste sighed and started moving, looking back to wink at me before she stood. Elise rose quickly, and Kriss followed, giving my leg a little squeeze as she hopped off the bed. Elise gave Maxon a curtsy as she left, while Kriss paused to straighten his lapel. Celeste walked up, as strong as I'd ever seen her, and whispered something into Maxon's ear.

When she was done, he smiled. "I don't think that will be necessary."

"Good." She left, closing the door behind her, and I stood to take whatever was coming.

"What was that about?" I asked, nodding toward the door.

"Oh, Celeste was making it clear that if I hurt you, she'd make me cry," he said with a smile.

I laughed. "I've been on the receiving end of those nails, so be careful there."

"Yes, ma'am."

I took in a breath, letting my smile fade. "So?"

"So?"

"Are you going to do it?"

Maxon grinned and shook his head. "No. It was an intriguing thought for a moment, but I don't want to start over. I like my imperfect girls." He shrugged, his face content. "Besides, Father doesn't know about August, or what the Northern rebels' goals are, or any of that. His solutions are shortsighted. Jumping ship now would be just that."

I sighed in relief. I'd hoped that Maxon cared about me enough not to let me go, but after sitting with the girls, I didn't want to see that happen to them either.

"Besides," he added, seeming pleased, "you should have seen the press."

"Why? What happened?" I begged, moving closer.

"They were impressed with you once again. I don't think even I quite understand the mood of the country right now. It's as if . . . it's as if they know things could be different. The way he governs the country is the same way he governs me. He feels no one is capable of making the right decisions but him, so he forces his opinions on people. And, after reading Gregory's diaries, it sounds like it's been that way for a while.

"But no one wants that anymore. People want a choice." Maxon shook his head. "You're terrifying to him, but he can't expel you. They *adore* you, America."

I swallowed. "Adore?"

He nodded. "And . . . I feel similarly. So, no matter what he says or does, don't lose faith. This isn't over."

I placed my fingers on my lips, shocked by the news. The Selection would continue, the girls and I still had our chance, and, based on Maxon's report, the people were approving of me more and more.

But for all the good news, one thing was still pressing on me.

I looked down at the blanket, almost afraid to ask. "I know this will sound stupid . . . but who's the French king's daughter?"

Maxon was silent for a moment before he sat down on the bed. "Her name is Daphne. Before the Selection, she was the only girl I really knew."

"And?"

He huffed out a soundless laugh. "And a little late in the game I discovered her feelings for me went a little bit deeper than friendship. But I didn't return those feelings. I couldn't."

"Was there something wrong with her or—"

"America, no." Maxon reached for my hand, forcing me to look at him. "Daphne is my friend. That's all she ever could be. I spent my life waiting for you, for all of you. This was my chance to find a wife, and I've known that for as long as I can remember. Romantically, my interactions with Daphne were nonexistent. I'd never have thought to mention her name to you, and I'm certain the only reason Father did was to give you yet another opportunity to doubt yourself."

I bit my lip. The king knew my weaknesses too well.

"I watch you do it, America. You compare yourself to my mother, to the other Elite, to a version of yourself you think you ought to be, and now you're about to do the same thing with a person you didn't know existed until a few hours ago."

It was true. I was already wondering if she was prettier than me, smarter than me, and if she said Maxon's name with a ridiculously flirtatious accent.

"America," he said, cupping my face in his hand. "If she had mattered, I would have told you. The same way you would with me."

My stomach turned. I hadn't been completely honest with Maxon. But with his eyes right there, staring so deeply into mine, it was easy to dismiss all that. I could forget about everything surrounding us when he looked at me like that. And so I did.

I fell into Maxon's arms, holding him tightly. There was no place in the world I wanted to be more.

CHAPTER 21

CELESTE HAD BECOME THE CHAMPION of our newfound sisterhood. It was her idea to drag all our maids and a bunch of big mirrors down to the Women's Room and essentially spend the day making one another over. There wasn't much point, seeing as there was no way any of us could do a better job than the palace staff, but it was fun all the same.

Kriss held the ends of my hair across my forehead. "Have you ever considered getting bangs?"

"A couple of times," I admitted, fluffing the fringe hanging just above my eyes. "But my sister usually ends up annoyed with hers, so I change my mind."

"I think you'd look cute," Kriss said enthusiastically. "I cut some for my cousin once. I could do yours if you want."

"Yeah," Celeste chimed in. "Let her near your face with scissors, America. Great idea."

We all burst into laughter. I even noticed a tiny giggle from the other end of the room. I glanced over to see the queen pursing her lips together tightly as she attempted to read the file in front of her. I was worried she'd find all this a bit improper, but, honestly, I wasn't sure I'd ever seen her so happy.

"We should take pictures!" Elise said.

"Anyone got a camera?" Celeste asked. "I'm a pro at this."

"Maxon does!" Kriss shouted. "Come here for a minute," she said to a maid, waving her over encouragingly.

"Hold on," I said, grabbing some paper. "Okay, okay. 'Your Highest of Highnesses, the ladies of the Elite require, immediately, the least fancy of your cameras for . . .'"

Kriss giggled, and Celeste shook her head.

"Oh! A study in feminine diplomacy," Elise added.

"Is that a real thing?" Kriss asked.

Celeste tossed her hair. "Who cares?"

Maybe twenty minutes later, Maxon knocked on the door and pushed it open an inch. "Can I come in?"

Kriss ran over. "No. We just want the camera." And she snatched it from his hand and closed the door in his face.

Celeste fell on the floor, laughing.

"What are you doing in there?" he called. But we were all too busy doubling over to answer.

There were lots of poses behind the shrubs and a thousand kisses blown, and Celeste showed us all how to "find the light."

As Kriss and Elise lay down on the couch and Celeste

climbed above them to snap more photos, I looked over and saw the satisfied smile on the queen's face. It felt wrong that she wasn't a part of this. I snatched up one of the brushes and walked over to her.

"Hello, Lady America," she greeted.

"Could I brush your hair?"

Several emotions played across her face, but she only nodded and spoke quietly. "Of course."

I walked behind her and picked up a handful of her absolutely gorgeous hair. I raked the brush down again and again, watching the other girls as I did so.

"It does my heart good to see you all getting along," she commented.

"Me, too. I like them." I was quiet for a while. "I'm sorry about the Convicting. I know I shouldn't have done that. I just . . ."

"I know, dear. You explained it all beforehand. It's a difficult task. And you did seem to have a sickly bunch."

I realized then how out of the loop she was. Or maybe she simply chose to believe the best about her husband at all costs.

As if she could read my thoughts, she spoke. "I know you think Clarkson's harsh, but he's a good man. You have no idea how stressful it is to be in his shoes. We all deal with it in our own ways. He has a temper sometimes; I need lots of rest; Maxon jokes it off."

"He does, doesn't he?" I said, laughing.

"The question is, how would you handle it?" She turned

her head. "I think your passion is one of your best features. If you could learn to control it, you could be a wonderful princess."

I nodded. "I'm sorry I let you down."

"No, no, dear," she said, turning forward. "I see potential in you. I worked in a factory when I was your age. I was dirty and hungry, and sometimes I was angry. But I had an undying crush on the prince of Illéa, and when I got the chance to make him my own, I learned to check those feelings. There's a lot to be done from here, but it might not happen the way you want it to. You need to learn to accept that, okay?"

"Yes, Mom," I joked.

She looked back at me, her face like stone.

"I mean, ma'am. Ma'am."

Her eyes started glistening, and she blinked a few times, turning forward again. "If it ends as I suspect it will, Mom will be just fine."

And then it was my turn to blink back the tears. It wasn't like I was ever going to replace my mother; but it felt special to be accepted, with all my flaws, by the mother of the person I might marry.

Celeste turned and saw us, and she ran over. "You're so cute! Smile."

I leaned down, wrapping my arms around Queen Amberly, and she reached up to touch my hands. After that, we all took turns crowding around her, getting her to finally make one silly face for the camera. The maids helped take pictures so we could all be in some together; and, by the end of it, I could easily say that was my best day in the palace. I didn't know if that would hold though. Christmas was right around the corner.

My maids were fixing my hair after Elise's last terrible attempt at an up-do when there was a knock on the door.

Mary rushed to answer it, and a guard whose name I didn't know came into the room. I'd seen him around a lot, almost exclusively at the king's side.

My maids curtsied as he walked closer, and I was more than a little anxious when he stopped in front of me.

"Lady America, the king requires your presence at once," he said coolly.

"Is anything wrong?" I asked, stalling.

"The king will answer your questions."

I swallowed. Every awful thing ran through my head. My family was in danger. The king had found a way to punish me quietly for all the ways I'd wronged him. He'd discovered we'd sneaked out of the palace. Or, perhaps worst of all, someone had figured out my connection to Aspen, and we were both about to pay for it.

I tried to shake the fear out of my system. I didn't want any of it to show in front of King Clarkson.

"I'll follow you then." I stood and started walking behind the guard, giving one last glance to the girls as I left. When I saw the worry on their faces, I wished I hadn't.

We went down the hall and started up the stairs to the

third floor. I didn't quite know what to do with my hands, and I kept touching my hair or my dress or lacing my fingers together.

When we were about halfway down the hall, I saw Maxon, and that helped. He paused just outside a room, waiting for me. There was no concern in his eyes, but he was better at hiding his fear than I was.

"What's this about?" I whispered.

"Your guess is as good as mine."

The guard took his place outside the door as Maxon escorted me inside. In the wide room, there were shelves of books along one wall. On easels, several maps were set up. There were at least three separate ones of Illéa, with markers in different colors. At a wide desk, the king sat with a piece of paper in his hand.

As he noticed Maxon and me enter the room, the king straightened.

"What exactly have you done with the Italian princess?" King Clarkson demanded, staring at me.

I froze. The money. I'd forgotten all about that. Conspiring to sell weapons to people he viewed as enemies was worse than any of the other scenarios for which I'd been preparing.

"I'm not sure what you mean," I lied, looking to Maxon. Even though he knew everything, he remained calm.

"We have been trying to make an alliance with the Italians for decades, and all of a sudden the royal family is quite interested in having us visit. However"—the king picked up the letter, searching for a specific section—"ah, here. 'While it would be more than an honor to have Your Majesty and your family grace us with your company, we hope that Lady America will also be able to visit with you. After meeting all the Elite, we can't imagine anyone following in the queen's footsteps quite like her.'"

The king raised his eyes back to me. "What have you done?"

Realizing I'd dodged something huge, I relaxed marginally. "All I've done was try to be polite toward the princess and her mother when they've visited. I didn't know she liked me so much."

King Clarkson rolled his eyes. "You're subversive. I've been watching you, and you're here for something; and it sure as hell isn't him."

Maxon turned to me at those words. I wished I hadn't seen the flicker of doubt in his eyes. I shook my head. "That's not true!"

"Then how did a girl of no means, no connections, and no power manage to get this country within the reach of something it's been trying to achieve for years? How?"

In my heart, I knew that there were factors here that he was oblivious to. But it was Nicoletta who had offered assistance to me, who had asked if she could do anything for a cause she wanted to support. If he'd accused me of something that was actually my fault, his rising voice would have been frightening. As it was, he came across like a child.

In response, I spoke quietly. "You were the ones who

assigned us to entertain your foreign guests. I never would have met any of those women otherwise. And she's the one who wrote, inviting me to come. I didn't beg for a trip to Italy. Maybe if you were simply more welcoming, you'd have had your alliance with Italy years ago."

He stood forcefully. "Watch. Your. Mouth."

Maxon put an arm around me. "Perhaps it's best you left, America."

I happily started moving, keen to be anywhere the king wasn't. But that was not what King Clarkson had in mind.

"Stop. I have more," he insisted. "This changes things. We can't reset the Selection and risk upsetting the Italians. They have a lot of influence. If we can get them, they'll open a lot of doors for us."

Maxon nodded, not upset at all. He had already made the choice to keep us here, but we had to play along and let the king think he was in control.

"We'll simply have to draw out the Selection," he concluded. My heart plummeted. "We have to give the Italians time to accept the other options as viable without offending them. Perhaps we should schedule a trip over there soon, give everyone an opportunity to shine."

He looked so pleased with himself, so proud of his solution. I wondered how far he would go. Prep Celeste, maybe. Or arrange for some private time with Kriss and Nicoletta. I wouldn't put it past him to make me look bad deliberately, the way he had tried to in the Convicting. If he went to all the lengths he could without openly incriminating himself,

I wasn't sure I had much of a chance.

And forget the political side of it. More time meant more opportunities to embarrass myself.

"Father, I'm not sure that would help," Maxon interjected. "The Italian ladies have already met all the candidates. If they're showing a preference for America, it must have come from something they like in her that wasn't visible in the others. You can't simply make that exist."

The king looked at Maxon, venom in his eyes. "Are you declaring your choice right now then? Is the Selection over?"

My pulse stopped altogether.

"No," Maxon answered, as if the very thought was ridiculous. "I'm just not sure what you're suggesting is the right course."

King Clarkson propped his chin on his hand, looking back and forth between Maxon and me, staring at us like some equation he couldn't solve.

"She has yet to prove herself trustworthy. Until that time, you cannot choose her." The king's face was unyielding.

"And how do you suggest she does that?" Maxon countered. "What exactly do you need in order to be satisfied?"

The king raised his eyebrows, seeming amused at his son's questions. After a moment of consideration, he pulled a small file out of his drawer.

"Even excluding your recent stunt on the *Report*, there seems to be a bit of unrest these days between the castes. I've been wanting to find a way to . . . aid in soothing the opinions of the moment; but it occurred to me that someone as fresh and young and, dare I say, popular as you are might do better at this than I would."

Pushing the file across the desk, he continued. "It seems the people follow your tunes. Perhaps you would sing one of mine for them."

I opened the folder and read the papers. "What is this?"

"Just some service announcements we'll be making soon. We know, of course, the caste makeup of each province and all the communities within them, so we'll be sending specific ones to certain areas. Encouraging them."

"What is it, America?" Maxon asked, confused by his father's words.

"They're like . . . commercials," I answered. "Advertisements to be happy with your own caste, not to associate closely with those outside it."

"Father, what's this about?"

The king leaned back in his chair, relaxing. "It's nothing serious. I'm merely trying to quell the unrest. If I don't do it, you'll have an uprising on your hands by the time I pass down the crown."

"How so?"

"The lower castes tend to get unruly from time to time—it's natural. But we have to subdue the anger and squash the ideas of usurping power quickly, before they unite and undo our great nation."

Maxon stared at his father, still not fully comprehending his words. If Aspen hadn't clued me in to sympathizers, I might have been the same way. The king was planning to divide and conquer: make the castes absurdly grateful for what they had—even if they were being treated like they didn't matter—and tell them not to associate with those outside of their castes, for they certainly wouldn't understand the plight of anyone outside their own.

"This is propaganda," I spat, remembering the word from Dad's tattered history book.

The king tried to soothe me. "No, no. It's a suggestion. It's reinforcement. It's a way of looking at the world that will keep our country happy."

"Happy? So you want me to tell some Seven that . . ."—I hunted for the words on the sheet—"'your task is possibly the greatest of our nation. You toil with your body and build the very roads and buildings that make our land.'" I searched for more. "'No Two or Three could equal your talent, so turn your eyes away from them on the street. No need to speak with those who may rank higher than you by caste but are beneath you in your contribution.'"

Maxon turned from me to his father. "Surely, that will alienate our people."

"On the contrary. It will help settle them into their places and make them feel that the palace has their best interests at heart."

"Do you?" I shot.

"Of course I do!" the king yelled.

His outburst made me take a few steps back.

"People need to be led by the bit, with blinders on like horses. If you do not guide their steps, they run astray, straight into what's worst for them. You may not like these little speeches, but they'll do more, *save* more, than you know."

My heart was still slowing as he finished speaking, and I stood silently with the papers in my hands.

I knew he was worried. Every time he got a report of something happening beyond his control, he crushed it. He lumped all change together, calling it treason before inspecting it. His answer this time was to have me do what Gregory did and isolate his people.

"I can't say it," I whispered.

He responded calmly. "Then you cannot marry my son."

"Father!"

King Clarkson held up a hand. "We're at that point, Maxon. I've let you have your way, and now we must negotiate. If you want this girl to stay, then she must be obedient. If she cannot follow through with the simplest of tasks, my only conclusion is that she doesn't love you. If that's the case, I can't see why you would want her in the first place."

I locked eyes with the king, hating him for putting the thought in Maxon's head.

"Do you? Do you love him at all?"

This wasn't how I was going to say it. Not at the end of an ultimatum, not for business.

The king tilted his head. "How sad, Maxon. She needs to think about it."

Do not cry. Do not *cry.*

"I'll give you some time to find out where you stand. If you won't do this, then rules be damned, *I'll* be kicking you out by Christmas Day. What a special gift that will be for your parents."

Three days.

He smiled. I set the folder on his desk and left, trying not to break into a run. All I needed was another excuse for him to say I was flawed.

"America!" Maxon yelled. "Stop!"

I kept walking until he grabbed me by the wrist, forcing me to pause.

"What the hell was that?" he demanded.

"He's insane!" I was on the verge of tears, but I held them in. If the king came out and saw me that way, I'd never live it down.

Maxon shook his head. "Not him. You. Why didn't you agree to do it?"

I looked at him, gob-smacked. "It's a trick, Maxon. Everything he's doing is a trick."

"If you had said yes, I would have ended this now."

Incredulous, I fired back. "Two seconds before, you had the chance to end it and didn't. How is this my fault?"

"Because," he answered, his whole demeanor urgent, "you are denying me your love. It's the only thing I've wanted in this entire competition, and you still hold back. I keep waiting for you to say it, and you won't. If you couldn't say it out loud in front of him, fine. But if you had simply agreed, that would have been good enough for me."

"And why would I when, for as far as we've come, he could still push me out? While I'm humiliated over and over again, and you stand by? That's not love, Maxon. You don't even know what love is."

"The hell I don't! Do you have any idea what I've been through—"

"Maxon, you were the one who said you wanted to stop arguing. So stop giving me reasons to argue with you!"

I stormed away. What was I still doing here? I kept torturing myself for someone who had no idea what it meant to be faithful to one person. And he never would, because his whole concept of romance revolved around the Selection. He wouldn't ever understand.

As I was about to hit the stairwell, I was whipped back again. Maxon held me tightly, both of his hands gripping my arms. Surely he could see how furious I still was, but in the seconds that had passed, his demeanor had shifted completely.

"I'm not him," he said.

"What?" I demanded, trying to free myself.

"America, stop." I huffed and quit struggling. Without any other options, I looked into Maxon's eyes. "I'm not him, all right?"

"I don't know what you mean."

He sighed. "I know that you spent years pouring yourself into another person who you thought was going to love you forever; and when he was faced with the realities of the world, he abandoned you." I froze, taking in his words. "I'm not him, America. I have no intentions of giving up on you."

I shook my head. "You can't see it, Maxon. He might

have let me down, but at least I knew him. After all this time, I still feel like there's a gap between us. The Selection has forced you to hand over your affection in slices. I'll never really have all of you. None of us will."

When I shrugged myself free this time, he didn't fight me.

CHAPTER 22

I DIDN'T REMEMBER MUCH OF the *Report*. I sat on my pedestal, thinking as every second passed that I was that much closer to being sent home. Then it dawned on me that staying wasn't much better. If I caved and read those horrible messages, the king would win. Maybe Maxon did love me, but if he wasn't man enough to say it out loud, then how could he ever protect me from the most frightening thing in my life: his father.

I would always be bending to King Clarkson's will; and for all the support Maxon had from the Northern rebels, behind these walls, he would be alone.

I was angry at Maxon, and I was angry at his father, and I was angry at the Selection and everything that came with it. All the frustration knotted itself around my heart to the point where it made no sense, and I wished more than anything that I could talk to the girls about what was going on.

That wasn't possible though. It wouldn't make anything better for me, and it would only make things worse for them. Sooner or later, I'd have to face my concerns by myself.

I peeked to my left, looking down the row of the Elite. I realized that whoever stayed would have to face this without the rest of us. The pressures the public would set on us, demanding to be a part of our lives, as well as the commands of the king, ever seeking to use anyone within reach as a tool in his plans—all on the shoulders of one girl.

I tentatively reached out for Celeste's hand, fingers brushing against hers. The second she felt them, she took hold, looking into my eyes with concern.

What's wrong? she mouthed.

I shrugged.

And so she just held my hand.

After a minute, she seemed to get a little sad, too. While the men in suits prattled on, she stretched out, reaching for Kriss's hand. Kriss didn't question it, and it took her only seconds to extend her hand for Elise's.

And there we were, in the background of it all, holding on to one another. The Perfectionist, the Sweetheart, the Diva . . . and me.

I spent the next morning in the Women's Room, being as obedient as I could. Several of the extended family members were in town, ready to spend Christmas Day in style. Tonight there was supposed to be a magnificent dinner and carol singing. Typically Christmas Eve was one of my favorite times of the year, but I felt too unsettled to even get excited.

There was a fantastic meal that I didn't taste and beautiful gifts from the public that I barely saw. I was crushed.

As the relatives started getting tipsy on eggnog, I slipped away, not up to pretending to be jolly. By the end of the night, I'd either have to agree to do King Clarkson's ridiculous commercials or let him send me home. I needed to think.

Back in my room, I sent my maids away and sat at my table, considering. I didn't want to do this. I didn't want to tell the people to be satisfied with what they had, even if it was nothing. I didn't want to discourage people from helping one another. I didn't want to eliminate the possibility of more, to be the face and voice of a campaign that said, "Be still. Let the king run your life. That's the best you can hope for."

But . . . didn't I love Maxon?

A second later, a knock came at the door. I reluctantly went to answer it, dreading King Clarkson's cold eyes as he followed through on his ultimatum.

I opened the door to Maxon. He stood there wordlessly.

And all my anger made sense. I wanted everything *from* him and everything *for* him, because I wanted every *piece of* him. It was infuriating that everyone had to have their hands on this—the girls, his parents, even Aspen. So many conditions and opinions and obligations surrounded us, and

I hated Maxon because they came with him.

And I loved him even so.

I was about to agree to do those awful announcements when he quietly held out his hand.

"Come with me?"

"Okay."

I closed the door behind me and followed Maxon down the hall.

"You have a point," he started. "I am afraid to show all of you every piece of me. You get some, Kriss gets others, and so on. And I've based that on what feels appropriate for each of you. With you, I always like coming to you, to your room. It's as if I'm stepping into a bit of your world, and if I do that enough, I can get all of you. Does that make sense?"

"Kind of," I said as we turned up the stairs.

"But that's not really fair, or even accurate. You explained to me once that these are our rooms, not yours. Anyway, I thought it was time I show you another piece of my world, maybe the last one where you're concerned."

"Oh?"

He nodded as we stopped in front of a door. "My room."

"Really?"

"Only Kriss has seen it, and that was a bit of an impulse. I'm not unhappy I showed her, but I feel as if it pushed things forward quickly. You know how private I can be."

"I do."

He wrapped his fingers around the handle. "I've wanted to share this with you, and I think it's well past the time.

It's not exactly something special, but it's mine. So, I don't know, I just want you to see it."

"Okay." I could tell he was feeling bashful, like maybe he'd built it up to be a bigger deal than it was, or maybe he'd regret showing me at all.

He took a deep breath and opened the door, letting me walk in first.

It was huge. The paneling was dark, some wood I wasn't familiar with lining the whole space. On the far wall, a wide fireplace stood, waiting to be used. The whole thing must have been for show since it never seemed to get cold enough here to justify a fire.

His bathroom door was cracked open, and I could see a porcelain tub on the elaborately tiled floor. He had his own collection of books and a table near the fireplace that looked like it was intended for dining rather than work. I wondered how many lonely meals he'd had here. Near the doors that opened to his private balcony, a glass case full of guns sat, perfectly lined up. I'd forgotten his love of hunting.

His bed, also made from a dark wood, was massive. I wanted to go and touch it, to see if it felt as good as it looked.

"Maxon, you could fit a football team in there," I teased.

"Tried it once. Not as comfortable as you'd think."

I turned to swat at him, glad to see him in a playful mood. It was then, looking past his smiling face, that I saw the pictures. I inhaled sharply, taking in the beautiful display behind him.

On the wall by Maxon's door was a vast collage, wide

enough to be wallpaper for my room back home. There didn't appear to be any sort of order to it, just image upon image piled up for him to enjoy.

I could see photos that surely had to have been taken by him, because they were of the palace, which was where he was almost all the time. Close-ups of tapestries, shots of the ceiling he must have lain flat on the carpet to get, and so many pictures of the gardens. There were others, maybe of places he hoped to see or had at least visited. I saw an ocean so blue it didn't seem possible. There were a few bridges, and one of a wall-like structure that looked like it went on for miles.

But above all this, I saw my face a dozen times over. There was the picture of me that was taken for my Selection application, and the one of Maxon and me taken for the magazine when I wore that sash. We seemed happy there, as if it was all a game. I'd never seen that photo, or the one from the article on Halloween. I remembered Maxon standing behind me while we looked at designs for my costume. While I'm staring at the sketch, Maxon's eyes are slightly turned toward me.

Then there were the photos he took. One of me shocked when the king and queen of Swendway visited and he'd quickly yelled out "Smile." One of me sitting on the set for the *Report*, laughing at Marlee. He must have been hiding behind the blinding lights, stealing little images of us when we were all just being ourselves. And there was another one of me in the night, standing on my balcony and looking at the moon.

The other girls were in them, too, the remaining ones

more than the others; but every once in a while I'd see Anna's eyes peek out from under a landscape or Marlee's smile hiding in a corner. And though they were just taken, pictures of Kriss and Celeste posing in the Women's Room were up there, too, next to Elise pretending to faint on a couch and me with my arms wrapped around his mother.

"Maxon," I breathed. "It's beautiful."

"You like it?"

"I'm in awe of it. How many of these did you take?"

"Nearly all of them, but ones like this," he said, pointing to one of the pictures used in the magazines, "I asked for." He pointed again. "I took this one in the very southern part of Honduragua. I used to think it was interesting, but now it makes me sad."

The image was of some pipes spilling smoke into the sky. "I used to look at the air, but now I remember how much I hated the smell of it. And people live in that all the time. I was so self-absorbed."

"Where is this?" I asked, pointing to the long brick wall.

"New Asia. It used to be to the north of what was the Chinese border. They called it the Great Wall. I hear it was once quite spectacular, but now it's mostly gone. It runs less than halfway through the middle of New Asia. That's how much they've expanded."

"Wow."

Maxon put his hands behind his back. "I was really hoping you would like it."

"I do. So much. I want you to make me one."

"You do?"

"Yes. Or teach me to. I can't even tell you how often I wished I could catch snippets of my life and hold on to them like this. I have a few torn pictures of my family and the new one with my sister's baby, but that's all. I've never even thought of keeping a journal or writing things down. . . . I feel like you make so much more sense now."

This was the center of who he was. I could feel the things that were permanent, such as his constant confinement in the palace and the brief bits of traveling. But there were also elements that shifted. The girls and I were on the wall so much because we'd taken over his world. Even as we left, we weren't really gone.

I stepped over and laced an arm behind his back. He did the same to me, and we stood there quietly for a minute, taking it all in. And then something that should have been obvious the whole time suddenly came to me.

"Maxon?"

"Yes?"

"If things were different and you weren't the prince, and you could pick what you did for a living, would this be it?" I pointed to the collage.

"Taking pictures, you mean?"

"Yes."

He barely needed a second to think. "Absolutely. For art or even just family portraits. I'd do advertising, pretty much whatever I could. I'm very passionate about it. I think you can see that though."

"I can." I smiled, happy with this knowledge.

"Why do you ask?"

"It's just . . ." I moved to look at him. "You'd be a Five."

Maxon slowly took in my words, and he smiled quietly. "That makes me happy."

"Me, too."

Suddenly, decisively, Maxon faced me, taking my hands in his.

"Say it, America. Please. Tell me you love me, that you want to be mine alone."

"I can't be yours alone with all the other girls here."

"And I can't send them home until I'm sure of your feelings."

"And I can't give you what you want while I know that tomorrow you could be doing this with Kriss."

"Doing what with Kriss? She's already seen my room, I told you."

"Not that. Just pulling her away, making her feel like . . ."

He waited. "How?" he whispered.

"Like she's the only one who matters. She's crazy about you. She's told me so. And I don't think it's one-sided."

He sighed, searching for the words. "I can't tell you she means nothing. I can tell you that you mean more."

"How am I supposed to be sure of that if you can't send her home?"

A devilish smirk came to his face. He moved his lips to my ear. "I can think of a few other ways to show you how you make me feel," he whispered.

I swallowed, both frightened and hopeful he'd say more. His body was now up against mine, his hand low on my back, holding me to him. The other hand pushed my hair off my neck. I trembled as he ran his open lips over a tiny patch of skin, his breath so very tempting.

It was as if I forgot how to use my limbs. I couldn't hold on to him or think of how to move. But Maxon took care of that, backing me up a few steps so I was pressed against his collection of pictures.

"I want you, America," he murmured into my ear. "I want you to be mine alone. And I want to give you everything." His lips kissed their way across my cheek, stopping at the corner of my mouth. "I want to give you things you didn't know you wanted. I want"—he breathed into me—"so desperately to—"

A loud knock came at the door.

I was so lost in Maxon's touch and words and scent that the sound was jarring. We both turned toward the door, but Maxon quickly put his lips back on mine.

"Don't move. I fully intend to finish this conversation." He kissed me slowly, then pulled away.

I stood there gasping for air. I told myself this was probably a bad idea, to let him kiss me into a confession. But, I reasoned, if there was ever a way to cave, this was it.

He opened the door, shielding me from the visitor. I ran my hands through my hair, trying to pull myself together.

"Sorry, Your Majesty," someone said. "We're looking for Lady America, and her maids said she would be with you."

I wondered how my maids had guessed, but I was pleased they seemed so in tune with me. Maxon's brow furrowed as he looked toward me and opened the door all the way to allow the guard to walk through. He came in, and his eyes had the air of inspecting me, like he was double-checking. Once he was satisfied, he leaned over Maxon's shoulder and whispered something.

Maxon's shoulders slumped, and he brought his hand to his eyes as if he was unable to deal with the news.

"Are you all right?" I asked, not wanting him to suffer alone.

He turned toward me, sympathy in his face. "I'm so sorry, America. I hate to be the one to tell you this. Your father has died."

I didn't quite understand the words for a minute. But no matter how I arranged them in my head, they all led to the same unthinkable conclusion.

And then the room tilted, and Maxon's expression became urgent. The last thing I felt was Maxon's arms keeping me from hitting the floor.

CHAPTER 23

"—UNDERSTAND. SHE'LL WANT TO VISIT her family."

"If she does, it can only be for a day at the most. I don't approve of her, but the people are fond of her, not to mention the Italians. It would be very inconvenient if she died."

I opened my eyes. I was on my bed, but not under my covers. I saw out of the corner of my eye that Mary was in the room with me.

The shouting voices were muted, and I realized that was because they were just outside my door.

"That won't be enough. She loved her father dearly; she'll want time," Maxon argued.

I heard something like a fist hitting a wall, and Mary and I both jumped at the sound. "Fine," the king huffed. "Four days. That's it."

"What if she decides not to come back? Even though this wasn't rebel caused, she might want to stay."

"If she's dumb enough to want that, then good riddance. She was supposed to give me an answer about those announcements anyway, and if she's not willing, then she can stay home."

"She said she would. She told me earlier tonight," Maxon lied. But he knew, didn't he?

"About time. As soon as she returns, we'll get her in the studio. I want this done by the New Year." His tone was irritated, even as he got what he wanted.

There was a pause before Maxon dared to speak. "I want to go with her."

"Like hell you will!" King Clarkson yelled.

"We're down to four, Father. That girl might be my wife. Am I supposed to send her alone?"

"Yes! If she dies, it's one thing. If you die, it's a whole other issue. You're staying here!"

I thought the fist hitting the wall this time was Maxon's. "I am not a commodity! And neither are they! I wish for once you would look at me and see a person."

The door opened quickly, and Maxon came in. "I'm so sorry," he said, walking over and sitting on the bed. "I didn't mean to wake you."

"Is it real?"

"Yes, darling. He's gone." He gently took my hand, looking pained. "There was a problem with his heart."

I sat up and threw myself into Maxon's arms. He held me tightly, letting me weep into his shoulder.

"Daddy," I cried. "Daddy."

"Hush, darling. It'll be all right," Maxon soothed. "You'll fly out tomorrow morning to go pay your respects."

"I didn't get to say good-bye. I didn't . . ."

"America, listen to me. Your father loved you. He was proud you'd done so well. He wouldn't hold this against you."

I nodded, knowing he was right. Practically everything my dad had told me since I'd come here was about how proud he was.

"This is what you need to do, okay?" he instructed, wiping tears off my cheeks. "You need to sleep as best as you can. You'll fly out tomorrow and stay at home for four days with your family. I wanted to get you more time, but Father is quite insistent."

"It's okay."

"Your maids are making an appropriate dress for the funeral, and they'll pack everything you need. You're going to have to take one of them with you, and a few guards. Speaking of which," he said, standing to acknowledge the figure standing in the open door. "Officer Leger, thank you for coming."

"Not at all, Your Majesty. I apologize for being out of uniform, sir."

Maxon reached out and shook Aspen's hand. "Least of my

concerns right now. I'm sure you know why you're here."

"I do." Aspen turned to me. "I'm very sorry for your loss, miss."

"Thank you," I mumbled.

"With the elevated rebel activity, we're all concerned about Lady America's safety," Maxon started. "We've already had some local officers dispatched to her home and to the sites being used over the next few days, and there are still palace-trained guards there, of course. But with her actually in the house, I think we should send more."

"Absolutely, Your Majesty."

"And you're familiar with the area?"

"Very, sir."

"Good. You'll be heading up the team going with her. Pick whomever you like, between six and eight guards."

Aspen raised his eyebrows.

"I know," Maxon conceded. "We're stretched tight right now, but at least three of the palace guards we've sent to her house have already abandoned their posts. And I want her to be as safe as, if not safer than, she is here."

"I'll take care of it, sir."

"Excellent. There will also be a maid going with her; watch her as well." He turned to me. "Do you know who you want to go?"

I shrugged, unable to think straight.

Aspen spoke on my behalf. "If I may, I know Anne is your head maid, but I remember Lucy getting along well with your sister and mother. Maybe it would be good for them to see a friendly face right now."

I nodded. "Lucy."

"Very good," Maxon said. "Officer, you don't have much time. You'll be leaving after breakfast."

"I'll get to work, sir. See you in the morning, miss," Aspen said. I could tell he was having a hard time keeping his distance, and, in that moment, I wanted nothing more than for him to comfort me. Aspen really knew my dad, and I wanted someone who understood him like I did to miss him with me.

Once Aspen left, Maxon came to sit with me again.

"One more thing before I go." He reached for my hands, holding them tenderly. "Sometimes when you're upset, you tend to be impulsive." He looked at me, and I actually smiled a little at the accusing look in his eyes. "Try to be sensible while you're away. I need you to take care of yourself."

I rubbed the back of his hands with my thumbs. "I will. I promise."

"Thank you." A sense of peace encircled us, the way it did sometimes. Even though my world would never be the same now, for that moment, with Maxon holding me, the loss didn't ache so much.

He leaned his head toward mine until our foreheads touched. I heard him draw in a breath as if he might say something and then change his mind. After a few seconds, he did it again. Finally, Maxon leaned back and shook his head and kissed my cheek. "Stay safe."

Then he left me alone in my sadness.

It was cold in Carolina, the humidity from the ocean coming inland and making the chill in the air damp. Secretly, I'd hoped for snow, but it didn't happen. I felt guilty for wanting anything at all.

Christmas Day. I'd spent the last few weeks imagining it several different ways. I thought maybe I'd be here, eliminated and home. We'd all be around our tree, dejected that I wasn't a princess but blissfully happy to be together. I'd also considered opening gifts under the massive tree at the palace, eating myself sick, and laughing with the other girls and Maxon, for one day every corner of the competition suspended to celebrate.

Never could I have imagined I'd be bracing myself for the task of putting my father in the ground.

As the car pulled up to my street, I started to see the masses. Though people ought to be home with their families, they instead crowded outside in the cold. I realized they were hoping to catch a glimpse of me, and I felt a little sick. People pointed as we passed, and some local news crews took footage.

The car stopped in front of my house, and the people waiting started cheering. I didn't understand. Didn't they know why I was here? I walked up the cracked sidewalk with Lucy by my side and six guards surrounding us. No chance was being taken.

"Lady America!" people called.

"Can I have your autograph?" someone screamed, and others joined in.

I kept moving, looking ahead. For once, I felt I could excuse myself from being theirs. I lifted my head to the lights hanging off the roof. Dad did that. Who was going to take them down?

Aspen, at the head of my entourage, knocked on the front door and waited. Another guard came to answer and he and Aspen spoke quickly before we were allowed inside. It was hard to get all of us down the hall, but once the space opened into the living room, I immediately felt something . . . wrong.

This wasn't home anymore.

I told myself I was crazy. Of course this was home. It was just the unfamiliarity of how this was unfolding. Everyone was here, even Kota. But Dad was gone, so it was only natural that it wouldn't seem quite right. And Kenna was holding a baby who I'd never seen in real life before. I'd have to get used to that.

And while Mom was in an apron and Gerad was in his pajamas, I was dressed for dinner at the palace: hair up, sapphires on my ears, and layers of luxurious fabrics draping to my heeled shoes. It felt as if I wasn't welcome for a moment.

But May hopped to her feet and ran to hug me, crying

into my shoulder. I held her back. I remembered that this might be a strange adjustment, but this was the only place I could be right now. I had to be with my family.

"America," Kenna said, standing with her child in her arms. "You look so beautiful."

"Thanks," I muttered, embarrassed.

She gave me a one-armed hug, and I peeked into the blankets at my sleeping niece. Astra's little face was serene as she slept, and every few seconds she'd unclench her tiny fist or fidget just a bit. She was breathtaking.

Aspen cleared his throat. "Mrs. Singer, I'm very sorry for your loss."

Mom gave him a tired smile. "Thank you."

"I'm sorry we're not here under better circumstances, but with Lady America home, we're going to have to be quite diligent about security," he said, a ring of authority in his voice. "We're going to have to ask everyone to stay in this house. I know it'll be tight, but it's only for a few days. And the guards have been provided an apartment nearby so we can rotate easily. We're going to try to be as out of the way as possible.

"James, Kenna, Kota, we're prepared to leave for your homes to pick up your necessities whenever you're ready to go. If you need some time to make a list, that's fine. We're on your schedule."

I smiled a little, happy to see Aspen this way. He'd grown so much.

"I can't stay away from my studio," Kota said. "I have

deadlines. There are pieces due."

Aspen, still professional, answered him. "Any materials you need can come to the studio here." He pointed toward our converted garage. "We'll make as many trips as necessary."

Kota crossed his arms and mumbled. "That place is a dump."

"Fine," Aspen said firmly. "The choice is yours. You can either work in the dump, or you can risk your life at your apartment."

The tension in the air was awkward, and very unnecessary at the moment. I decided to break it. "May, you can sleep with me. Kenna and James can have your room."

They nodded.

"Lucy," I whispered. "I want you near us. You might have to sleep on the floor, but I want you close by."

She stood a bit taller. "I wouldn't be anywhere else, miss."

"Where am I supposed to sleep?" Kota demanded.

"With me," Gerad offered, though he didn't seem excited about it.

"Absolutely not!" Kota scoffed. "I'm not sleeping on a bunk bed with a child."

"Kota!" I said, stepping away from my sisters and Lucy. "You can sleep on the couch or in the garage or in the tree house for all I care; but if you don't check your attitude, I'll send you back to your apartment right now! Have some gratitude for the security you've been offered. Need I remind you that tomorrow we're burying our father? Either stop the bickering or go home." I turned on my heel and headed down the hall. Without checking, I knew Lucy was right behind me, suitcase in hand.

I opened the door to my room, waiting for her to come in with me. Once her skirts swished past the frame, I slammed it shut, heaving a sigh.

"Was that too much?" I asked.

"It was perfect!" she replied with delight. "You might as well be the princess already, miss. You're ready for it."

CHAPTER 24

THE NEXT DAY PASSED IN a blur of black dresses and hugs. Lots of people I'd never even seen before came to Dad's funeral. I wondered if I just didn't know all his friends or if they were here because I was.

A local pastor gave the service, but for security reasons, the family was asked not to stand and speak. There was a reception, far more elaborate than anything we could have ever hoped for. Though no one told me so, I was sure Silvia or some other palace employee had a hand in making this as easy for us and as beautiful as possible. For safety, it was short, but that was fine with me. I wanted to let him go as painlessly as I could.

Aspen stayed near me at all times, and I was grateful for his presence. I couldn't have trusted anyone with my life as I could him.

"I haven't cried since I left the palace," I said. "I thought I'd be a wreck."

"It hits at funny times," he replied. "I fell apart for a few days after my father died, before I realized I had to get it together for everyone else's sake. But sometimes when something would happen and I'd want to tell my dad about it, the whole thing would hit me in the chest again, and I'd break down."

"So . . . I'm normal?"

He smiled. "You're normal."

"I don't know a lot of these people."

"They're all local. We checked identification. It's probably a bit higher of a number because of who you are, but I think your dad made a painting for the Hampshires, and I saw him speaking to Mr. Clippings and Albert Hammers in the market area more than once. It's hard to know everything about people close to you, even the people you love the most."

I sensed there was something more in that sentence, something I was supposed to respond to. I just couldn't right now.

"We need to get used to this," he said.

"To what? Everything feeling awful?"

"No," he answered, shaking his head. "Nothing is the same anymore. Everything that ever made sense is shifting."

I laughed humorlessly. "It is, isn't it?"

"We've got to stop being afraid of the change." He looked at me, eyes pleading. I couldn't help but wonder what change he meant.

"I'll confront the change. But not today." I walked away, embracing more strangers, trying to comprehend that I couldn't talk to my dad anymore about how confused I was feeling.

After the funeral, we tried to keep the spirits up. There were presents left over from Christmas to open since no one had been in the mood for a big gift-giving spree. Gerad was given special permission to play ball in the house, and Mom spent most of the afternoon next to Kenna, holding Astra. Kota was beyond pleasing, so we let him go off into the studio without bothering to check up on him. It was May I worried about the most. She kept saying her hands wanted to work, but she didn't want to go into the studio and not see Dad there.

In an inspired moment, I pulled her and Lucy into my room for some playtime. Lucy was a willing subject as May brushed out her hair, giggling as the makeup brushes tickled her cheeks.

"You do this to me every day!" I complained lightly.

May really had a talent for arranging hair, her artist's eyes ready to work with any medium. While May wore one of the maid uniforms even though it was too big for her, we put dress after dress on Lucy. We settled on a blue one, long and delicate, pinning it in the back so it fit.

"Shoes!" May cried, running to find a matching pair.

"My feet are too wide," Lucy complained.

"Nonsense," May insisted, and Lucy obediently sat on the bed while May tried the most bizarre forms of shoe application on the planet.

Lucy's feet really were too big, but with every attempt she laughed herself into a stupor at May's antics, and I was doubled over watching it all. We were so loud, it was only a matter of time until someone came to see what was going on.

After three quick knocks, I heard Aspen's voice through the door. "Is everything all right in there, miss?"

I ran over and opened the door wide. "Officer Leger, look at our masterpiece." I gave a wide sweep of my arm toward Lucy, and May pulled her up, her poor bare feet hidden under the dress.

Aspen looked at May in her baggy uniform and laughed and then took in Lucy, looking like a princess. "An amazing transformation," he said, grinning from ear to ear.

"Okay, I think we should put your hair all the way up now," May insisted.

Lucy rolled her eyes jokingly toward Aspen and me and let May drag her back to the mirror.

"Was this your idea?" he asked quietly.

"Yes. May looked so lost. I had to distract her."

"She looks better. And Lucy looks happy, too."

"It does as much for me as it does for them. It feels like, if we can do things that are silly or even just typical, I'll be okay."

"You will be. It'll take time, but you'll be okay."

I nodded. But then I started thinking about Dad again, and I didn't want to cry now. I took a deep breath and moved on.

"It seems wrong that I'm the lowest caste left in the Selection," I whispered back to him. "Look at Lucy. She's as pretty and sweet and smart as half of the girls who were in that pool of thirty-five, but this is the best she'll ever have. A few hours in a borrowed dress. It's not right."

Aspen shook his head. "I've gotten to know all your maids pretty well over the last few months, and she's a really special girl."

Suddenly a promise I'd made came back to me.

"Speaking of my maids, I need to talk to you about something," I said, dropping my voice.

Aspen stiffened. "Oh?"

"I know this is awkward, but I need to say it all the same."

He swallowed. "Okay."

I bashfully looked him in the eye. "Would you ever consider Anne?"

His expression was strange, as if he was simultaneously relieved and amused. "Anne?" he whispered incredulously. "Why her?"

"I think she likes you. And she's a really sweet girl," I said, trying to hide the depth of Anne's feelings but build her up at the same time.

He shook his head. "I know you want me to think about the possibility of other people, but she's not at all the kind of girl I'd want to be with. She's so . . . rigid."

I shrugged. "I thought Maxon was like that until I got to know him. Besides, I think she's had it rough."

"So? Lucy's had it rough, and look at her," he said, nodding his head toward her laughing reflection.

I took a guess. "Did she tell you how she ended up at the palace?"

He nodded. "I've always hated the castes, Mer; you know that. But I'd never heard of them being manipulated that way, to acquire slaves."

I sighed, looking over at May and Lucy, this stolen moment of joy in the middle of sorrow.

"Prepare yourself for words you thought you'd never hear," Aspen warned, and I looked up at him, waiting. "I'm actually really glad Maxon met you."

I coughed out something close to a laugh.

"I know, I know," he said, rolling his eyes but smiling. "But I don't think he would have ever stopped to wonder about the lower castes if it wasn't for you. I think just you being there has changed things."

We looked at each other for a moment. I remembered our conversation in the tree house, when he urged me to sign up for the Selection, hoping I'd have a chance for something better. I didn't know yet if I'd gotten something better for myself—it was still hard to tell—but the thought of maybe giving something better to everyone else in Illéa . . . that possibility meant more to me than I could say.

"I'm proud of you, America," Aspen said, looking from me to the girls by the mirror. "Really proud." He moved into the hallway, back to his rounds. "Your father would be, too."

CHAPTER 25

THE NEXT DAY WAS ANOTHER sentence of house arrest. From time to time, I'd hear the floor creak, and I'd turn my head, thinking that Dad would walk out of the garage, paint in his hair like always. But knowing that wasn't going to happen didn't feel as bad when I could hear May's voice or smell Astra's baby powder. The house felt full, and that was enough for now—its own kind of comfort.

I'd decided Lucy shouldn't wear her uniform while she was here, and after a little protesting, I wiggled her into some of my old clothes that were too small for me but too big for May. Since Mom was busy distracting herself by cooking and serving everyone and I'd decided to tone down my look to sit around the house, Lucy's main job was to play with May and Gerad, a task she took on happily.

We were all gathered in the living room, busying ourselves in our own ways. I had a book in hand, and Kota was hogging the television, reminding me of Celeste. I smiled, betting she was doing exactly that now.

Lucy, May, and Gerad were playing a card game on the floor, each one laughing when they won a round. Kenna was propped up against James on the couch, and baby Astra was finishing a bottle in his arms. It was easy to see the exhaustion in his face, but also the absolute pride in his beautiful wife and daughter.

It was almost as if nothing had changed. Then I'd see Aspen out of the corner of my eye in his uniform, standing watch over us, and remember that, in reality, nothing would ever be the same.

I heard Mom sniffling before I saw her coming down the hall. I turned my head and watched her walk toward us, holding a handful of envelopes.

"How are you feeling, Mom?" I asked.

"I'm fine. I just can't believe he's gone." She swallowed, forcing herself not to cry again.

It was strange. There had been so many times when I had doubted Mom's devotion to Dad. I'd never caught the glimpses of affection between them that I'd seen in other couples. Even Aspen, when everything was on the verge of being real but still very much a secret, showed me he loved me more than Mom did Dad.

But I could tell that this was more than the worry of

raising May and Gerad alone getting to her, or stress over money. Her husband was gone, and nothing would ever make that right.

"Kota, could you turn off the TV for a minute? And Lucy, honey, could you take May and Gerad into America's room? I have some things to discuss with the others," she said quietly.

"Of course, ma'am," Lucy replied, and turned to May and Gerad. "Let's go then."

May didn't look happy about being excluded from whatever was going on, but she chose not to put up a fight. I wasn't sure if it was because of Mom's heavy demeanor or her love for Lucy, but either way I was glad.

Once they were gone, Mom turned to the rest of us. "You know your father's condition was something that ran in the family. I think he could tell he only had a little time left, because about three years ago, he sat down and started writing these letters to you, to all of you." She looked down to the envelopes in her hands.

"He made me promise that if anything ever happened, I'd give them to you. I have ones for May and Gerad, but I'm not sure they're old enough. I haven't read them or anything. They were meant for you, so . . . I thought this would be a nice time to read them. This is Kenna's," she said, handing over a letter. "Kota." He sat up straighter and took his. Mom walked over to me. "And America."

I took my letter, unsure whether I wanted to open it or not. These were my last words from my father, the good-bye I thought I'd lost. I ran my hand over my name on the envelope, thinking of my father dashing the pen across it. He dotted the *i* in my name with some kind of squiggle. I smiled to myself, trying to guess what made him decide to do that and not caring at the same time. Maybe he knew I'd need to smile.

But then I looked at it closer. That little mark had been added later. The ink on my name had mostly faded, but that scribble was darker, fresher than the rest.

I flipped over the envelope. The seal had been broken and taped back together.

I glanced over to Kenna and Kota, who were both diving into the words. They seemed engrossed, so they hadn't known that these existed before this moment. That meant either Mom was lying and had read mine or Dad had opened this again.

That was all it took for me to decide I had to know what he'd left for me. I carefully picked at the retaped seal and pulled open the envelope.

There was a letter on faded paper and then a short, quick note on bright white paper. I wanted to read the short note, but I was afraid I wouldn't understand it without reading the long one first. I pulled out the letter and took in Dad's words in the sunlight by the window.

AMERICA,
     MY SWEET GIRL. I'M HAVING A HARD TIME EVEN STARTING THIS LETTER BECAUSE I FEEL LIKE THERE'S SO MUCH TO TELL YOU. THOUGH I LOVE ALL MY CHILDREN EQUALLY, YOU HAVE A SPECIAL

PLACE IN MY HEART. KENNA AND MAY BOTH LEAN ON YOUR MOTHER, KOTA IS SO INDEPENDENT THAT GERAD IS DRAWN TO HIM, BUT YOU HAVE ALWAYS COME TO ME. WHEN YOU SCRAPED YOUR KNEES OR WERE PICKED ON BY THE UPPER KIDS, MY ARMS WERE ALWAYS THE ONES YOU WANTED. IT MEANS THE WORLD TO ME TO KNOW THAT, AT LEAST FOR ONE OF MY CHILDREN, I WAS THEIR ROCK.

BUT EVEN IF YOU DIDN'T LOVE ME THE WAY THAT YOU DO, WITHOUT ANY SORT OF WORRY OR RESTRAINT, I'D STILL BE INCREDIBLY PROUD OF YOU. YOU'RE COMING INTO YOUR OWN AS A MUSICIAN, AND THE SOUNDS OF YOU PLAYING YOUR VIOLIN OR JUST SINGING AROUND THE HOUSE ARE THE LOVELIEST, MOST SOOTHING SOUNDS IN ALL THE WORLD. I WISH I COULD GIVE YOU A BETTER STAGE, AMERICA. YOU DESERVE SO MUCH MORE THAN STANDING IN THE SHADOWS AT STUFFY PARTIES. I KEEP HOPING YOU'LL BE ONE OF THE LUCKY ONES, THE BREAKOUTS. I THINK KOTA HAS A CHANCE AT IT, TOO. HE'S GIFTED AT WHAT HE DOES. BUT I FEEL LIKE KOTA WOULD FIGHT FOR IT, AND I'M NOT SURE YOU HAVE THAT INSTINCT IN YOU. YOU WERE NEVER A CUTTHROAT KIND OF GIRL, THE WAY SOME OF THE OTHER LOWERS CAN BE. AND THAT'S PART OF WHY I LOVE YOU, TOO.

YOU'RE GOOD, AMERICA. YOU'D BE SURPRISED AT HOW RARE THAT IS IN THIS WORLD. I'M NOT SAYING YOU'RE PERFECT; HAVING DEALT WITH SOME OF YOUR TEMPER TANTRUMS, I KNOW THAT'S FAR FROM THE TRUTH! BUT YOU'RE KIND, AND YOU ACHE FOR THINGS TO BE FAIR. YOU'RE GOOD, AND I SUSPECT YOU SEE THINGS IN THIS WORLD THAT NO ONE ELSE SEES, NOT EVEN ME.

AND I WISH I COULD TELL YOU HOW MUCH I SEE.

AS I'VE BEEN WRITING THESE LETTERS TO YOUR BROTHERS AND SISTERS, I'VE FELT THE NEED TO PASS ON WISDOM. I SEE IN THEM,

EVEN IN LITTLE GERAD, THE THINGS IN THEIR PERSONALITIES THAT COULD MAKE EVERY YEAR MORE DIFFICULT IF THEY DON'T MAKE THE EFFORT TO FIGHT AGAINST THE HARDNESS IN LIFE. I DON'T QUITE FEEL THAT URGE WITH YOU.

I SENSE THAT YOU WON'T LET THE WORLD PUSH YOU INTO A LIFE YOU DON'T WANT. MAYBE I'M WRONG, SO LET ME AT LEAST SAY THIS: FIGHT, AMERICA. YOU MIGHT NOT WANT TO FIGHT FOR THE THINGS THAT MOST OTHERS WOULD FIGHT FOR, LIKE MONEY OR NOTORIETY, BUT FIGHT ALL THE SAME. WHATEVER IT IS THAT YOU WANT, AMERICA, GO AFTER IT WITH ALL THAT YOU HAVE IN YOU.

IF YOU CAN DO THAT, IF YOU CAN KEEP FROM LETTING FEAR MAKE YOU SETTLE FOR SECOND BEST, THEN I CAN'T ASK FOR ANYTHING MORE FROM YOU AS A PARENT. LIVE YOUR LIFE. BE AS HAPPY AS YOU CAN BE, LET GO OF THE THINGS THAT DON'T MATTER, AND FIGHT.

I LOVE YOU, KITTEN. SO MUCH THAT I CAN'T FIND THE WORDS TO SAY IT. I COULD PAINT IT MAYBE, BUT I CAN'T FIT A CANVAS IN THIS ENVELOPE. EVEN THEN IT WOULD NEVER DO YOU JUSTICE. I LOVE YOU BEYOND PAINT, BEYOND MELODIES, BEYOND WORDS. AND I HOPE YOU WILL ALWAYS FEEL THAT, EVEN WHEN I'M NOT AROUND TO TELL YOU SO.

LOVE, DAD

I wasn't sure at what point I had started crying, but it was hard to make out the last of the letter. I wished so badly I'd had a chance to tell him I loved him the same way. And for a minute there, I could feel it, that warmth of absolute acceptance.

I looked up and saw that Kenna was crying, too, still trying to make her way through the letter. Kota looked confused as he flipped past the pages, seeming to go over them again.

Turning away, I pulled out the little note, hoping it wasn't nearly as touching as his letter. I wasn't sure I could take any more of that today.

AMERICA,

I'M SORRY. WHEN WE VISITED, I WENT TO YOUR ROOM AND FOUND ILLÉA'S DIARY. YOU DIDN'T TELL ME IT WAS THERE; I JUST FIGURED IT OUT. IF THERE'S ANY TROUBLE FROM THIS, THE BLAME IS MINE. AND I'M SURE THERE WILL BE REPERCUSSIONS BECAUSE OF WHO I AM AND BECAUSE OF WHO I TOLD. I HATE TO BETRAY YOU THAT WAY, BUT TRUST THAT I DID IT HOPING THAT YOUR FUTURE AND EVERYONE ELSE'S COULD BE BETTER.

LOOK UNTO THE NORTH STAR,
YOUR EVERLASTING GUIDE.
LET TRUTH, HONOR, ALL THAT'S RIGHT,
BE ALWAYS BY YOUR SIDE.
LOVE YOU,
SHALOM

I stood there for several minutes, trying to riddle this out. Repercussions? Who he was and who he had told? And what was with that poem?

Slowly, August's words came back to me, that my display on the *Report* wasn't how they knew the diaries existed and how they knew more of what was inside than I'd exposed. . . .

Who I am . . . who I told . . . look unto the North Star . . .

I stared at Dad's signature and remembered the way he signed the letters he'd sent me at the palace. I always thought the way he wrote his *o*'s looked funny. They were eight-point stars: North Stars.

The scribble over the *i* in my name. Did he want it to mean something to me, too? Did it already mean something because we'd talked to August and Georgia?

August and Georgia! His compass: eight points. The designs on her jacket weren't flowers at all. Both different but absolutely stars. The boy Kriss got at the Convicting. That wasn't a cross on his neck.

This was how they identified their own.

My father was a Northern rebel.

I felt as if I'd seen the star in other places. Maybe walking in the market or even in the palace. Had this been staring me in the face for years?

Stricken, I looked up; Aspen was waiting there, his eyes holding questions he couldn't ask aloud.

My dad was a rebel. A half-destroyed history book hidden in his room, friends at his funeral I knew nothing about . . . a daughter named America. If I'd paid attention at all, I would have seen it years ago.

"That's it?" Kota asked, sounding offended. "What the hell am I supposed to do with that?"

I turned away from Aspen, focusing on Kota.

"What's wrong?" Mom asked, coming back into the room with some tea.

"Dad's letter. He left me this house. What am I supposed to do with this dump?" He stood up, gripping the pages in his hand.

"Kota, Dad wrote that before you moved out," Kenna explained, still emotional. "He was trying to provide for you."

"Well, he failed then, didn't he? When have we ever not been hungry? This house sure as hell wouldn't have changed things. I did that for myself." Kota threw the papers across the room, and they flitted to the floor haphazardly.

Running his fingers through his hair, he huffed out a sigh. "Do we have any liquor in this place? Aspen, go get me a drink," he demanded, not even looking in Aspen's direction.

I turned and saw Aspen's face as a thousand emotions flickered across it: irritation, sympathy, pride, acceptance. He started toward the kitchen.

"Stop!" I commanded. Aspen paused.

Kota looked up, frustrated. "That's what he does, America."

"No, he doesn't," I spat. "You might have forgotten, but Aspen's a Two now. It would do you better to get *him* something to drink. Not just for his status, but for everything he's been doing for all of us."

A sly smirk fell across Kota's face. "Huh. Does Maxon know? Does he know this is still going on?" he asked, waving a lazy finger between the two of us.

My heart stopped beating.

"What would he do, you think? The caning thing's been done, and lots of people say that girl didn't get it bad enough for what she did." Kota placed his satisfied hands on his hips, staring us down.

I couldn't speak. Aspen didn't either, and I wondered if our silence was helping us or condemning us.

Finally Mom broke the silence. "Is it true?"

I needed to think; I needed to find the right way to explain this. Or a way to fight it, because really, it wasn't true . . . not anymore.

"Aspen, go check on Lucy," I said. He started walking until Kota protested.

"No, he stays!"

I lost it. "I say he goes! Now sit!"

The tone in my voice, unlike anything I had ever heard before, startled everyone. Mom plopped down immediately, shocked. Aspen made his way down the hall, and Kota slowly, begrudgingly sat as well.

I tried to focus.

"Yes, before the Selection, I was dating Aspen. We were planning on telling everyone once we saved up the money to get married. Before I left, we broke it off, and then I met Maxon. I care about Maxon, and even though Aspen is with me a lot, nothing is happening there." *Anymore,* I amended in my head.

Then I turned to Kota. "If you think, even for a second, you can twist my past into something and try to blackmail me with it, think again. You once asked if I told Maxon about you, and I did. He knows exactly what a spineless, ungrateful jackass you are."

Kota pressed his lips together, ready to boil over. I spoke quickly.

"And you should know that he adores me," I said grandly. "If you think he'd take your word over mine, you might be surprised by how quickly my suggestion of putting a cane to your hands would happen if I chose to make it so. You want to test me?"

He clenched his fists, clearly debating. If I was right and his hands got injured, that would be the end of his career.

"Good," I said. "And if I hear you say another unkind word about Dad, I might do it anyway. You were damn lucky to have a father who loved you so much. He left you the house, and he could have taken it away after you left, but he didn't. He still had hope for you, which is more than I can say."

I stormed off, heading into my room and slamming the door. I'd forgotten that Gerad, May, Lucy, and Aspen would be waiting for me there.

"You were dating Aspen?" May asked.

I gasped.

"You were a little loud," Aspen said.

I looked to Lucy. There were tears in her eyes. I didn't want to make her keep another secret, and clearly it pained her to think about it. She was so honest and loyal, how could I ask her to choose between me and the family she was sworn to serve?

"I'll tell Maxon when we go back," I said to Aspen. "I thought I was protecting you, I thought I was protecting myself, but all I've been doing is lying. And if Kota knows, then maybe other people do. I want to be the one to tell him."

CHAPTER 26

I SPENT THE REST OF the day hiding in my room. I didn't want to see Kota's accusing face or deal with Mom's questions. The worst was Lucy. She looked so sad to find out that I'd kept this secret from her. I didn't even want her serving me, and it seemed she was mostly fine with helping Mom however she could or playing with May.

I had too much to think about to have her around anyway. I kept rehearsing my speech to Maxon. I was trying to figure out the best way to confess this news. Should I leave out anything Aspen and I had done at the palace? If I did and he asked about it, would that be worse than me admitting to it in the first place?

And then I would get distracted thinking about Dad, wondering just what he'd said and done over the years. Were all those people I didn't know at his funeral really other rebels?

Could there possibly be that many?

Should I tell Maxon about that? Would he want me if he knew my family had rebel ties? It seemed as if some of the other Elite were there because of who they were linked to. What if my link undid me? It seemed unlikely now that we were so close to August, but still.

I wondered what Maxon was doing now. Working, maybe. Or finding a way to avoid it. I wasn't there for him to take walks with or sit with. I wondered if Kriss was taking my place.

I covered my eyes, trying to think. How was I supposed to get through all this?

There was a knock on my door. I didn't know if what was coming would make things better or worse, but I told the visitor to come in anyway.

Kenna walked in, and, for the first time since I'd come home, Astra was nowhere in sight.

"You okay?"

I shook my head, and the tears came. She walked in and sat beside me on the bed, wrapping an arm around me.

"I miss Dad. His letter was so . . ."

"I know," she said. "He hardly even spoke when he was here. But he left us with all these words. Part of me is glad. I don't know if I would remember it all if he hadn't written it down."

"Yeah." In that I had the answer to a question I was afraid to ask. No one else knew Dad had been a rebel.

"So . . . you and Aspen?"

"It's over, I swear."

"I believe you. When you're on TV, you should see the way you look at Maxon. Even that other girl, Celeste?" She rolled her eyes.

I smiled to myself.

"She tries to look like she's in love with him, but you can see it's not real. Or at least not as real as she wishes it was."

I snorted. "You have no idea how right you are on that one."

"I was wondering how long that had been happening. With Aspen, I mean."

"Two years. It started after you got married and Kota moved out. We'd been meeting in the tree house about once a week. We were saving up to get married."

"You were in love then?"

Shouldn't I have been able to answer right away? Shouldn't I have been able to tell her that I knew without a doubt that I'd loved Aspen? But now it didn't really seem that way. Maybe it was, but time and distance made it look different.

"I think so. But it doesn't feel . . ."

"It doesn't feel like things with Maxon?" she guessed.

I shook my head. "It just seems so strange now. For the longest time, Aspen was the only person I could imagine being with. I was ready to be a Six. And now?"

"And now you're five minutes away from being the next princess?" Her deadpan voice made the whole thing funny, and I laughed with her at the drastic change in my life.

"Thanks for that."

"That's what sisters are for."

I looked into her eyes and sensed that this hurt her somehow. "Sorry I didn't tell you sooner."

"You're telling me now."

"It wasn't because I didn't trust you. It was part of what made it special, I think. Keeping him a secret." Saying it out loud, I realized that it was true. Yes, I had feelings for him, but there were other things that surrounded us that made having Aspen that much sweeter: the secrecy, the rush of being touched, the thought of having something worth working toward.

"I understand, America, I really do. I just hope you never felt like you *had* to keep it a secret. Because I'm here for you."

I exhaled, and so many of my worries seemed to leave with that breath. At least for a moment. I propped my head on Kenna's shoulder, and it was nice to be able to think.

"So, is anything going on between you and Aspen anymore? How does he feel about you?"

I sighed, sitting up. "He keeps trying to tell me something, something about how he's always loved me. And I know I should tell him that it doesn't matter and that I love Maxon, but . . ."

"But?"

"What if Maxon picks someone else? I can't walk away from this with nothing. At least if Aspen still thinks there's a chance, maybe we could try again when everything's over."

She stared at me. "You're using Aspen as a safety net?"

I buried my head in my hands. "I know, I know. It's awful, isn't it?"

"America, you're better than that. And if you've ever cared about him at all, you need to tell him the truth just as badly as you need to tell Maxon the truth."

A knock came at the door. "Come in."

I blushed a little as Aspen walked in the doorway, a dejected Lucy close behind.

"You need to get dressed and packed," he said.

"Is something wrong?" I stood up, suddenly tense.

"All I know is that Maxon wants you back at the palace immediately."

I sighed, confused. I was supposed to have one more day. Kenna wrapped her arm around me again and gave me a tiny squeeze before heading back to the living room. Aspen left, and Lucy merely grabbed her uniform and went to the bathroom to change, closing the door behind her.

Alone again, I thought over everything. Kenna was right. I already knew how I felt about Maxon, and it was time to do what Dad had told me to do, what I'd meant to be doing this whole time: I was going to fight.

And because it felt like the bigger task, I would talk to Maxon first. Once that was settled, no matter the outcome, then I would figure out what to say to Aspen.

It had happened so slowly that it took me a while to realize how much we'd changed. But I'd known for weeks and had still kept my feelings to myself. I had to do the right thing and tell him so. I had to let go of Aspen.

I reached into my suitcase, hunting for the bundle at the bottom. Once I found the ball of fabric, I unrolled it, taking out my jar. The penny wasn't so lonely in there now with the bracelet, but that didn't matter.

I took the jar and placed it on my windowsill, leaving it where it should have stayed a long time ago.

I spent the majority of the plane ride going over my confession to Maxon. I was dreading this, but we could only move forward if he knew the truth.

I looked up from my comfy seat near the rear of the plane. Aspen and Lucy were sitting toward the front on opposite sides of the aisle, deep in conversation. Lucy looked upset still, and she seemed to be giving Aspen some sort of instructions. He was quiet as he took in her words, nodding at her suggestions. She retreated into her seat, and Aspen stood. I ducked back, hoping he didn't notice me spying.

I tried to look very interested in my book until he approached.

"The pilot says another half hour or so," he informed me.

"All right. Good."

He hesitated. "I'm sorry about everything with Kota."

"You don't have anything to be sorry for. He's just mean."

"No, I do. Years ago he teased me for having a crush on you, and I brushed it off; but I think he saw through it. He must have been paying attention since then. I should have been more careful or something. I should have—"

"Aspen."

"Yes?"

"It'll be fine. I'm going to tell Maxon the truth, and I'm going to take responsibility for this. You've got people at home depending on you. If something happens to you—"

"Mer, you tried to keep me from this, and I was too stubborn to listen. It's my fault."

"No, it's not."

He took a deep breath. "Listen . . . I need to tell you something. I know it's going to be difficult, but you need to know. When I told you I'd always love you, I meant it. And I—"

"Stop," I pleaded. I knew I had to tell him the truth, but I could only deal with one confession at a time. "I can't handle this right now. I just had my world turned upside down, and I'm about to do something I'm terrified to do. I need you to give me some room right now."

Aspen didn't look happy with this decision, but he let me make it all the same.

"As you wish, my lady." He walked away, and I felt even worse than I had before.

CHAPTER 27

WALKING BACK INTO THE PALACE felt impossibly right. A maid I'd never seen before was there to take my coat, and Aspen was next to a guard, explaining quietly that he'd give a full report on the trip in the morning. I started up the stairs, but another maid stopped me.

"Don't you want to go to the reception, miss?"

"Excuse me?" Was I supposed to have some fantastic homecoming or something?

"In the Women's Room, my lady. I'm sure they're waiting for you."

That was less of an explanation than I was hoping for, but I climbed back down the stairs and headed around the corner to the Women's Room. Strolling down the familiar halls was more comforting than I could have imagined. Of course I still missed my dad, but it was nice not to see things that made me think of him everywhere I turned. The only thing that would have made this homecoming better was Maxon walking here with me.

I was toying with the possibility of sending for him when I heard the wild noise coming from the Women's Room. I was confused by the sound. By the volume, half of Illéa was waiting in there.

Tentatively, I opened the door. The second Tiny—what was she doing here?—caught a glimpse of my hair, she called out to the room.

"She's here! America's back!"

The room exploded with cheers, and I was so confused. Emmica, Ashley, Bariel . . . everyone was here. I hunted, but I knew it was pointless. Marlee wouldn't be invited to this.

I was rushed by Celeste, who embraced me tightly. "Ahh, you bitch, I *knew* you'd make it!"

"What?" I asked.

She didn't get her words out fast enough. A split second later, Kriss was hugging me and half screaming in my ear. The smell on her breath said she'd been drinking quite a bit, and the glass in her hand confirmed she wasn't planning on stopping.

"It's us!" she yelled. "Maxon's announcing his engagement tomorrow! It's one of us!"

"Are you sure?"

"Elise and I got the boot last night, but he sent for all the girls to come back and celebrate, so we stayed," Celeste confirmed. "Elise isn't taking it well; you know how it is with her family. She thinks she failed."

"What about you?" I asked nervously.

She shrugged and smiled. "Eh."

I laughed at that, and a moment later a drink was shoved in my hand.

"To Kriss and America, the last girls standing!" someone yelled.

I was dizzy with the news. He'd decided to end it, to send everyone home. And he did it while I was away. Did that mean he missed me? Did that mean he realized he was fine without me?

"Drink!" Celeste insisted, tipping the glass back for me. I downed the champagne and came up coughing. Between the jet lag, the emotional stress of the last few days, and the sudden intake of alcohol, I was immediately giddy.

I watched as girls danced on the couches, celebrating even though they had lost. Celeste was in a corner with Anna; it looked as if she was apologizing repeatedly for her actions. Elise crept in quietly and came to offer me a hug before retreating again. It was a blur of excitement, and I found myself happy even though I wasn't totally certain of the outcome in front of me.

I turned around, and Kriss was suddenly there, embracing me.

"Okay," she said. "Let's promise that tomorrow, no matter what, we'll be happy for each other."

"I think that's a good plan," I shouted over the din. I laughed and lowered my eyes. In that quick second, a serious realization flooded me. That flash of silver on her neck suddenly meant so much more than it had a few days ago.

I sucked in a breath, and she looked at me with an expression that asked what was wrong. Even though it was rude and abrupt, I pulled her out of the room and down the hall.

"Where are we going?" she asked. "America, what's wrong?"

I dragged her around the corner and into the ladies' bathroom, double-checking to make sure we were alone before speaking.

"You're a rebel," I accused.

"What?" she said, a little too rehearsed. "You're crazy." But her hand fluttered to her neck, giving her away.

"I know what that star means, Kriss, so don't lie to me," I said calmly.

After a calculated pause she sighed. "I haven't done anything illegal. I'm not mounting protests anywhere; I just support the cause."

"Fine," I spat. "But how much of your part in the Selection is you wanting Maxon and how much is your group wanting one of their own on the throne?"

She was quiet for a moment, choosing her words. Clenching her jaw, she walked over to the door and locked it. "If you must know, yes, I was . . . *presented* to the king as an option. I'm sure you've guessed by now that the lottery was a joke."

I nodded.

"The king was—and still is—unaware of how many Northerners were promoted while the choice was being made. I was the only one of all the hopefuls to make it through, and, at first, I was completely dedicated to my cause. I didn't understand Maxon, and it didn't seem like he wanted me at all. But then I got to know him, and I was really sad about him not taking an interest in me. After Marlee left and you lost your hold on him, I saw him in a totally new light.

"You might think that my motives for coming here were wrong, and maybe you're right. But my reasons for being here *now* are completely different. I love Maxon, and I'm still fighting for him. And we can do great things together. So if you're thinking about trying to blackmail me or sell me out, forget it. I'm not backing down. Do you understand me?"

Kriss had never spoken so forcefully, and I didn't know if the reason was her absolute faith in her words or the heavy amount of champagne. She looked so fierce at the moment, I wasn't sure what to say.

I wanted to tell her that Maxon and I could do great things, too, that we'd probably already done more than she could guess. But now wasn't the time to brag. Besides, she and I had a lot in common. I came here for my family; she came here for a family of sorts. That got us through the doorway and into Maxon's heart. What good would it do us to tear each other apart now?

She took my silence as an agreement to behave, and she relaxed her stance.

"Good. Now, if you'll excuse me, I'm going back to the party."

Giving me a cold stare, she swept out of the room, leaving me torn. Should I keep my mouth shut? Should I at least let someone know? Was this even a bad thing?

I sighed and left the bathroom. I wasn't in the mood to celebrate anymore, so I took the back stairway up to my room.

Even though I wanted to see Anne and Mary, I was glad no one was there. I flopped onto the bed and tried to think. So Kriss was a rebel. Nothing dangerous, according to her, but I still wondered what that meant exactly. She must be who August and Georgia were talking about. What had ever made me think it was Elise?

Had Kriss helped them get into the palace? Had she pointed them in the direction of things they had been looking for? I had my secrets in the palace, but I'd never stopped to think about what the other girls could be hiding. I should have though.

Because what could I say now? If there was something real between Maxon and Kriss, any attempt to expose her would look like a desperate last effort to win. And even if that worked, that wasn't how I wanted to get Maxon.

I wanted him to know I loved him.

A knock came at the door, and I considered not answering it. If it was Kriss coming to explain more or one of the girls trying to drag me downstairs, that wasn't anything I wanted to deal with. Eventually, I heaved myself upright and went to the door.

Maxon stood there with a stuffed envelope and a small, gift-wrapped package.

In the second it took us to register that we were in the same place again, it felt as if the whole space charged with a magical kind of electricity, making me acutely aware of just how much I missed him.

"Hi," he said. He seemed a little stunned, as if he couldn't think of anything more to say.

"Hi."

We stared.

"Do you want to come in?" I offered.

"Oh. Um, yes, I do." Something was off. He was different, nervous maybe.

I stood aside, making room for him to enter. He looked around the space as if it had changed somehow since the last time he saw it.

He turned to gaze at me. "How are you feeling?"

I realized he probably meant about my dad, and I reminded myself that the end of the Selection wasn't the only shift in my world right now. "Okay. It doesn't really feel like he's gone, especially now that I'm here. I feel like I could write him a letter, and he'd still get it."

He gave me a sympathetic smile. "How's your family?"

I sighed. "Mom is holding it together, and Kenna is a rock. It's mostly May and Gerad I'm worried about. Kota couldn't have been any meaner about the whole thing. It's like he didn't love him at all, and I don't understand that," I confessed. "You met my dad. He was so sweet."

"He was," Maxon agreed. "I'm glad I at least got to meet him. I can see bits of him in you, you know."

"Really?"

"Absolutely!" He put his parcels in one hand, holding me with his free one. He walked me over to the bed, sitting next to me. "Your sense of humor, for one. And your tenacity. When he and I spoke during his visit, he grilled me. It was nerve-racking, but kind of funny at the same time. You've never just let me off the hook either.

"Of course, you have his eyes and I think his nose, too. And I can see your optimism beaming out sometimes. He gave me that impression as well."

I soaked up the words, holding on to all the parts of me that were like him. And here I thought Maxon didn't know him.

"All I'm saying is, it's okay to be sad about this, but you can be sure the best of him is still around," he concluded.

I threw my arms around him, and he held me with his free hand. "Thank you."

"I mean it."

"I know you do. Thanks." I moved back beside him and decided to change the subject before I got too emotional. "What's this all about?" I asked, nodding toward his full hand.

"Oh." Maxon fumbled with his thoughts a moment.

"These are for you. A late Christmas present."

He held up the envelope, thick with folded papers. "I can't believe I'm actually giving this to you, and you have to wait to look at them until I'm not here, but . . . it's for you to keep."

"Okay," I said questioningly as he set the envelope on my bedside table.

"This is a little less embarrassing," he added playfully, handing me the gift. "Sorry the wrapping is so bad."

"It's fine," I lied, trying not laugh at the crooked seams and tearing at the paper on the back.

Inside, the gift was a frame holding a picture of a house. Not just any house, but a beautiful one. It was a warm yellow color with plush grass that I wanted to put my feet in just from looking at the print. The windows were tall and wide on both stories, with trees offering shade to a section of the lawn. One tree even had a swing hanging from it.

I tried not to look at the house but at the photo itself. I was sure that this little piece of art was something Maxon made himself, though I couldn't guess when he'd gotten out of the palace to find its subject.

"It's beautiful," I admitted. "Did you take it yourself?"

"Oh, no." He laughed, shaking his head. "The picture isn't the gift; the house is."

I tried to let that sink in. "What?"

"I thought you'd want your family close by. It's a short drive away, with plenty of room. Your sister and her little family would even be comfortable there, I think."

"Wha . . . I . . ." I stared at him, searching for clarification.

Patient as ever, Maxon gave me the explanation he thought I already understood. "You told me to send everyone home. I did. I had to keep one other girl—those are the rules—but . . . you said that if I could prove I loved you . . ."

". . . It's me?"

"Of course it's you."

I was speechless. I laughed in shock and started giving him kisses and giggling between each one. Maxon, so pleased with the affection, took every kiss and laughed along with me.

"We're getting married?" I yelled, kissing him again.

"Yes, we're getting married." He chuckled and let me attack him in my excitement. I realized then that I was in his lap. I didn't remember getting there.

I kissed him on and on . . . and somewhere in there the laughing stopped. After a while, the smiling dwindled. The kisses turned from playful to something much deeper. When I pulled away and looked into his eyes, they were intense, focused.

Maxon held me close, and I could feel his heart racing against my chest. Guided by a deep hunger for him, I pushed his suit coat down his back, and he helped me as best as he could while holding on to me. I let my shoes fall to the floor, thudding a little song on their way down. I felt Maxon's legs shift underneath me as he slipped his off as well.

Without breaking our kiss, he lifted me, crawling deeper onto the bed and laying me down gently somewhere near the middle. His lips traveled down my neck as I loosened his tie, throwing it somewhere near our shoes.

"You're breaking a lot of rules, Miss Singer."

"You're the prince. You can just pardon me."

He chuckled darkly, his lips at my throat, my ear, my cheek. I untucked his shirt, fumbling with the buttons. He helped with the last few, sitting up to toss it aside. The last time I'd seen Maxon without his shirt on, I didn't get to really appreciate it because of the circumstance. But now . . .

I ran my fingers lightly down his stomach, admiring how strong he was. When my hand got to his belt, I gripped it and pulled him back down. He came willingly, dragging a hand up my leg, resting it comfortably on my thigh underneath the layers of my dress.

I was going crazy, wanting so much more of him, aching to know if he'd let me have it. Without even thinking, I reached around and dug my fingers into his back.

Immediately, he stopped kissing me, pulling back to look at me.

"What?" I whispered, terrified to break this moment.

"Does it . . . does it repulse you?" he asked nervously.

"What do you mean?"

"My back."

I ran a hand down his cheek, staring directly into his eyes, wanting to leave him with no doubt about how I felt.

"Maxon, some of those marks are on your back so they wouldn't be on mine, and I love you for them."

He stopped breathing for a second. "What did you say?"

I smiled. "I love you."

"One more time, please? I just—"

I took his face in both of my hands. "Maxon Schreave, I love you. I love you."

"And I love you, America Singer. With all that I am, I love you."

He kissed me again, and I let my hands move to his back, and this time he didn't pause. He moved his hands beneath me, and I felt his fingers playing with the back of my dress.

"How many damn buttons does this thing have?" he complained.

"I know! It's—"

Maxon sat up, placing his hands along the bust line of my dress. With one firm pull, he ripped my dress down the front, exposing the slip underneath.

There was a charged silence as Maxon took that in. Slowly, his eyes returned to mine. Without breaking that contact, I sat up, sliding the sleeves of my dress down my back. It took a little bit of work to get it all off; and, by the end of it, Maxon and I were kneeling on my bed, my hardly covered chest pressed to his, kissing slowly.

I wanted to stay up all night with him, to explore this new feeling we'd discovered. It felt as if everything else in the world was gone . . . until we heard a crash in the hall. Maxon stared at the door, seeming to expect it to burst open at any second. He was tense, more frightened than I'd ever seen him.

"It's not him," I whispered. "It's probably one of the girls stumbling to her room, or a maid cleaning something. It's okay."

He finally released a breath I didn't see he was holding and fell back onto the bed. He draped an arm over his eyes, frustrated or exhausted or maybe both.

"I can't, America. Not like this."

"But it's okay, Maxon. We're safe here." I lay down beside him, cuddling onto his free shoulder.

He shook his head. "I want to let all the walls down with you. You deserve that. And I can't now." He looked over to me. "I'm sorry."

"It's okay." But I couldn't hide my disappointment.

"Don't be sad. I want to take you on a proper honey-moon. Someplace warm and private. No duties, no cameras, no guards." He wrapped his arms around me. "It will be so much better that way. And I can really spoil you."

It didn't sound so bad to wait when he put it that way, but as always, I pushed back. "You can't spoil me, Maxon. I don't want anything."

We were nose to nose by then. "Oh, I know. I don't intend on giving you things. Well," he amended, "I do intend on giving you things, but that's not what I mean. I'm going to love you more than any man has ever loved a woman, more than you ever dreamed you could be loved. I promise you that."

The kisses that followed were sweet and hopeful, like our first ones. I could feel it, the promise he'd just made, starting now. And I was afraid and excited by the possibility of being loved so much.

"Maxon?"

"Yes?"

"Would you stay with me tonight?" I asked. Maxon raised an eyebrow, and I giggled. "I'll behave, I promise. Just . . . would you sleep here?"

He looked to the ceiling, debating. Finally he caved. "I will. But I'll need to leave early."

"Okay."

"Okay."

Maxon took off his pants and socks, neatly stacking his clothes so they wouldn't be too wrinkled in the morning. He crawled back into the bed, snuggling up with his stomach against my back. One of his arms he laced under my neck and the other he gently wrapped around me.

I loved my bed at the palace. The pillows were like clouds, and the mattress cradled me into it. I was never too warm or too cold under my covers, and the feeling of my nightgown against my skin was almost as if I was wearing air.

But I'd never felt so settled as I did with Maxon's arms around me.

He placed a gentle kiss behind my ear. "Sleep well, my America."

"I love you," I said quietly.

He held me a little tighter. "I love you."

I lay there, letting the happiness of the moment sink into me. It seemed only seconds later that Maxon's breathing was slow and steady. He was already asleep.

Maxon never slept.

I must have made him feel safer than I'd imagined. And, after all my worries about how his father acted toward me, he made me feel safe, too.

I sighed, promising myself that we'd talk about Aspen tomorrow. It would need to happen before the ceremony, and I felt sure I knew how to explain things in the best way. For now, I would enjoy this tiny bubble of peace and rest securely in the arms of the man I loved.

CHAPTER 28

I woke to the feeling of Maxon sliding an arm around me. Somewhere in the night, I ended up with my head on his chest, and the slow sound of his heartbeat was echoing in my ear.

Without a word, he kissed my hair and went to hold me closer. I couldn't believe this was happening. I was here with Maxon, together, waking up in my bed. This morning he would be giving me a ring. . . .

"We could wake up like this every day," he mumbled.

I giggled. "You're reading my mind."

He sighed contentedly. "How are you feeling, my dear?"

"I feel like punching you for calling me 'my dear' mostly." I poked his bare stomach.

Smiling, he crawled to sit over me. "Fine then. My darling? My pet? My love?"

"Any of those would work, so long as you've reserved it solely for me," I said, my hands mindlessly wandering his chest, his arms. "What am I supposed to call you?"

"Your Royal Husbandness. It's required by law, I'm afraid." His own hands glided over my skin, finding a delicate spot on my neck.

"Don't!" I said, shying away.

His responding smile was triumphant. "You're ticklish!"

Despite my protests, he started running his fingers all over me, making me shriek at the playful touching.

Nearly as quickly as I began squealing, I stopped. A guard rushed through the door, gun drawn.

This time I screamed, pulling up the sheet to cover myself. I was so frightened that it took me a moment to realize the determined eyes of the guard belonged to Aspen. It felt as if my face caught on fire, I was so humiliated.

Aspen looked stricken. He couldn't even put a sentence together as his eyes flashed back and forth between Maxon in his underwear and me draped in a sheet to cover mine.

My shock was finally broken by a deep laugh.

For as terrified as I was, Maxon was the picture of ease. In fact, he seemed pleased at being caught. His voice was a little smug as he spoke. "I assure you, Leger, she's perfectly safe."

Aspen cleared his throat, unable to look either of us in the eye. "Of course, Your Majesty." He bowed and left, closing the door behind him.

I fell over, moaning into my pillow. I would never live that down. I should have told Aspen how I felt on the plane when I had the chance.

Maxon came to hug me. "Don't be so embarrassed. It's not as if we were naked. And it's bound to happen in the future."

"It's so humiliating," I wailed.

"To be caught in bed with me?" The pain in his voice was clear. I sat up and faced him.

"No! It's not you. It's just, I don't know, this was supposed to be private." I ducked my head and played with a piece of the blanket.

Tenderly, Maxon stroked my cheek. "I'm sorry." I looked up at him, his voice too sincere to ignore. "I know it's going to be hard for you, but people will always be looking at our lives now. For the first few years, there will probably be a lot of interference. All the kings and queens have had only children. Some by choice, I'm sure; but after the difficulty my mother had, they'll want to make sure we can even have a family."

He stopped talking, his eyes having moved from my face to a spot on the bed.

"Hey," I said, cupping his cheek. "I'm one of five, remember? I have really good genes in that department. It'll be all right."

He gave me a weak smile. "I really hope so. Partly because, yes, we're duty bound to produce heirs. But also . . . I want everything with you, America. I want the holidays and the birthdays, the busy seasons and lazy weekends. I want peanut butter fingerprints on my desk. I want inside jokes and fights and everything. I want a life with you."

Suddenly the last few minutes were erased from my mind. The growing warmth in my chest was pushing everything else away.

"I want that, too," I assured him.

He smiled. "How about we make it official in a few hours?"

I shrugged. "I guess I don't have any other plans today."

Maxon tackled me on the bed, covering me with kisses. I would have let him kiss me like that for hours, but Aspen seeing us together was enough. There was no way I'd be able to stop my maids from gushing if they saw this.

He got dressed, and I pulled on my robe. It should have felt funny, maybe, this little moment in the afterward. All I could think about, though, as I watched Maxon cover his scars with his shirt, was how incredible this was. This thing I'd never wanted to happen was making me so happy.

Maxon gave me one last kiss before opening the door and heading on his way. It was harder to part with him than I thought it would be. I told myself it was only for a few hours and that the wait would be so worth it.

Before I closed the door, I heard Maxon whisper, "The lady would appreciate your discretion, officer."

There was no response, but I could imagine Aspen's solemn nod. I stood behind the closed door, debating what to say, wondering if I should even say anything. Minutes passed, but I knew I had to face Aspen. I couldn't move forward with everything that was going to happen today without talking to him first. I drew in a breath and nervously opened the door. He tilted his head toward the hallway listening for voices. Finally Aspen turned his accusing eyes my way, and the weight of his stare broke me.

"I'm so sorry," I breathed.

He shook his head. "It's not as if I didn't know it was coming. It was just a shock."

"I should have told you," I said, stepping into the hall.

"It doesn't matter. I just can't believe you slept with him."

I put my hands on his chest. "I didn't, Aspen. I swear."

And then, at the last possible moment, everything was ruined.

Maxon stepped around the corner, holding Kriss by the hand. His eyes locked on to me, body pressed into Aspen with the intensity of my defense. I backed away, but not quickly enough. Aspen turned to face Maxon, prepared to give an excuse but still too stunned to speak.

Kriss's mouth dropped open, and she quickly covered it with a hand. Looking into Maxon's shocked eyes, I shook my head, trying to explain without words that this was all a misunderstanding.

It was only a second before Maxon regained his cool demeanor. "I found Kriss in the hall and was coming to explain my choice to you both before the cameras showed up, but it seems we have other things to discuss."

I looked at Kriss and was at least consoled by the fact that there was no triumph in her eyes. On the contrary, she looked sad for me.

"Kriss, would you please return to your room? Quietly?" Maxon instructed.

She curtsied and disappeared down the hall, eager to get away from the situation. Maxon took a deep breath before looking at us again.

"I knew it," he said. "I told myself I was crazy, because surely you would have told me if I was right. You were supposed to be honest with me." He rolled his eyes. "I cannot believe I didn't trust myself. From that first meeting, I knew it. The way you looked at him, how distracted you were. That damn bracelet you wore, the note on the wall, all those times when I thought I had you and then suddenly lost you again . . . it was you," he said, turning to Aspen.

"Your Majesty, this is my fault," Aspen lied. "I pursued her. She made it perfectly clear that she had no intentions of being in a relationship with anyone but you, but I went after her anyway."

Without responding to Aspen's excuses, he walked right up to him, looking him in the eye. "What's your name? Your first name?"

He swallowed. "Aspen."

"Aspen Leger," he said, testing the words. "Get out of my sight before I send you to New Asia to die."

Aspen's breath caught. "Your Majesty, I—"

"GO!"

Aspen looked at me once, then turned and walked away.

I stood there, silent and still, afraid to risk a peek into Maxon's eyes. When I finally did, he nudged his chin toward my room, and I went in, with him following me. I turned to see him close the door and run his hand through his hair one time. He moved to face me, and I saw his eyes catch on the unmade bed. He laughed humorlessly to himself.

"How long?" he asked quietly, still in control.

"Do you remember that fight—" I started.

Maxon erupted. "We've been fighting since the day we met, America! You'll have to be more specific!"

I shook where I stood. "After Kriss's party."

His eyes widened. "So basically since he got here," he said, something like sarcasm in his voice.

"Maxon, I'm so sorry. At first I was protecting him, and then I was protecting myself. And after Marlee was caned, I was afraid to tell you the truth. I couldn't lose you," I pleaded.

"Lose me? Lose *me*?" he asked, astonished. "You're going home with a small fortune, a new caste, and a man who is still pursuing you! I'm the one losing here today, America!"

The words took my breath away. "I'm going home?"

He looked at me as if I was an idiot for asking. "How many times am I supposed to let you break my heart, America? Do you think I'd honestly marry you, make you my princess, when you've been lying to me for most of our relationship? I refuse to torture myself for the rest of my life. You might have noticed, I get plenty of that already."

I erupted into sobs. "Maxon, please. I'm sorry; it's not what it looked like. I s-swear. I love you!"

He sauntered up to me, his eyes dead. "Of all the lies

you've told me, that's the one I resent the most."

"It's not—" The look in his eyes silenced me.

"Have your maids do their best. You should go out in style."

He walked past me, out the doorway and out of the future I'd held in my hands only a few minutes before. I turned back to the room, holding my stomach as if the core of my body was about to crack from the pain. I went over to the bed, rolling onto my side, no longer able to stand.

I cried, hoping to get the ache out of my body before the ceremony. How was I supposed to face that? I looked to the clock to see how much time I had . . . and saw the thick envelope Maxon had given me last night.

I decided this was the last piece of him I would ever have, so I opened the seal, desperate.

CHAPTER 29

December 25, 4:30 p.m.

Dear America,

It's been seven hours since you left. Twice now I've started to go to your room to ask how you liked your presents and then remembered you weren't here. I've gotten so used to you, it's strange that you aren't around, drifting down the halls. I've nearly called a few times, but I don't want to seem possessive. I don't want you to feel like I'm a cage to you. I remember how you said the palace was just that the first night you came here. I think, over time, you've felt freer, and I'd hate to ruin that freedom. I'm going to have to distract myself until you come back.

I decided to sit and write to you, hoping maybe it would feel like I was talking to you. It sort of does. I can imagine you sitting here, smiling at my idea, maybe shaking your head at me as if to say I'm being silly. You do that sometimes, did you know? I like that expression on you. You're the only person who wears it in a way that doesn't come across like you think I'm completely hopeless. You smile at my idiosyncrasies, accept that they exist, and continue to be my friend. And, in seven short hours, I've started to miss that.

I wonder what you've done in that time. I'm betting by now you've flown across the country, made it to your home, and are safe. I hope you are safe. I can't imagine what a comfort you must be to your family right now. The lovely daughter has finally returned!

I keep trying to picture your home. I remember you telling me it was small, that you had a tree house, and that your garage was where your father and sister did all their work. Beyond that I've had to resort to my imagination. I imagine you curled up in a hug with your sister or kicking around a ball with your little brother. I remember that, you know? That you said he liked to play ball.

I tried to imagine walking into your house with you. I would have liked that, to see you where you grew up. I would love to see your brother run around or be embraced by your mother. I think it would be comforting to sense the presence of people near you, floorboards creaking and doors shutting. I would have liked to sit in one part of the house and still probably be able to smell the kitchen. I've always imagined that real homes are full of the aromas of whatever's being cooked. I wouldn't do a scrap of work. Nothing having to do with armies or budgets or negotiations. I'd sit with you, maybe try to work on my photography while you played the piano. We'd be Fives together, like you said. I could join your family for dinner, talking over one another in a collection of conversations instead of whispering and waiting our turns. And maybe I'd sleep in a spare bed or on the couch. I'd sleep on the floor beside you if you'd let me.

I think about that sometimes. Falling asleep next to you, I mean, like we did in the safe room. It was nice to hear your breaths as they came and went, something quiet and close, keeping me from feeling so alone.

This letter has gotten foolish, and I think you know how I detest looking like a fool. But still I do. For you.

Maxon

December 25, 10:35 p.m.
Dear America,

It's nearly bedtime, and I'm trying to relax, but I can't. All I can think about is you. I'm terrified you're going to get hurt. I know someone would tell me if you weren't all right, and that has led to its own kind of paranoia. If anyone comes up to me to deliver a message, my heart stops for a moment, fearing the worst: You are gone. You're not coming back.

I wish you were here. I wish I could just see you.

You are never getting these letters. It's too humiliating.

I want you home. I keep thinking of your smile and worrying that I'll never see it again.

I hope you come back to me, America.
Merry Christmas.
Maxon

December 26, 10:00 a.m.
Dear America,

Miracle of miracles, I've made it through the night. When I finally woke up, I convinced myself I was worried for nothing. I vowed that I would focus on work today and not fret so much about you.

I got through breakfast and most of a meeting before thoughts of you consumed me. I told everyone I was sick and am now hiding in my room, writing to you, hoping this will make me feel like you're home again.

I'm so selfish. Today you will bury your father, and all I can think of is bringing you here. Having written that out, seeing it in ink, I feel like an absolute ass. You are exactly where you need to be. I think I already said this, but I'm sure you're such a comfort to your family.

You know, I haven't told this to you and I ought to have, but you've gotten so much stronger since I met you. I'm not arrogant enough to believe that has anything to do with me, but I think this experience has changed you. I know it's changed me. From the very beginning you had your own brand of fearlessness, and that has been polished into something strong. Where I used to imagine you as a girl with a bag full of stones, ready to throw them at any foe who crossed her path, you have become the stone itself. You are steady and able. And I bet your family sees that in you. I should have told you that. I hope you come home soon so I can.

Maxon

December 26, 7:40 p.m.
Dear America,

I've been thinking of our first kiss. I suppose I should say first kisses, but what I mean is the second, the one I was actually invited to give you. Did I ever tell you how I felt that night? It wasn't just getting my first kiss ever; it was getting to have that first kiss with you. I've seen so much, America, had access to the corners of our planet. But never have I come across anything so painfully beautiful as that kiss. I wish it was something I could catch with a net or place in a book. I wish it was something I could save and share with the world so I could tell the universe: this is what it's like; this is how it feels when you fall.

These letters are so embarrassing. I'll have to burn them before you get home.

Maxon

December 27, noon
America,

I might as well tell you this since your maid will tell you anyway. I've been thinking of the little things you do. Sometimes you hum or sing when you walk around the palace. Sometimes when I come up to your room, I hear the melodies you've saved up in your heart spilling out the doorway. The palace seems empty without them.

I also miss your smell. I miss your perfume drifting off your hair when you turn to laugh at me or your scent radiating on your skin when we walk through the garden. It's intoxicating.

So I went to your room to spray your perfume on my handkerchief, another silly trick to make me feel like you were here. And as I was leaving your room, Mary caught me. I'm not sure what she was looking after since you're not here; but she saw me, shrieked, and a guard came running in to see what was wrong. He had his staff gripped, and his eyes flashed threateningly. I was nearly attacked. All because I missed your smell.

December 27, 11:00 p.m.
My Dear America,

I've never written a love letter, so forgive me if I fail now. . . .

The simple thing would be to say that I love you. But, in truth, it's so much more than that. I want you, America. I need you.

I've held back so much from you out of fear. I'm afraid that if I show you everything at once, it will overwhelm you, and you'll run away. I'm afraid that somewhere in the back of your heart is a love for someone else that will never die. I'm afraid that I will make a mistake again, something so huge that you retreat into that silent world of yours. No scolding from a tutor, no lashing from my father, no isolation in my youth has ever hurt me so much as you separating yourself from me.

I keep thinking that it's there, waiting to come back and strike me. So I've held on to all my options, fearing that the moment I wipe them away, you will be standing there with your arms closed, happy to be my friend but unable to be my equal, my queen, my wife.

And for you to be my wife is all I want in the world. I love you. I was afraid to admit it for a long time, but I know it now.

I would never rejoice in the loss of your father, the sadness you've felt since he passed, or the emptiness I've experienced since you left. But I'm so grateful that you had to go. I'm not sure how long it would have taken for me to figure this out if I hadn't had to start trying to imagine a life without you. I know now, with absolute certainty, that is nothing I want.

I wish I was as true an artist as you so that I could find a way to tell you what you've become to me. America, my love, you are sunlight falling through trees. You are laughter that breaks through sadness. You are the breeze on a too-warm day. You are clarity in the midst of confusion.

You are not the world, but you are everything that makes the world good. Without you, my life would still exist, but that's all it would manage to do.

You said that to get things right one of us would have to take a leap of faith. I think I've discovered the canyon that must be leaped, and I hope to find you waiting for me on the other side.

I love you, America.

Yours forever,

Maxon

CHAPTER 30

THE GREAT ROOM WAS PACKED. For once, instead of the king and queen being the focal point of the room, it was Maxon. On a slightly raised platform, Maxon, Kriss, and I sat at an ornate table. I felt as if our positioning was deceitful. I was on Maxon's right. I always thought being on someone's right was a good thing, an honored position. But so far he'd spent the entire time speaking to Kriss. As if I didn't already know what was coming.

I tried to seem happy as I looked around the room. It was packed. Gavril, of course, was in a corner, speaking into a camera, narrating the events as they happened.

Ashley smiled and waved, and beside her Anna winked at me. I gave them a nod, still too nervous to speak. Toward the back of the room, in deceptively clean clothes, August, Georgia, and some of the other Northern rebels sat at a table by themselves. Of course Maxon would want them here to meet his new wife. Little did he know she was one of their own.

They surveyed the room tensely, as if they feared any second a guard would recognize them and attack. The guards didn't seem to be paying attention though. In fact, this was the first time I'd ever seen them look so poorly focused, eyes meandering around the room, several of them on edge. I'd even noticed that one or two hadn't shaved and looked a little rough. It was a big event though. Maybe they were just rushed.

My eyes flitted over to Queen Amberly, speaking with her sister Adele and her gaggle of children. She looked radiant. She'd been waiting for this day for so long. She would love Kriss like her own. For a moment, I was so jealous of that fact.

I turned and scanned the faces of the Selected again, and this time my eyes landed on Celeste. I could see the clear question in her eyes: What are you so worried about? I gave her a minuscule shake of my head, letting her know that I'd lost. She sent me a thin smile and mouthed the words *It'll be okay*. I nodded, and I tried to believe her. She turned away, laughing at something someone said; and I finally looked to my right, taking in the face of the guard stationed closest to our table.

Aspen was distracted though. He was looking around the room like so many of the other men in uniform, but he seemed to be trying to think of something. It was as if he was doing a puzzle in his head. I wished he would look my way, maybe try to explain wordlessly what he was worried about, but he didn't.

"Trying to arrange a time to meet later?" Maxon asked, and I whipped my head back.

"No, of course not."

"It's not like it matters. Kriss's family will be here this afternoon for a small celebration, and yours will be here to take you home. They don't like for the last loser to be alone. She tends to get dramatic."

He was so cold, so distant. It was as if it wasn't even Maxon at all.

"You can keep that house if you want. It's been paid for. I'd like my letters back though."

"I read them," I whispered. "I loved them."

He huffed as if it was a joke. "Don't know what I was thinking."

"Please don't do this. Please. I love you." My face was crumpling.

"Don't. You. Dare," Maxon ordered through gritted teeth. "You put on a smile, and you wear it to the last second."

I blinked away the tears and gave a weak smile.

"That'll do. Don't let that slip until you leave the room, do you understand?" I nodded. He looked into my eyes. "I'll be glad when you're gone."

After he spat out those last words, his smile returned and

he faced Kriss again. I stared into my lap a minute, slowing my breathing and putting on a brave face.

When I brought my eyes up again, I didn't dare to look directly at anyone. I didn't think I could honor Maxon's last wish if I did. Instead, I focused on the walls of the room. It was because of that I noticed when most of the guards stepped away from them at some signal I didn't see. Pieces of red fabric were pulled out of their pockets and tied across their foreheads.

I watched in confusion as a red-marked guard walked up behind Celeste and put a bullet squarely through the back of her head.

The screaming and gunfire exploded at once. Guttural shouts of pain filled the room, adding to the cacophony of chairs screeching, bodies hitting walls, and the stampede of people trying to escape as fast as they could in their heels and suits. The men shouted as they fired, making the whole thing far more terrifying. I watched, stunned, seeing death more times in a handful of seconds than ought to be possible. I looked for the king and queen, but they were gone. I was gripped with fear, unsure if they'd escaped or been captured. I looked for Adele, for her children. I couldn't see them anywhere, and that was even worse than losing sight of the king and queen.

Beside me, Maxon was trying to calm Kriss. "Get on the floor," he told her. "We're going to be fine."

I looked to my right for Aspen and was in awe for a

moment. He was on one knee, taking aim, firing deliberately into the crowd. He must have been very sure of his target to do that.

Out of the corner of my eye, I saw a flicker of red. Suddenly a rebel guard was standing in front of us. As I thought the words *rebel guard*, it all clicked into place. Anne had told me this had happened once before, when the rebels had gotten the guards' uniforms and had sneaked into the palace. But how?

As Kriss let out another cry, I realized that the guards who were sent to our houses hadn't abandoned their posts at all. They were dead and buried, their clothes stolen and standing in front of us.

Not that this information did me any good now.

I knew that I should run, that Maxon and Kriss should run if they were going to make it. But I was frozen as the menacing figure raised his gun and directed it at Maxon. I looked up at Maxon, and he looked to me. I wished I had time to speak. I turned away, back to the man.

A look of amusement crossed his face. As if he suspected this would be much more entertaining for himself and much more painful for Maxon, he slid his gun ever so slightly to his left and aimed it at me.

I didn't even think to scream. I couldn't move at all, but I saw the blur of Maxon's suit coat as he leaped toward me.

I fell to the ground, but not in the direction I thought I would. Maxon missed me, flying across in front of me. When

I hit the floor, I looked up to see Aspen. He'd sprinted to the table and pushed over my chair, crashing on top of me.

"I got him!" someone shouted. "Find the king!"

I heard several shouts of delight, pleased with the declaration. And screaming. So much screaming. As I came out of my stupor, the sounds crashed into my ears again. Other chairs and bodies clamored to the floor. Guards yelled out orders. Shots were fired, and the sickening pops pierced my ears. It was pure pandemonium.

"Are you hurt?" Aspen demanded over the commotion.

I think I shook my head.

"Don't move."

I watched as he stood, widened his stance, and aimed. He fired several times, eyes focused and body at ease. By the angle of his shots, it looked like more rebels were trying to get close to us. Thanks to Aspen, they failed.

After a quick survey, he popped down again. "I'm going to get her out of here before she really loses it."

He crawled over me and grabbed Kriss, who was covering her ears and crying in earnest. Aspen pulled her face up and slapped her. She was stunned into silence long enough to listen to his orders and follow him from the room, shielding her head as she went.

It was getting quieter. People must be leaving now. Or dying.

And then I noticed a very still leg hanging out from under the tablecloth. Oh, God! Maxon!

I scurried under the table to find Maxon breathing with great labor, a large red stain growing across his shirt. There was a wound below his left shoulder, and it looked very serious.

"Oh, Maxon," I cried. Unsure of what else to do, I balled up the hem of my dress in my hands and pressed it to the bullet wound. He winced a bit. "I'm so sorry."

He reached up his hand and covered mine. "No, I'm sorry," he said. "I was about to ruin both our lives."

"Don't talk right now. Just focus, okay?"

"Look at me, America."

I blinked a few times and pulled my gaze up to his eyes. Through the pain, he smiled at me.

"Break my heart. Break it a thousand times if you like. It was only ever yours to break anyway."

"Shhh," I urged.

"I'll love you until my very last breath. Every beat of my heart is yours. I don't want to die without you knowing that."

"Please don't," I choked.

He took his hand off mine and laced it through my hair. The pressure was light, but it was enough for me to know what he wanted. I bent to kiss him. It was every kiss we'd ever had, all the uncertainty, all the hope.

"Don't give up, Maxon. I love you; please don't give up."

He took an unsteady breath.

Aspen ducked under the table then, and I squealed in fear before I realized who it was.

"Kriss is in a safe room, Your Majesty," Aspen said, all business. "Your turn. Can you stand?"

He shook his head. "A waste of time. Take her."

"But, Your Majesty—"

"That's an order," he said as forcefully as he could manage.

Maxon and Aspen stared at each other for a long second.

"Yes, sir."

"No! I won't go!" I insisted.

"You'll go," Maxon said, sounding tired.

"Come on, Mer. We'll have to hurry."

"I'm not leaving!"

Quickly, as if he might suddenly be fine, Maxon reached up to Aspen's uniform and clutched it in his hands. "She lives. Do you understand me? Whatever it takes, she lives."

Aspen nodded and grabbed my arm harder than I thought possible.

"No!" I cried. "Maxon, please!"

"Be happy," he breathed, squeezing my hand one last time as Aspen dragged me away, screaming.

As we got to the door, Aspen pushed me up against the wall. "Shut up! They'll hear you. The sooner I get you to a safe room, the sooner I can come back for him. You have to do whatever I say, got it?"

I nodded.

"Okay, stay low and quiet," he said, pulling out his gun again and dragging me into the hall.

We looked up and down, and saw someone running away

from us at the far end of the corridor. Once he was gone we moved. Around the corner we stumbled upon a guard on the ground. Aspen checked his pulse and shook his head. He reached over and grabbed the guard's gun, and handed it to me.

"What am I supposed to do with this?" I whispered, terrified.

"Fire it. But make sure you know if it's a friend or a foe before you do. This is mayhem."

It was a tense few minutes of ducking into corners and checking safe rooms that were already taken and locked. It seemed that most of the action had moved upstairs or outside, because the pops of gunshots and faceless screams were muffled by walls. Still, each time we heard a whisper of a sound, we paused before moving.

Aspen peeked around a corner. "This is a dead end, so keep a lookout."

I nodded. We moved quickly to the end of the short hallway, and the first thing I noticed was the bright sun coming in through the window. Didn't the sky know the world was falling apart? How could the sun shine today?

"Please, please, please," Aspen whispered, reaching for the lock. Mercifully, it opened. "Yes!" He sighed, pulling back the door, blocking half the hall from view.

"Aspen, I don't want to do this."

"You have to. You have to be safe, for so many people. And . . . I need you to do something for me."

"What?"

He fidgeted. "If something happens to me . . . I need you to tell—"

Over his shoulder, a hint of red came from behind the corner at the end of the hall. I jerked the gun up and pointed it past Aspen, firing at the figure. Not a second later, Aspen pushed me into the safe room and slammed the door, leaving me alone in the dark.

CHAPTER 31

I DON'T KNOW HOW LONG I sat there. I kept listening for something outside the door, even though I knew it was useless. When Maxon and I had been locked in a safe room a few weeks ago, we couldn't hear a single sound from the outside world. And there had been so much destruction then.

Still, I hoped. Maybe Aspen was okay and would open the door at any second. He couldn't be dead. No. Aspen was a fighter; he'd always been a fighter. When hunger and poverty threatened him, he pushed back. When the world took away his dad, he made sure his family survived. When the Selection took me, when the draft took him, he didn't let it stop him from hoping. Compared to all that, a bullet was tiny, insignificant. No bullet was taking down Aspen Leger.

I pressed my ear up to the door, praying for a word, a breath, anything. I focused, listening for something that sounded like Maxon's labored breathing as he lay dying underneath the table.

I pinched my eyes together, begging God to keep him alive. Certainly, everyone in the palace would be looking for Maxon and his parents. They would be the first ones helped. They wouldn't let him die; they couldn't.

But was it past hope?

He'd looked so pale. Even the last squeeze of my hand was weak.

Be happy.

He loved me. He really loved me. And I loved him. In spite of everything that should have kept us apart—our castes, our mistakes, the world around us—we were supposed to be together.

I should be with him. Especially now, while he lay dying. I shouldn't be hiding.

I stood up and started feeling around the walls for the light switch. I slapped the steel until I found it. I surveyed the space. It was smaller than the other room I'd been in. It had a sink but no toilet, just a bucket in one corner. A bench was pressed up against the wall by the door, and a shelf with some packets of food and blankets lined the back. And then finally, on the floor, the gun sat cold and waiting.

I didn't even know if this would work, but I had to try. I pulled the bench over to the middle of the room and tipped it on its side with the wide seat propped up toward the door. I crouched below it, checking the height, and realized that wasn't going to be much cover. It would have to do though.

As I stood, I tripped over my stupid dress. Huffing, I hunted on the shelves. The thin knife was probably for opening and dividing food, but it worked on the material just fine. Once my dress was cut into an uneven hem around my knees, I took some of the fabric and made a makeshift belt and tucked the knife in it for good measure.

I pulled the blankets over myself, expecting there to be some sort of shrapnel. Looking one more time around the room, I tried to see if there was anything I should take with me, something I could repurpose. No. This was it.

Ducking behind the bench, I aimed the gun at the lock, took a steadying breath, and fired.

The sound echoed in the tiny space, scaring me even though I'd been expecting it. Once I was sure that the bullet wasn't ricocheting around the room, I went up to check the door. Above the lock, a small crater sat, exposing rough layers of metal. I was upset that I'd missed, but at least I knew this might work. If I hit the lock enough times, maybe I could get out of here.

I hid behind the bench and tried again. Shot after shot hit the door, but never in the same place. After a while, I got frustrated and stood up straight, hoping it would help. All I managed to do was get my arms cut by pieces of the door flying back at me.

It wasn't until I heard the hollow click that I realized I'd used all the bullets and was stuck. I threw down the gun and ran over to the door. I hit it with all the force of my body.

"Move!" I rammed into it again. "MOVE!"

I hit the door with my fists, accomplishing nothing. "No! No, no, no! I have to get out!"

The door stood there, silent and severe, mocking my heartbreak with its stillness.

I slid down to the floor, crying now that I knew there was nothing I could do. Aspen might be a lifeless body only feet away from me, and Maxon . . . surely by now he was gone.

I curled my legs to my chest and rested my head against the door.

"If you live," I whispered, "I'll let you call me your dear. I won't complain, I promise."

And then I was left to wait.

Every so often I'd try to guess at the time, though I had no way of knowing if I was right. Each sluggish minute was maddening. I'd never felt so powerless, and the worry was killing me.

After an eternity, I heard the click of the lock. Someone was coming for me. I didn't know if it was a friend or not, so I pointed the empty gun at the door. It would at least look intimidating. The door creaked open, and the light from the window glared in. Did that mean it was still the same day? Or was it the next? I held my aim though I had to squint to do so.

"Don't shoot, Lady America!" a guard pleaded. "You're safe!"

"How do I know that? How do I know you're not one of them?"

The guard looked down the hall, acknowledging an approaching figure. August stepped into the light, followed closely by Gavril. Though his suit was practically destroyed, his pin—which I now realized looked an awful lot like a North Star—still hung proudly on his bloody lapel.

No wonder the Northern rebels knew so much.

"It's over, America. We got them," August confirmed.

I sighed, overwhelmed with relief, and dropped the gun.

"Where's Maxon? Is he alive? Did Kriss make it?" I asked Gavril before focusing again on August. "There was an officer; he brought me here. His name is Officer Leger; have you seen him?" The words tumbled out almost too quickly to be understood.

I was feeling funny, light-headed.

"I think she's in shock. Take her to the hospital wing, quickly," Gavril ordered, and the guard scooped me up easily.

"Maxon?" I asked. No one answered. Or maybe I was gone by then. I couldn't remember.

When I woke up, I was on a cot. I could feel the stings of my many cuts now, but as I picked up my arm to inspect it, the cuts were all clean, and the larger ones were bandaged. I was safe.

I sat up and looked around, and realized I was in a tiny office. I inspected the desk and the diplomas on the wall and discovered it was Dr. Ashlar's. I couldn't stay here. I needed answers.

When I opened the door, I discovered why I'd been tucked away. The hospital wing was packed. Some of the less injured were placed two to a bed, and others were on the floor between them. It was easy to tell that the worst were in beds toward the back of the room. Despite the number of people, the space was remarkably quiet.

I scanned the area, looking for familiar faces. Was it good not to find them here? What did that mean?

Tuesday was in a bed, holding on to Emmica as they cried quietly. I recognized a few of the maids, but only vaguely. They nodded their heads at me as I passed, as if I somehow deserved it.

I started losing hope as the crowd started to thin. Maxon wasn't here. If he was, he'd have a swarm of people around him, jumping to meet his every need. But I'd been placed in a side room. Maybe he had, too?

I saw a guard, and his face was scarred from what I couldn't guess. "Is the prince down here somewhere?" I asked quietly.

Solemnly, he shook his head.

"Oh."

A bullet wound and a broken heart would seem like two different injuries. But I could feel myself bleeding out just as surely as Maxon had. No amount of pressure or stitching would ever fix this; nothing would ever stop the ache.

I didn't break into a scream, though it felt as if something similar was happening inside. I just let the tears fall. They didn't wash anything away, but they felt like a promise.

Nothing will ever replace you, Maxon. And I sealed our love away.

"Mer?"

I turned and saw a bandaged figure in one of the last beds in the wing. Aspen.

My breathing hitched as I took unsteady steps toward him. His head was bandaged, and there was blood staining its way through. His chest was bare and bruised in several places, but the worst part was his leg. A thick cast was wrapped around the bottom, and several bandages were sloppily placed over gashes on his thigh. Wearing nothing but some shorts and a bit of a sheet over his other leg, it was easy to see how badly he'd been wounded.

"What happened?" I whispered.

"I'd rather not relive the details. I made it for a long time, and I took out maybe six or seven of them before one got my leg. The doctor says I'll probably be able to walk on it, but I'll need a cane. At least I'm alive."

A tear continued silently down my cheek. I was so grateful and scared and hopeless, I couldn't help it.

"You saved my life, Mer."

My eyes flew from his leg to his face.

"The shot you took spooked that rebel and gave me just enough time to fire. If you hadn't done it, he would have shot me in the back, and that would have been it. Thank you."

I wiped my eyes. "It was you who saved my life. You always have. It's about time I started paying you back."

He smiled. "I do have a tendency for heroics, don't I?"

"You always wanted to be someone's knight in shining armor." I shook my head, thinking over everything he'd ever done for anyone he loved.

"Mer, listen to me. When I said that I'd always love you, I meant it. And I think if we had stayed in Carolina, we would have gotten married, and we would have been happy. Poor, but happy." He smiled sadly. "But we didn't stay in Carolina. And you've changed. I have, too. You were right when you said that I'd never given anyone else a chance, and why would I have ever bothered except for all this happening?

"It's my instinct to fight for you, Mer. It took me a long time to see that you didn't want me to do that anymore. But once I did, I realized I didn't want to fight for you either."

I stared at him, stunned.

"You'll always have a piece of my heart, Mer, but I'm not in love with you anymore. I think sometimes that you still need me or want me, but I don't know if that's right. You deserve better than me being with you because I feel obligated."

I sighed. "And you deserve better than being someone I settle for."

He held out his hand to me and I took it. "I don't want you to be mad at me."

"I'm not. It's good to know you're not mad at me. Even if he is dead, I still love him."

Aspen's forehead creased. "Who's dead?"

"Maxon," I breathed, ready to cry again.

There was a pause. "Maxon's not dead."

"What! But that guard said he wasn't here and—"

"Of course he's not here. He's the king. He's recovering in his room."

I lunged to hug him, and he grunted at the impact of my embrace; but I was too happy to be cautious. Then the happy and sad news mixed together.

I stepped back slowly. "The king died?"

Aspen nodded. "The queen, too."

"No!" I shuddered, blinking again. *She said I could call her Mom.* What was Maxon going to do without her?

"Actually, if it hadn't been for the Northern rebels, Maxon might not have made it either. They were really the tipping point."

"They were?"

I could see the wonder and appreciation in his eyes. "We should have had rebels training us. They fight differently. They knew what to do. I recognized August and Georgia in the Great Room. They had backup outside the palace walls. Once they realized something was wrong, well, they already have a talent for getting into the palace quickly. I don't know where they got the artillery from, but we'd all be gone without them."

I could hardly take in all this. I was still putting the pieces together when the opening door disturbed the quiet murmurs in the wing. A worried face surveyed the room, and though her dress was torn and her hair was tumbling down around her face, I recognized her immediately.

Before I could call out to her, Aspen did. "Lucy!" he cried, sitting up. I knew the motion had to hurt him, but there was no sign of pain in his face.

"Aspen!" She gasped and ran across the wing, hopping over people as necessary. She fell into his arms, kissing his face over and over. While he'd grunted in pain when I'd hugged him, it was clear that in this moment, Aspen wasn't feeling anything but pure happiness.

"Where were you?" he demanded.

"Fourth floor. They're only now reaching the rooms up there. I came as fast as I could. What happened?" Though she was usually so panicked after rebel attacks, Lucy seemed focused now, seeing only Aspen.

"I'm fine. What about you? Do you need to see the doctor?" Aspen looked around, trying to find someone to help.

"No, I don't even have a scratch," she promised. "I was just worried about you."

Aspen stared into Lucy's eyes with absolute devotion. "Now that you're here, everything's right."

She stroked his face, careful not to disturb his bandages.

He put a hand behind her neck and gently pulled her to him, kissing her deeply.

No one needed a knight more than Lucy, and no one could protect her better than Aspen.

They were so lost in each other; they didn't notice me walk away, heading off to find the one person I really wanted to see.

CHAPTER 32

LEAVING THE HOSPITAL WING, I got my first look at the palace. It was hard to process the destruction. So much broken glass strewn across the floor, glittering hopefully in the sunlight. Ruined paintings, parts of the wall blown out, and menacing red stains on the carpets reminded me of how close we'd all been to death.

I started up the stairs, trying to avoid eye contact with anyone. As I passed from the second floor to the third, I noticed an earring on the floor. I couldn't help but wonder if its owner was still alive.

I made my way to the landing and saw a number of guards as I walked toward Maxon's room. I supposed it was unavoidable. If I had to, maybe I'd call out to him. Maybe he'd tell them to let me pass . . . just like the night we met.

The door to Maxon's room was open, and people buzzed

in and out, bringing in papers or taking away platters. Six guards lined the wall leading up to the door, and I braced myself for the brush-off. But as I got closer, one of the guards noticed me. He squinted, as if double-checking that I was who he thought I was. Beside him, another guard recognized me, and one by one they bowed, deeply and reverently.

One of the guards by the door extended an arm. "He's been waiting for you, my lady."

I tried to be someone deserving of the honor they were giving me. I stood taller as I walked, though my scratched arms and cut-off dress did nothing to help. "Thank you," I said with a gentle nod.

A maid rushed past as I went in. Maxon was on his bed, the left side of his chest padded with gauze under his plain cotton shirt. His left arm was in a sling, and he used his right to hold up the paper some adviser was explaining to him.

He looked so normal there, dressed down, hair a mess. But at the same time, he looked like so much more than he had been before. Was he sitting a little taller? Had his face somehow become more serious?

He was so clearly the king.

"Your Majesty," I breathed, falling into a low curtsy. Standing, I saw the quiet smile in his eyes.

"Set the papers here, Stavros. Would everyone please leave the room? I need to speak with the lady."

Everyone circling around him bowed and headed toward the hall. Stavros quietly placed the papers on Maxon's bedside table, and as he passed, he winked at me. I waited until the door closed before I moved.

I wanted to run to him, to fall into his embrace and stay there forever. But I moved slowly, worried that maybe he regretted his last words to me.

"I'm so sorry about your parents."

"It doesn't seem real yet," he said, motioning that I should sit on the bed. "I keep thinking that Father is in his study, and Mom's downstairs, and any minute one of them will come in here with something for me to do."

"I know exactly what you mean."

He gave me a sympathetic smile. "I know you do." He reached out and put his hand on mine. I took that as a good sign and held his hand back. "She tried to save him. A guard told me a rebel had my father in his sights, but she ran behind him. She went down first, but they got Father immediately after."

He shook his head. "She was always selfless. To her very last breath."

"You shouldn't be so surprised. You're a lot like her."

He made a face. "I'll never be quite as good as her. I'm going to miss her so much."

I rubbed his hand. She wasn't my mother, but I would miss her as well.

"At least you're safe," he said, not looking into my eyes. "At least there's that."

There was a long stretch of silence, and I didn't know what to say. Should I bring up what he said? Should I ask about Kriss? Would he even want to think about any of this now?

"There's something I want to show you," he suddenly announced. "Mind you, it's a bit rough, but I think you'll still like it. Open the drawer here," he instructed. "It should be on the top."

I pulled out the drawer in his bedside table, noticing a pile of typed papers right away. I gave Maxon a questioning look, but he just nodded toward the writing.

I started reading the document, trying to process what it said. I got to the end of the first paragraph and then reread it, sure I was mistaken.

"Are you . . . you're going to dissolve the castes?" I asked, looking up to Maxon.

"That's the plan," he answered, smiling. "I don't want you to get too excited. This will take a long time to do, but I think it will work. You see," he said, turning the pages of the vast file and pointing to a paragraph. "I want to start from the bottom. I'm planning on eliminating the Eight label first. There's a lot of construction we need to do; and I feel like, with a little bit of work, the Eights could be absorbed into the Sevens. After that, it gets tricky. There's got to be a way to get rid of the stigmas that come along with the numbers, but that's my goal."

I was awestruck. I'd only ever known a world in which I wore my caste like a piece of clothing. And here I was, holding something saying that those invisible lines we'd drawn between people could finally be erased.

Maxon's hand touched mine. "I want you to know that this is all your doing. Since the day you called me into the hallway and told me about being hungry, I've been working on this. It was one of the reasons I got so upset after you did your presentation; I had a quieter way of reaching the exact same goal. But of all the things I wanted to do for my country, this would have never crossed my mind if I hadn't known you."

I took in a breath and gazed at the pages again. I thought over the years of my life, so short and fast. I'd never expected to do more than sing in the background of people's house parties and maybe get married one day. I thought about what this would mean for the people of Illéa, and I was beside myself. I felt both humbled and proud.

"There's something else," Maxon said hesitantly as I continued to take in the words in front of me. Then suddenly, on top of the papers, Maxon slid over an open box with a ring resting in it, shining in the light cascading through his windows.

"I've been sleeping with that darn thing under my pillow," he said, sounding playfully irritated. I looked up to him, not saying anything, as I was still too stunned to speak. I was sure he could read the questions in my eyes, but he had his own to address. "Do you like it?"

A web of thin gold vines crawled up, forming the circle of the ring, holding at the top two gems—one green, one purple—that kissed at the crown of it. I knew the purple one was my birthstone, so the green one must be his. There we were, two little spots of light growing together, inseparable.

I meant to speak and opened my mouth several times to try. All I could manage to do was smile, blink back my tears, and nod.

Maxon cleared his throat. "Twice now I've tried to do this on a grand scale and failed spectacularly. As it is, I can't even get on one knee. I hope you won't mind if I just speak to you plainly."

I nodded. I still couldn't find a word in my entire body.

He swallowed and shrugged his uninjured shoulder. "I love you," he said simply. "I should have told you a long time ago. Maybe we could have avoided so many stupid mistakes if I had. Then again," he added, beginning to smile, "sometimes I think it was all those obstacles that made me love you so deeply."

Tears pooled in the corners of my eyes, balancing on my lashes.

"What I said was true. My heart is yours to break. As you already know, I'd rather die than see you in pain. In the moment I was hit, when I fell to the floor sure my life was ending, all I could think about was you."

Maxon had to stop. He swallowed, and I could see he was as close to tears as I was. After a moment, he continued.

"In those seconds, I was mourning everything I'd lost. How I'd never get to see you walk down an aisle toward me, how I'd never get to see your face in our children, how I'd never get to see streaks of silver in your hair. But, at the same time, I couldn't be bothered. If me dying meant you living"—he did his one-shoulder shrug again—"how could that be anything but good?"

At that, I lost my control, and the tears came in earnest. How had I ever thought that I knew what it meant to be loved before this very second? Nothing had come close to this feeling radiating in my heart, filling every inch of me with absolute warmth.

"America," Maxon said sweetly, forcing me to wipe my eyes and face him. "I know you see a king here, but let me be clear; this isn't a command. This is a request, a plea. I beg you; make me the happiest man alive. Please do me the honor of becoming my wife."

I couldn't get out how much I wanted this. But where my voice failed, my body succeeded. I crawled into Maxon's arms, holding on to him tightly, certain that nothing could ever pull us apart. When he kissed me, I felt my life settle into place. I had found everything I'd ever wanted—things I didn't even know I was looking for—here in Maxon's arms. And if I had him to guide me, to hold me, then I could take on the world.

It seemed too soon our kiss slowed, and Maxon pulled back to look into my eyes. I saw it in his face. I was home. And I finally found my voice.

"Yes."

EPILOGUE

I TRY NOT TO SHAKE, but it does no good. Any girl would do the same. The day is big, the dress is heavy, and the eyes watching are uncountable. Brave as I ought to be, I tremble.

I know that once the doors open, I will see Maxon waiting for me, so while all the last-second details are settled around me, I hold on to that promise and try to relax.

"Oh! This is our cue," Mom says, noting the change in the music. Silvia waves my family over. James and Kenna are ready to go. Gerad is running around, already wrinkling his suit, and May keeps trying desperately to get him to stand in one place for two seconds back-to-back. Even if he is a bit rumpled, they all look surprisingly regal today.

As happy as I am that everyone who loves me is with me, I can't help but feel an ache that Dad isn't here. I feel him, though, whispering how much he loves me, how proud he is, how lovely I look. I knew him so well that I feel like I can pick out the exact words he would say to me today; and I hope it stays like that always, that he'll never really be gone.

I'm so lost in my daydreams that May sneaks up on me. "You look beautiful, Ames," she says, reaching up to touch the intricate high collar of my dress.

"Mary outdid herself, didn't she?" I answer, touching parts of the dress myself. Mary is the only one of my original maids still with me. When the dust settled, we found out so many more lives were lost than we'd guessed at first. While Lucy made it through the attack and chose to retire, Anne was simply gone.

Another empty place today that ought to be filled.

"My gosh, Ames, you're shaking." May grabs my hands and tries to still them, laughing at my nerves.

"I know. I can't help it."

"Marlee," May calls. "Come help me calm America down."

My one and only bridesmaid walks over, her eyes as bright as ever; and with the two of them surrounding me, I do start to feel less tense.

"Don't worry, America; I'm sure he'll show up," she teases. May laughs, and I swat at them both.

"I'm not worried he'll change his mind! I'm afraid I'll trip or mispronounce his name or something. I have a talent for messing things up," I lament.

Marlee puts her forehead on mine. "Nothing could mess up today."

"May!" Mom hisses.

"Okay, Mom's losing it. See you up there." She gives me a ghost kiss on my cheek, making sure not to leave a lipstick smudge, and goes on her way. The music plays, and they walk together around the corner and down the aisle that's waiting for me.

Marlee steps back. "Am I next?"

"Yes. I love this color on you, by the way."

She juts out her hip, posing in the gown. "You have great taste, Your Majesty."

I suck in a breath. "No one's called me that yet. Oh, goodness, that's going to be my name to pretty much everyone." I try to adjust to the words quickly. The coronation is part of the wedding. First the vows to Maxon, then the ones to Illéa. Rings, then crowns.

"Don't start getting nervous again!" she insists.

"I'm trying! I mean, I knew it was coming; it's just a lot for one day."

"Ha!" she exclaims as the music shifts. "Wait until tonight."

"Marlee!"

Before I can scold her, she scampers away, winking as she goes, and I'm forced to giggle. I'm so glad to have her back in my life. I officially made her one of my attendants, and Maxon did the same for Carter. It was a clear sign to the public of what was coming with Maxon's reign, and I was happy to see how many people welcomed the change.

I listen, waiting. I know the notes are coming soon, so I

take one last chance to straighten my dress.

It's truly magnificent. The white gown is fitted through my hips, flitting out in waves to the floor. The lace sleeves are short and lead to a high collar that genuinely makes me look like a princess. Over the dress, a sleeveless capelike coat flows out behind me, making a train. I'll take it off for the reception, where I intend to dance with my husband until I can't stand anymore.

"Ready, Mer?"

I turn to Aspen. "Yes. I'm ready."

He holds an arm out for me, and I put mine through his. "You look incredible."

"You clean up pretty nice yourself," I comment. And though I smile, I know he sees my nervousness.

"There's nothing to worry about," he assures me, that confident smile making me believe that whatever he says is true, same as always.

I take in a deep breath and nod. "Right. Just don't let me fall, okay?"

"Don't worry. If you look unsteady, I'll hand you this." He holds up the deep-blue cane, specially made to match his dress uniform, and the idea makes me laugh.

"There we go," he says, happy to see me genuinely smile.

"Your Majesty?" Silvia asks. "It's time." Her tone is slightly awed.

I give her a nod, and Aspen and I make our way to the doors.

"Knock 'em dead," he says just before the music rises and

we're revealed to the guests.

All the fear rushes back. Though we tried to keep the guest list small, hundreds of people line the aisle that will take me to Maxon. And as they all rise to greet me, I can't see him.

I just need to see his face. If I can find those steady eyes, I'll know I can do this.

I smile, trying to stay calm, graciously nodding at our guests, thanking them for their presence here today. But Aspen knows.

"It's okay, Mer."

I look to him, and the encouragement in his expression helps.

I keep moving.

It's not the most graceful parade down the aisle. It's also not the fastest. With Aspen's leg so injured, we have to hobble our way slowly to the front. But who else could I have asked? Who else *would* I have asked? Aspen had shifted to fill a desperate place in my life. Not my boyfriend, not my friend, but my *family*.

I had expected him to say no, afraid it was somehow an insult. But he'd said he was honored and embraced me when I'd asked.

Devoted and true, even to the very end. That's my Aspen.

Finally I see a familiar face in the crowd. Lucy is there, sitting with her father. She beams with pride for me, though really she can hardly tear her eyes off Aspen. He stands a little taller as we pass her. I know that soon it will be her turn, and I'm looking forward to it. Aspen couldn't have made a better choice.

Beside her, filling up the closest rows, are the other Selected girls. It was brave of them to come back for me, considering not everyone who should be here is. Still, they smile, even Kriss, though I can see the sadness in her eyes. I'm shocked by how much I wish Celeste was here. I can imagine her rolling her eyes and then winking, or something like that. Making some wisecrack that was almost snotty but not quite. I really, really miss her.

I miss Queen Amberly, too. I can only imagine how happy she would have been today, finally getting a daughter. I feel as if marrying Maxon makes it okay for me to love her that way, like a mother. I'm certain I always will.

And then there's my mom and May holding on to each other so tightly they look as if they're supporting each other. Around them are so many smiles. It's almost overwhelming how loved I feel.

I'm so distracted by their faces that I forget how close I am to the end of the aisle. As I turn forward . . . he's there.

And then it seems as if no one else is here at all.

No cameras filming, no bulbs flashing. It's just us. It's just Maxon and me.

He's wearing his crown, and the suit with the blue sash and the medals. What did I say the first time he wore it? Something about hanging him up with the chandeliers, I think. I smile, remembering the long journey that got us here, standing at the altar.

Aspen's last few steps are slow but steady. When we reach our destination, I turn to him. Aspen gives me one last smile, and I reach over to kiss his cheek, saying good-bye to so many things. We share a look for a moment, and he takes my hand and puts it in Maxon's, giving me away.

They nod to each other, nothing but respect in their faces. I don't think I could ever understand all that's passed between them, but it feels peaceful in that moment. Aspen steps back, and I step forward, arriving at the one place I never thought I'd be.

Maxon and I move close to each other as the ceremony starts.

"Hello, my dear," he whispers.

"Don't start," I warn in return, and we're both left smiling.

He holds my hands as if they're the only things pinning him to the earth, and I focus on that as I prepare myself for the words coming, the promises I'll never break. It's magical, really, the power this day has.

But even now I know this isn't a fairy tale. I know that we'll have hard times, confusing times. I know that things won't always happen the way we want them to and that we'll have to work to remember that we chose this. It won't be perfect, not all the time.

This isn't happily ever after.

It's so much more than that.

ACKNOWLEDGMENTS

CAN YOU JUST PUT YOUR hand on the page and pretend I'm giving you a high five? Seriously. How else do I thank you for reading my books? I hope you've had as much fun with America's story as I have, and I'll never be able to express how happy I am that you took the time to go through it with me. You're keen. Thank you so much!

First of all, a huge thank-you to Callaway. It still makes my day when I see your "Husband of the #1 *New York Times* bestselling author Kiera Cass" email signature, and I'm so glad you're proud of me. Thanks for being my biggest supporter through this whole journey. Love you!

Thank you, Guyden and Zuzu, for being such great kids and letting mommy run off to her office to work. You're wonderful little people, and I love you bunches.

To Mimoo, Poopa, and Uncle Jody, thanks for all your encouragement, and the same goes for Mimi, Papa, and Uncle Chris. Lots of little things couldn't have happened without your help, so thank you for being there, not just for me, but for our whole little family.

To the best agent ever, Elana Roth Parker. I wanted you to want me so bad! Thanks for your faith and hard work and for just plain old being cool. If I was ever in a street fight, I'd want you right there beside me. I mean that in the best way possible. *HUGS*

To Erica Sussman, my fantastic editor. So much of this story worked because of you. Thank you so much for taking me on. I'm crazy about you and your purple pens and your smiley faces! I feel bad for any author who has to work with an editor that isn't you. Absolutely the best!

To everyone at HarperTeen, for being so brilliant and for working so hard. You were the place I longed to call home, and I can't believe how good you are to me! Thank you so much!

To Kathleen, who takes care of all the foreign rights. Thanks for getting my books (and me!) all over the world! It's still unbelievable.

To Samantha Clark, for running the Kiera Cass fan page on Facebook without ever being asked to do it or complaining about any work it brings her way. So, so cool of you! Thank you!

To everyone who runs a Selection-based Twitter, Tumblr, or Facebook account. Half of the time I can't read the language you're posting in, and that alone is insane to me! Thanks for being diligent and creative and for talking to me. For realsies, you guys are the best!

To Georgia Whitaker, for making a really rad video and earning her name a spot in the book. Thanks for letting me borrow it!

Who am I forgetting? Like a thousand people, I just know it . . .

To Northstar church (which I *swear* I started going to years after *The Selection* was born), thanks for being home to the Cass family and for your constant encouragement.

To FTW . . . I don't even know what to say. You guys are ridiculous, and I love you.

To The Fray, One Direction, Jack's Mannequin, Paramore, Elbow, and a slew of other musicians, thanks for keeping me inspired over the years. You were fuel for these stories.

As well as Coke Zero and low-fat Wheat Thins. Sometimes also Milk Duds. Very important to my survival over the years, so thanks.

Lastly, and most important, to God. Years ago, writing saved me from a very dark time in my life. It wasn't on my radar at all, but it became my lifeline. I believe it was grace that brought this into my life, and even on the most stressful days, my job makes me happy. I feel blessed a thousand times over and even though I write for a living, I still can't find the words to express my gratitude. Thank you.

Twenty years ago, her mother won the crown.
Now Eadlyn will enter a Selection of her own. . . .

Turn the page for a sneak peek
at the fourth book in
THE SELECTION SERIES

CHAPTER 1

I COULD NOT HOLD MY breath for seven minutes. I couldn't even make it to one. I once tried to run a mile in seven minutes after hearing some athletes could do it in four but failed spectacularly when a side stitch crippled me about halfway in.

However, there was one thing I managed to do in seven minutes that most would say is quite impressive: I became queen.

By seven tiny minutes I beat my brother, Ahren, into the world, so the throne that ought to have been his was mine. Had I been born a generation earlier, it wouldn't have mattered. Ahren was the male, so Ahren would have been the heir.

Alas, Mom and Dad couldn't stand to watch their firstborn be stripped of a title by an unfortunate but rather lovely set of breasts. So they changed the law, and the people rejoiced, and I was trained day by day to become the next ruler of Illéa.

What they didn't understand was that their attempts to make my life fair seemed rather *unfair* to me.

I tried not to complain. After all, I knew how fortunate I was. But there were days, or sometimes months, when it felt like far too much was piled on me, too much for any one person, really.

I flipped through the newspaper and saw that there had been yet another riot, this time in Zuni. Twenty years ago, Dad's first act as king was to dissolve the castes, and the old system had been phased out slowly over my lifetime. I still thought it was completely bizarre that once upon a time people lived with these limiting but arbitrary labels on their backs. Mom was a Five; Dad was a One. It made no sense, especially since there was no outward sign of the divisions. How was I supposed to know if I was walking next to a Six or a Three? And why did that even matter?

When Dad had first decreed that the castes were no more, people all over the country had been delighted. Dad had expected the changes he was making in Illéa to be comfortably in place over the course of a generation, meaning any day now everything should click.

That wasn't happening—and this new riot was just the most recent in a string of unrest.

"Coffee, Your Highness," Neena said, setting the drink on my table.

"Thank you. You can take the plates."

I scanned the article. This time a restaurant was burned to the ground because its owner refused to promote a waiter to a position as a chef. The waiter claimed that a promotion had been promised but was never delivered, and he was sure it was because of his family's past.

Looking at the charred remains of the building, I honestly didn't know whose side I was on. The owner had the right to promote or fire anyone he wanted, and the waiter had the right not to be seen as something that, technically, didn't exist anymore.

I pushed the paper away and picked up my drink. Dad was going to be upset. I was sure he was already running the scenario over and over in his head, trying to figure out how to set it right. The problem was, even if we could fix one issue, we couldn't stop every instance of post-caste discrimination. It was too hard to monitor and happening far too often.

I set down my coffee and headed to my closet. It was time to start the day.

"Neena," I called. "Do you know where that plum-colored dress is? The one with the sash?"

She squinted in concentration as she came over to help.

In the grand scheme of things, Neena was new to the palace. She'd only been working with me for six months, after my last maid fell ill for two weeks. Neena was acutely attuned to my needs and much more agreeable to be around, so I kept her on. I also admired her eye for fashion.

Neena stared into the massive space. "Maybe we should reorganize."

"You can if you have the time. That's not a project I'm interested in."

"Not when I can hunt down your clothes for you," she teased.

"Exactly!"

She took my humor in stride, laughing as she quickly sorted through gowns and pants.

"I like your hair today," I commented.

"Thank you." All the maids wore caps, but Neena was still creative with her hairdos. Sometimes a few thick, black curls would frame her face, and other times she twisted back strands until they were all tucked away. At the moment there were wide braids encircling her head, with the rest of her hair under her cap. I really enjoyed that she found ways to work with her uniform, to make it her own each day.

"Ah! It's back here." Neena pulled down the knee-length dress, fanning it out across the dark skin of her arm.

"Perfect! And do you know where my gray blazer is? The one with the three-quarter sleeves?"

She stared at me, her face deadpan. "I'm definitely rearranging."

I giggled. "You search; I'll dress."

I pulled on my outfit and brushed out my hair, preparing for another day as the future face of the monarchy. The outfit was feminine enough to soften me but strong enough that I'd be taken seriously. It was a fine line to walk, but I did it every day.

Staring into the mirror, I talked to my reflection.

"You are Eadlyn Schreave. You are the next person in line to run this country, and you will be the first girl to do it on your own. No one," I said, "is as powerful as you."

Dad was already in his office, brow furrowed as he took in the news. Other than my eyes, I didn't look much like him. Or Mom, for that matter.

With my dark hair, oval-shaped face, and a hint of a tan that lingered year round, I looked more like my grandmother than anyone else. A painting of her on her coronation day hung in the fourth-floor hallway, and I used to study it when I was younger, trying to guess at how I would look as I grew. Her age in the portrait was near to mine now, and though we weren't identical, I sometimes felt like her echo.

I walked across the room and kissed Dad's cheek. "Morning."

"Morning. Did you see the papers?" he asked.

"Yes. At least no one died this time."

"Thank goodness for that." Those were the worst, the ones where people were left dead in the street or went missing. It was terrible, reading the names of young men who'd been beaten simply for moving their families into a nicer neighborhood or women who were attacked for trying to get a job that in the past would not have been open to them.

Sometimes it took no time at all to find the motive and the person behind these crimes, but more often than not we were faced with a lot of finger-pointing and no real answers. It was exhausting for me to watch, and I knew it was worse for Dad.

"I don't understand it." He took off his reading glasses and rubbed his eyes. "They didn't want the castes anymore. We took our time, eliminated them slowly so everyone could adjust. Now they're burning down buildings."

"Is there a way to regulate this? Could we create a board to oversee grievances?" I looked at the photo again. In the corner, the young son of the restaurant owner wept over losing everything. In my heart I knew complaints would come in faster than anyone could address them, but I also knew Dad couldn't bear doing nothing.

Dad looked at me. "Is that what you would do?"

I smiled. "No, I'd ask my father what he would do."

He sighed. "That won't always be an option for you, Eadlyn. You need to be strong, decisive. How would you fix this one particular incident?"

I considered. "I don't think we can. There's no way to prove the old castes were why the waiter was denied the promotion. The only thing we can do is launch an investigation into who set the fire. That family lost their livelihood today, and someone needs to be held responsible. Arson is not how you exact justice."

He shook his head at the paper. "I think you're right. I'd like to be able to help them. But, more than that, we need to figure out how to prevent this from happening again. It's become rampant, Eadlyn, and it's frightening."

Dad tossed the paper into the trash, then stood and walked to the window. I could read the stress in his posture. Sometimes his role brought him so much joy, like visiting the schools he'd worked tirelessly to improve or seeing communities flourish in the war-free era he'd ushered in. But those instances were becoming few and far between. Most days he was anxious about the state of the country, and he had to fake his smiles when reporters came by, hoping that his sense of calm would somehow spread to everyone else. Mom helped shoulder the burden, but at the end of the day the fate of the country was placed squarely on his back. One day it would be on mine.

Vain as it was, I worried I would go gray prematurely.

"Make a note for me, Eadlyn. Remind me to write Governor Harpen in Zuni. Oh, and put to write it to Joshua Harpen, not his father. I keep forgetting he was the one who ran in the last election."

I wrote his instructions in my elegant cursive, thinking how pleased Dad would be when he looked at it later. He used to give me the worst time over my penmanship.

I was grinning to myself when I looked back at him, but my face fell almost immediately when I saw him rubbing his forehead, trying so desperately to think of a solution to these problems.

"Dad?"

He turned and instinctively squared his shoulders, like he needed to act strong even in front of me.

"Why do you think this is happening? It wasn't always like this."

He raised his eyebrows. "It certainly wasn't," he said, almost to himself. "At first everyone seemed pleased. Every time we removed a new caste, people held parties. It's only been in the last few years, since all the labels have officially been erased, that it's gone downhill."

He stared back out the window. "The only thing I can think is that those who grew up with the castes are aware of how much better this is. Comparatively, it's easier to marry or work. A family's finances aren't capped by a single profession. There are more choices when it comes to education. But those who are growing up without the castes and are still running into opposition . . . I guess they don't know what else to do."

He looked at me and shrugged. "I need time," he muttered. "I need a way to put things on pause, set them right, and press play again."

I noted the deep furrow in his brow. "Dad, I don't think that's possible."

He chuckled. "We've done it before. I can remember. . . ."

The focus in his eyes changed. He watched me for a moment, seeming to ask me a question without words.

"Dad?"

"Yes."

"Are you all right?"

He blinked a few times. "Yes, dear, quite all right. Why don't you get to work on those budget cuts. We can go over your ideas this afternoon. I need to speak with your mother."

"Sure." Math wasn't a skill that came to me naturally,

so I had to work twice as long on any proposals for budget cuts or financial plans. But I absolutely refused to have one of Dad's advisers come behind me with a calculator to clean up my mess. Even if I had to stay up all night, I always made sure my work was accurate.

Of course, Ahren was naturally good at math, but he was never forced to sit through meetings about budgets or rezoning or health care. He got off scot-free by seven stupid minutes.

Dad patted me on the shoulder before dashing out of the room. It took me longer than usual to focus on the numbers. I couldn't help but be distracted by the look on his face and the unmistakable certainty that it was tied to me.

CHAPTER 2

AFTER WORKING ON THE BUDGET report for a few hours, I decided I needed a break and retreated to my room to get a hand massage from Neena. I loved those little bits of luxury in my day. Dresses made to my exact measurements, exotic desserts flown in simply because it was Thursday, and an endless supply of beautiful things were all perks; and they were easily my favorite parts of the job.

My room overlooked the gardens. As the day shifted, the light changed to a warm, honey color, brightening the high walls. I focused on the heat and Neena's deliberate fingers.

"Anyway, his face got all funny. It was kind of like he disappeared for a minute."

I was trying to explain Dad's out-of-character departure this morning, but it was hard to get it across. I didn't even know if he found Mom or not, as he never came back to the office.

"Do you think he's sick? He does seem tired these days." Neena's hands worked her magic as she spoke.

"Does he?" I asked, thinking that Dad didn't seem tired exactly. "He's probably just stressed. How could he not be with all the decisions he has to make?"

"And someday that will be you," she commented, her tone a mix of genuine worry and playful amusement.

"Which means you will be giving me twice as many massages."

"I don't know," she said. "I think in a few years I might like to try something new."

I scrunched my face. "What else would you do? There aren't many positions better than working in the palace."

There was a knock on the door, and she didn't have a chance to answer the question.

I stood, throwing my blazer back on to look presentable, and gave a nod to Neena to let my guests in.

Mom came around the door, smiling, with Dad contentedly trailing her steps. I couldn't help but notice it was always this way. At state events or important dinners, Mom was beside Dad or situated right behind him. But when they were just husband and wife—not king and queen—he followed her everywhere.

"Hi, Mom." I walked over to hug her.

Mom tucked my hair behind my ear, smiling at me. "I like this look."

I stood back proudly and smoothed out my dress with my

hands. "The bracelets really set it off, don't you think?"

She giggled. "Excellent attention to detail." Every once in a while Mom let me pick out jewelry or shoes for her, but it was rare. Mom didn't find it as much fun as I did, and she didn't rely on the extras for beauty. In her case, she really didn't need it. I liked that she was classic.

Mom turned and touched Neena's shoulder. "You're excused," she said quietly.

Neena instantly curtsied and left us alone.

"Is something wrong?" I asked.

"No, sweetheart. We simply want to speak in private." Dad held out a hand and ushered us all to the table. "We have an opportunity to talk to you about."

"Opportunity? Are we traveling?" I adored traveling. "Please tell me we're finally going on a beach trip. Could it just be the six of us?"

"Not exactly. We wouldn't be going somewhere so much as having visitors," Mom explained.

"Oh! Company! Who's coming?"

They exchanged glances, then Mom continued talking. "You know that things are precarious right now. The people are restless and unhappy, and we cannot figure out how to ease the tension."

I sighed. "I know."

"We're seeking a way to boost morale," Dad added.

I perked up. Morale boosting typically involved a celebration. And I was always up for a party.

"What did you have in mind?" I started designing a new

dress in my head and dismissed it almost as quickly. That wasn't what needed my attention at the moment.

"Well," Dad started, "the public responds best to something positive with our family. When your mother and I were married, it was one of the best seasons in our country. And do you remember how people threw parties in the street when they found out Osten was coming?"

I smiled. I was eight when Osten was born, and I'd never forget how excited everyone got just over the announcement. I heard music playing from my bedroom practically until dawn.

"That was marvelous."

"It was. And now the people look to you. It won't be long before you're queen." Dad paused. "We thought that perhaps you'd be willing to do something publicly, something that would be exciting for the people but also might be very beneficial to you."

I narrowed my eyes, not sure where this was going. "I'm listening."

Mom cleared her throat. "You know that in the past, princesses were married off to princes from other countries to solidify our international relations."

"I did hear you use the past tense there, correct?"

She laughed, but I wasn't amused. "Yes."

"Good. Because Prince Nathaniel looks like a zombie, Prince Hector dances like a zombie, and if the prince from the German Federation doesn't learn to embrace personal hygiene by the Christmas party, he shouldn't be invited."

Mom rubbed the side of her head in frustration. "Eadlyn, you've always been so picky."

Dad shrugged. "Maybe that's not a bad thing," he said, earning a glare from Mom.

I frowned. "What in the world are you talking about?"

"You know how your mother and I met," Dad began.

I rolled my eyes. "Everyone does. You two are practically a fairy tale."

At those words their eyes went soft, and smiles washed over their faces. Their bodies seemed to tilt slightly toward each other, and Dad bit his lip looking at Mom.

"Excuse me. Firstborn in the room, do you mind?"

Mom blushed as Dad cleared his throat and continued. "The Selection process was very successful for us. And though my parents had their problems, it worked well for them, too. So . . . we were hoping. . . ." He hesitated and met my eyes.

I was slow to pick up on their hints. I knew what the Selection was, but never, not even once, had it been suggested as an option for any of us, let alone me.

"No."

Mom put up her hands, cautioning me. "Just listen—"

"A Selection?" I burst out. "That's insane!"

"Eadlyn, you're being irrational."

I glared at her. "You promised—*you promised*—you'd never force me into marrying someone for an alliance. How is this any better?"

"Hear us out," she urged.

"No!" I shouted. "I won't do it."

"Calm down, love."

"Don't talk to me like that. I'm not a child!"

Mom sighed. "You're certainly acting like one."

"You're ruining my life!" I ran my fingers through my hair and took several deep breaths, hoping it would help me think. This couldn't happen. Not to me.

"It's a huge opportunity," Dad insisted.

"You're trying to shackle me to a stranger!"

"I told you she'd be stubborn," Mom muttered to Dad.

"Wonder where she gets that from," he shot back with a smile.

"Don't talk about me like I'm not in the room!"

"I'm sorry," Dad said. "We just need you to consider this."

"What about Ahren? Can't he do it?"

"Ahren isn't going to be the future king. Besides, he has Camille."

Princess Camille was the heir to the French throne, and a few years ago she'd managed to bat her lashes all the way into Ahren's heart.

"Then make them get married!" I pleaded.

"Camille will be queen when her time comes, and she, like you, will have to ask her partner to marry her. If it was Ahren's choice, we'd consider it; but it's not."

"What about Kaden? Can't you have him do it?"

Mom laughed humorlessly. "He's fourteen! We don't have that kind of time. The people need something to be excited about now." She narrowed her eyes at me. "And, honestly, isn't it time you look for someone to rule beside you?"

Dad nodded. "It's true. It's not a role that should be shouldered alone."

"But I don't want to get married," I pleaded. "Please don't make me do this. I'm only eighteen."

"Which is how old I was when I married your father," Mom stated.

"I'm not ready," I urged. "I don't want a husband. Please don't do this to me."

Mom reached across the table and put her hand on mine. "No one would be doing anything to you. You would be doing something for your people. You'd be giving them a gift."

"You mean faking a smile when I'd rather cry?"

She gave me a fleeting frown. "That has always been part of our job."

I stared at her, silently demanding a better answer.

"Eadlyn, why don't you take some time to think this over?" Dad said calmly. "I know this is a big thing we're asking of you."

"Does that mean I have a choice?"

Dad inhaled deeply, considering. "Well, love, you'll really have thirty-five choices."

I leaped up from my chair, pointing toward the door.

"Get out!" I demanded. "Get! Out!"

Without another word they left my room.

Didn't they know who I was, what they'd trained me

for? I was Eadlyn Schreave. No one was more powerful than me.

So if they thought I was going down without a fight, they were sadly mistaken.

CHAPTER 3

I DECIDED TO TAKE DINNER in my room. I didn't feel like seeing my family at the moment. I was irate with all of them. At my parents for being happy, at Ahren for not picking up the pace eighteen years ago, at Kaden and Osten for being so young.

Neena circled me, filling my cup as she spoke. "Do you think you'll go through with it, miss?" she asked.

"I'm still trying to figure a way out."

"What if you said you were already in love with somebody?"

I shook my head as I poked at my food. "I insulted my three most likely candidates right in front of them."

She set a small plate of chocolates in the middle of the table, guessing correctly that I'd probably want those more than the caviar-garnished salmon.

"Perhaps a guard then? Happens to the maids often enough," she suggested with a giggle.

I scoffed. "That's fine for them, but I'm not that desperate."

Her laughter faded.

I saw immediately that I had offended her, but that was the truth. I couldn't settle for any old person, let alone a guard. Even considering it was a waste of time. I needed a way out of this whole situation.

"I don't mean it like that, Neena. It's just that people expect certain things from me."

"Of course."

"I'm done. You can go for the night; I'll leave the cart in the hallway."

She nodded and left without another word.

I grazed on the chocolates before completely giving up on the food and slipped into my nightgown. I couldn't reason with Mom and Dad right now, and Neena didn't understand. I needed to talk to the only person who might see my side, the person who sometimes felt like he was half of me. I needed Ahren.

"Are you busy?" I asked, cracking open his door.

Ahren was sitting at his desk, writing. His blond hair was end-of-the-day messy, but his eyes were far from tired, and he looked so much like the pictures of Dad when he was younger it was eerie. He was still dressed from dinner but had taken off his coat and tie, settling in for the evening. "Knock, for goodness' sake."

"I know, I know; but it's an emergency."

"Then get a guard," he snapped back, returning to his papers.

"That's already been suggested," I muttered to myself. "I'm serious, Ahren; I need your help."

Ahren peeked over his shoulder at me, and I could see he was already planning to give in. He used his foot to push out the seat next to him casually. "Step into my office."

Sitting, I sighed. "What are you writing?"

He quickly piled papers on top of the one he'd been working on. "A letter to Camille."

"You know you could simply phone her."

He grinned. "Oh, I will. But then I'll send her this, too."

"That makes no sense. What could you possibly have to talk about that would fill an entire phone call and a letter?"

He tilted his head. "For your information, they serve different purposes. The calls are for updates and to see how her day went. The letters are for the things I can't always say out loud."

"Oh, really?" I leaned over, reaching for the paper.

Before I could even get close, Ahren's hand gripped my wrist. "I will murder you," he vowed.

"Good," I shot. "Then you can be the heir, and you can go through a Selection and kiss your precious Camille good-bye."

He scrunched his forehead. "What?"

I slumped back into my chair. "Mom and Dad need to

boost morale. They've decided that, for the sake of Illéa," I said in mock patriotism, "I need to go through a Selection."

I was expecting abject horror. Perhaps a sympathetic hand on my shoulder. But Ahren threw back his head and laughed.

"Ahren!"

He continued to howl, pitching himself forward and hitting his knee.

"You're going to wrinkle your suit," I warned, which only made him laugh harder. "For goodness' sake, stop it! What am I supposed to do?"

"As if I know! I can't believe they think this would even work," he added, his smile still not fading.

"What's that supposed to mean?"

He shrugged. "I don't know. I guess I thought, if you ever did get married, it'd be down the line. I think everyone assumed that."

"And what is *that* supposed to mean?"

The warm touch I'd been hoping for finally came as he reached for my hand. "Come on, Eady. You've always been independent. It's the queen in you. You like to be in charge, do things on your own. I didn't think you'd partner up with anyone until you at least got to reign for a while."

"Not like I really had a choice in the first place," I mumbled, tilting my head to the floor but still looking to my brother.

He gave me a little pout. "Poor little princess. Don't want to rule the world?"

I swatted his hand away. "Seven minutes. It should have

been you. I'd much rather sit alone and scribble away instead of do all that stupid paperwork. And this ridiculous Selection nonsense! Can't you see how dreadful this is?"

"How did you get roped into this anyway? I thought they'd done away with it."

I rolled my eyes again. "It has absolutely nothing to do with me. That's the worst part. Dad's facing public opposition, so he's trying to distract them." I shook my head. "It's getting really bad, Ahren. People are destroying homes and businesses. Some have died. Dad isn't completely sure where it's coming from, but he thinks it's people our age, the generation that grew up without castes, causing most of it."

He made a face. "That doesn't make sense. How could growing up without those restrictions make you upset?"

I paused, thinking. How could I explain what we could only really guess at? "Well, I grew up being told I was going to be queen one day. That was it. No choice. You grew up knowing you had options. You could go into the military, you could become an ambassador, you could do plenty of things. But what if that wasn't really happening? What if you didn't have all the opportunities you thought you would?"

"Huh," he said, following. "So they're being denied jobs?"

"Jobs, education, money. I've heard of people refusing to let their kids get married because of old castes. Nothing is happening the way Dad thought it would, and it's nearly impossible to control. Can we force people to be fair?"

"And that's what Dad's trying to figure out now?" he asked, skeptical.

"Yes, and I'm the smoke-and-mirror act diverting their attention while he comes up with a plan."

He chuckled. "That makes much more sense than you suddenly being romantically inclined."

I cocked my head. "Let it go, Ahren. So I'm not interested in marriage. Why does that matter? Other women can stay single."

"But other women aren't expected to produce an heir."

I hit him again. "Help me! What do I do?"

His eyes searched mine, and I knew, as easily as I could read any emotion in him, that he saw I was terrified. Not irritated or angry. Not outraged or repulsed.

I was scared.

It was one thing to be expected to rule, to hold the weight of millions of people in my hands. That was a job, a task. I could check things off lists, delegate. But this was much more personal, one more piece of my life that ought to be mine but wasn't.

His playful smile disappeared, and he pulled his chair closer to mine. "If they're looking to distract people, maybe you could suggest other . . . opportunities. A possible marriage isn't the only choice. That said, if Mom and Dad came to this conclusion, they might have already exhausted every other option."

I buried my head in my hands. I didn't want to tell him I tried to offer up him as an alternative or that I thought Kaden might even be acceptable. I sensed he was right, that the Selection was their last hope.

"Here's the thing, Eady. You'll be the first girl to hold the throne fully in her own right. And people expect a lot from you."

"Like I don't already know that."

"But," he continued, "that also gives you a lot of bargaining power."

I raised my head marginally. "What do you mean?"

"If they really need you to do this, then negotiate."

I sat up straight, my mind running around in circles, trying to think of what I could ask for. There might be a way to get through this quickly, without it even ending in a proposal.

Without a proposal!

If I spoke fast enough, I could probably get Dad to agree to practically anything so long as he got his Selection out of it.

"Negotiate!" I whispered.

"Exactly."

I stood up, grabbed Ahren by his ears, and planted a kiss on his forehead. "You are my absolute hero!"

He smiled. "Anything for you, my queen."

I giggled, shoving him. "Thanks, Ahren."

"Get to work." He waved me toward the door, and I suspected he was actually more eager to get back to his letter than he was for me to come up with a plan.

I dashed from the room, heading to my own to fetch some paper. I needed to think.

As I rounded the corner, I ran smack into someone, falling backward onto the carpet.

"Ow!" I complained, looking up to see Kile Woodwork, Miss Marlee's son.

Kile and the rest of the Woodworks had rooms on the same floor as our family, a singularly huge honor. Or irritation, depending on how one felt about the Woodworks.

"Do you mind?" I snapped.

"I wasn't the one running," he answered, picking up the books he'd dropped. "You ought to be looking where you're going."

"A gentleman would offer his hand right now," I reminded him.

Kile's hair flopped across his eyes as he looked over at me. He was in desperate need of a cut and a shave, and his shirt was too big for him. I didn't know who I was more embarrassed for: him for looking so sloppy or my family for having to be seen with such a disaster.

What was especially irritating was that he wasn't always so scruffy, and he didn't have to be now. How hard would it be to run a brush through his hair?

"Eadlyn, you've never thought I was a gentleman."

"True." I pulled myself up without help and brushed off my robe.

For the last six months I had been spared Kile's less-than-thrilling company. He'd gone to Fennley to enroll in some accelerated course, and his mother had been lamenting his absence ever since the day he left. I didn't know what he was studying, and I didn't particularly care. But he was back now, and his presence was another stressor on an ever-growing list.

"And what would make such a lady run like that in the first place?"

"Matters you are far too dim to comprehend."

He laughed. "Right, because I'm such a simpleton. It's a miracle I manage to bathe myself."

I was about to ask if he did bathe, because he looked like he'd been running away from anything that resembled a bar of soap.

"I hope one of those books is a primer on etiquette. You seriously need a refresher."

"You're not queen yet, Eadlyn. Take it down a notch." He walked away, and I was furious with myself for not getting the last word.

I pressed on. There were bigger problems in my life right now than the state of Kile's manners. I couldn't waste my time quibbling with people or being distracted by anything that couldn't put the Selection to death.

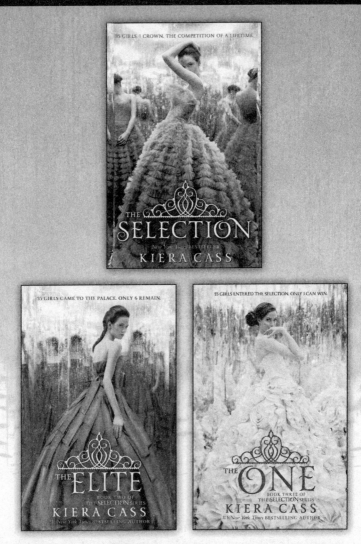

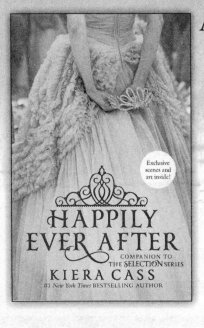